S0-BNZ-919

SOULSMITH

CRADLE : VOLUME TWO

WILL
WIGHT

HIDDEN
GNOME
PUBLISHING

SOULSMITH

Copyright © 2017 Hidden Gnome Publishing

Book and cover design by Patrick Foster Design

All rights reserved. No part of this book may be reproduced in any form by any electronic or mechanical means including photocopying, recording, or information storage and retrieval without permission in writing from the author.

ISBN 978-0-9896717-7-4 (print edition)

www.WillWight.com

will@willwight.com

twitter.com/willwight

To my brother Sam, for reading this.

PROLOGUE

INFORMATION REQUESTED: DISCIPLE TRAINING ON THE PATH OF THE ENDLESS SWORD.

BEGINNING REPORT...

When you're alone, first look for a weapon.

The master leaves his disciple with these words. The disciple kneels in the winter snow, shivering as the snow presses through her knees. Finding a weapon isn't her problem.

Thirteen swords are thrust into the snow around her, cold blades turned so that their razor edges touch her skin. With every shiver, she opens another cut. Her thighs, knees, and upper arms are sheathed in freezing blood.

At the edge of pain, exhaustion, and isolation, each of her thoughts becomes slippery. But she knows, clear and distinct as the ring of a bell, that her master has abandoned her here.

It's his favorite training technique: leaving her alone, where no one can save her, and forcing her to rely on her own knowledge to escape. It teaches her reliance, he says. A Path is only one person wide.

She knows he's always right. She's only Iron, not quite ten years old, and she can't question him.

But every time he walks away, he leaves her with the fear that *this* will be the time he doesn't come back.

She is surrounded by sword aura, silver and sharp in her spiritual vision, and she drinks it in to cycle it, to refine it until it becomes a part of her spirit. Her madra. She has done this constantly since he first left her kneeling in the snow, but it hasn't helped. She knows no technique she can use from this position, has no blade of her own through which she can channel the madra.

She tries to push her power out through her skin, but the swords only shake and open up new lines of blood.

When you're alone, first look for a weapon.

The Sword Sage is not a bad teacher, but he has a preference for cryptic riddles. She has already strained her eyes and even extended her hands—at least as far as she can, without slicing them open on the waiting blades—to search for weapons in the snow. She'd thought he might have hidden something for her, and that treasure will be the key to her escape.

She finds nothing. She kneels for hours, burning in the cold, throwing madra at the implacable weapons. She may as well have shouted at them.

As the morning climbs into afternoon, she has only one coherent thought left. Her master is not coming back. Why should he? A disciple who cannot learn is one not worth teaching. Her master deserves someone who can keep up with his instruction.

Someone who can be trusted.

Her unwelcome guest starts to stir, squirming against the seal that her master has placed upon it. It doesn't speak—it can't—but its presence reminds her that there is another source of power here. Another route she can take, besides sword madra. Another Path.

She will freeze to death before she takes it.

When her vision starts to dim, she knows that even her

Iron body is reaching its limits. She screams, shaking herself awake, and the fresh cuts on her body don't even hurt. She draws in as much sword aura as she can, flooding her system with borrowed power, though she won't be able to use it until she cycles it through her own spirit. Full to bursting, she pushes it all away from her.

Faintly, the swords ring like distant bells.

She stills herself, waiting for her tired thoughts to catch up.

When you're alone, first look for a weapon.

On the Path of the Endless Sword, she's learned to Enforce madra into a weapon so that it gathers aura as it moves, strengthening with time. She has learned to pour madra into a Striker's slash, severing a tree branch twenty paces away. She's even learned to crystallize her power into a Forged razor, though it still shatters like glass.

She still hasn't learned a Ruler technique, the ability to manipulate compatible aura in the world around her.

It's a weapon she hasn't seized.

Her madra echoes in time with her breath, gusting out and striking the circle of swords and the aura gathered there. The aura echoes with a pure note, sweet and clear in the winter afternoon.

The swords slide away.

SUGGESTED TOPIC: THE FATED FUTURE OF YERIN, THE SWORD SAGE'S DISCIPLE. CONTINUE?

DENIED, REPORT COMPLETE.

CHAPTER ONE

Lindon unwrapped the bandage from Yerin's forehead, examining the wound. It was red and angry, a long slash, but shallow. Her master's Remnant had cut her with the precision of a battlefield surgeon. She was already covered in scars so pale and thin they looked as though they were painted on her skin, and unless he missed his guess, she was going to end up with a fresh new set in a few months.

He tossed the crusty bandage into the fire—fuel wasn't terribly hard to come by out here, in the hills east of Mount Samara, but gathering sticks was torture on his injured back. He wouldn't give up any tinder, and burning their old bandages had the added benefit of removing blood scent from their trail. He doubted anyone would leave Sacred Valley to track them, but no one ever died from being too careful.

Yerin sat quietly, watching the fire, as Lindon dug into his pack at his feet. He liked to carry anything he even *might* need, so his pack bulged at the seams. Seated on a fallen tree as he was, the pack stood higher than his knees.

But he'd been glad he had it over the past five days. He pulled out another roll of clean gauze from a pocket, quickly tying it around Yerin's head. That cut on Yerin's forehead wasn't her worst, so by the time he was finished, she was wrapped like a fish packaged for market. And he wasn't much better.

"Apologies, but this is the last of the bandages," Lindon said, replacing another gauze wrapping on her elbow and tossing it into the fire. "I have a set of spare clothes that we can cut into strips."

"Won't need it," Yerin said. "Now that I've got something more than wind and wishes in my core, I'll cycle for a few more days and be all polished up." She rapped her knuckles on the back of her forearm with the air of someone knocking on wood, though it made the usual sound of flesh on flesh. "Iron body comes with all sorts of treats, depending on what sort you have. Copper's even easier. We'll break you through to Copper tonight, and that'll perk you up quick. Nothing does good for the flesh and blood like advancing a realm."

Lindon paused with the last strip of gauze in his hand. "Tonight?"

She turned to flash him a quick smile. "Unless you'd choose to wait."

As she turned, he had to dodge to avoid taking a thin steel arm to the face. The limb sprouted from her shoulder blade, a structure of Forged madra so dense that it felt like real steel, ending in a sword blade that dangled over her head like a scorpion's tail.

She grimaced, and the arm lurched awkwardly away from Lindon's cheek. "Haven't quite tamed that one yet, sorry."

His task was complete anyway, so he stood up from the log and moved around her. "Copper, you said. I'll be able to sense vital aura, won't I? Even...sword aura?"

He thought he understood Copper fairly well, having grown up primarily around children who had reached that stage, but from Yerin he'd learned that half of what he knew about the sacred arts was completely wrong. This was an opportunity for him to learn.

And perhaps to gain something more.

He'd split his core into two parts only days before, embarking on what he called the Path of Twin Stars. This gave him a natural defense against anyone attacking his spirit, but more importantly, he should *theoretically* be able to hold two types of madra in the same body. He could keep his own pure madra, while learning Yerin's Path as well.

Except thus far, every time he'd broached the topic, she had refused to teach him.

Yerin's eyes drifted to her own sword, which she'd taken from her master's body. "You need a master in truth, Lindon, and those aren't shoes I can fill." He started to protest, but she rode over him. "Listen. You ever heard anybody talk about Copper eyes?"

He shook his head.

"It's a saying I grew up with. Copper eyes see the world, Iron eyes see far, and Jade eyes see deep. Tells you what you're in for. At Copper, you see aura. You can begin taking it in, cycling it, turning it into madra. At Iron, you're forging the body you'll use for the rest of your life, and the actual eyes in your head get better. And when you hit Jade, you can use your spirit to...see. Sense. There's not a good word for it, really."

"What about Gold?" he asked eagerly.

She flicked a finger against the silvery steel blade hanging down into her face. "At Gold you hold a Remnant in your core, and you get a little something extra for your trouble. We call it a Goldsign, and it's the simple way to tell who's on what Path. Now shut it, we're talking about Copper."

Lindon settled down on a nearby rock, the fire crackling between them.

"Ten chances out of a dozen, you'll have to prepare for a stage before you advance," Yerin continued. "And what preparation you settle on depends on your Path. *My* master stuck me in a ring of swords to polish me up for Jade. He wouldn't let me out until I could push them away on my own. Strengthened me, turned me toward sword madra, prepared me to advance. Like eating a red pepper to prepare for a white one."

It sounded more like sadistic torture than sacred arts to Lindon, and though he didn't say anything, Yerin must have noticed the look on his face.

"Wasn't so bad," she said, tracing one of the paper-thin scars on her arm. "Taught me character. Anyway, the thrust of it is, I can't teach you. You're not following in my footsteps, so I don't know where to take you from here. Maybe if I knew more...but I don't. I'm just a Gold."

Hearing someone say they were 'just' a Gold was like hearing an emperor say his summer palace 'just' had a thousand rooms, but the idea that he wasn't ready for a Path sent chills up his back.

"So, if I understand you correctly, then I'm not...I mean, I'll never be..." He couldn't squeeze the words out.

She snapped her fingers in front of his eyes. "Are your ears open? What did I say? *I* don't know how to get you in condition for *my* Path. The Path of the Endless Sword is pretty choosy, but most Paths are not. I've met more than a few masters who wouldn't even look at a student before Iron."

Lindon breathed deeply again as the chills faded, but he didn't miss a word. "These masters are beyond Gold, you say. What kind of a realm is that?"

"Gold is a wide river to ford," she said dryly, "especially for somebody who hasn't so much as touched Copper. You want to advance, you'd best clear out your mind."

He took the opportunity to stretch his sore back and look around. Samara wasn't the last mountain they'd crossed since leaving Sacred Valley, and snow-capped peaks hid the halo that would be lighting up the Wei clan's night. Without the Thousand-Mile Cloud, the horse-sized pillow of opaque red fog that hovered off to the side of their campsite, they would never have made it through the mountains in only a few days.

Here in the foothills, they were nestled between two house-sized boulders and a scrubby bundle of trees. The late-summer wind was mild but unceasing, and it flowed down the mountain with a tinge of autumn chill. Their "campsite" was nothing more than a fire, a collapsed tree Yerin had dragged over for a bench, and a pair of thin blankets he'd placed on the ground.

Behind them rose the mountains he'd left behind. In front of them, the land lowered further until rolling hills spread out beneath them. Yerin called this place the Desolate Wilds, though it seemed more wild than desolate. The hills were carpeted in trees with scorch-black leaves, marred with the occasional strange-colored lights or patch of ash. The forest filled him with dread, as though he stared down into deep water with no idea what sort of monstrous creature might rise from the depths at any second.

Because there *were* creatures in those dark trees. He'd seen them.

"Before we start, if I may ask...Copper, will it help me survive down there?"

Yerin looked like someone who had lived alone in the wilderness for too long—she was thin and wiry, without an ounce of fat, and her traditional black sacred artist's robe was faded and tattered. Her hair was black as her robe and cut absolutely straight, which he suspected she did with her sword.

She was a survivor, she had been even before her master was murdered, and she looked the part. She knew what it took to make it out of a deadly wilderness alive, while he'd slept on a cloud-soft mattress since he was a child.

She shrugged one shoulder. "Going down there without Copper is like going in with a hood over your eyes. You'd lose your head without a glimpse of what buried you. Going in *with* Copper...well, at least you'll see what's eating you."

He knelt opposite her, so that their knees were almost touching. With both their backs straight, he was head and shoulders taller than she was. He slouched a little, almost on instinct—in his clan, an Unsouled who loomed over his betters would be asking for a beating.

Yerin didn't seem to notice or care. She continued, "Iron is better by miles. Your sacred arts will still be rotten, but you won't die to a stray breeze. Presuming we can find a few things tomorrow, like a covered place to sleep, we'll stay here until you hit Iron. We'll want to make you hit perfect Iron, so we can lag until end of winter. Come spring, we can move down into the trees."

Lindon's breath came a little too fast, and his stomach churned with sickening hope. He'd lived almost sixteen years yearning for Copper, and now she was saying he could reach Iron in just a few more months? It was like hearing her promise that, with a little more effort, he could sprout wings and fly around the sky like a bird.

His own *parents* were only Iron, and they'd been famous in the Wei clan when they were only a little older than him. Come spring, if he returned to Sacred Valley, how would they see him then?

Memory returned, of a vision he'd once seen: a colossal shadow wading through the mountains like a child wading through a creek, devastating the entire valley.

"Is that the soonest we can leave?" he asked, and she looked at him as though he'd proposed setting themselves on fire.

"So you know, you *can* rush to Iron, but you surely don't want to. Ruins your chances of reaching Lowgold. And the weakest sacred artist down there will be Lowgold, so even if you survived a stroll through the trees, it only takes one privileged son with a rotten temper to scatter your bones all through the trees."

"Pardon, but who is Lowgold?"

She stuck a finger at him as though threatening him with it. "You're proving my point for me. It's not a *who,* it's what you call the first rank of Gold."

"Rank?"

"I told you Gold was a wide river. The weakest Golds are Lowgold, then Highgold, and Truegold past that. The gap between each one is ten times wider than the gap between Copper and Iron, and if you were a shade quicker and two shades smarter, you'd hole up here for a handful of years until *you* hit Lowgold."

If he'd thought he was impressed before, this time his lungs froze. Gold? Even if it took him a few years, Suriel had told him he had three decades. Suddenly he didn't feel as though he were on such a tight schedule after all.

She waved a hand at him. "That's the sweetest view of events. Spine of the matter is, we're not trying to catch the tide. A year or two won't change much."

Part of that statement stuck out to Lindon like a burning bush. *We're* not trying to catch the tide. She'd included herself, as though she intended to stay with him.

That meant more to him than he was prepared to consider, carving into his heart with a sweet pain. For most of his life, even his family had only taken his side out of blood obligation. An Unsouled wasn't headed anywhere except straight into the ground, and no one wanted to travel with him on that journey.

Now, here was someone who had already fulfilled her oath—she'd taken him out of Sacred Valley safely. He'd half-expected her to walk off and leave him the second he'd finished bandaging her wounds.

But in five days, she still hadn't said a word of it.

Still kneeling, he bowed to her, pressing his fists together. "Gratitude," he said.

She flushed and rubbed the back of her neck. "Well, every path has a first step. Let's get you to Copper first. How's that Starlotus?"

He closed his eyes and visualized his madra. He could just barely feel the power trickling through his spiritual channels, which he always imagined as a dim blue-white light running throughout his body like blood running through veins. The energy pulsed in rhythm with his breath, spinning out from his core and returning after visiting his extremities.

Before this week, his core had been located in the same place as everyone else's: just below his navel, at his center of gravity, where people said the soul was located. Now, it was an inch to the right.

And to the left, it had a twin.

Both cores shone in his imagination, stretched like inflated bladders until they looked like the size of his fist. He could withdraw his madra into a core and cycle the other one, if he wanted to, but there was no point: both cores held an equal amount of the same madra. He'd cycled every night for the past five days, even using the parasite ring he'd stolen from the Heaven's Glory School, and hadn't gained an ounce of power since eating the Starlotus bud. He'd consumed one half of the flower to solidify his foundation in one core, and the other half went to the other. Now, according to Yerin, both cores had reached their capacity.

So it was time to advance.

"The flower's madra has settled down," he reported, eyes still shut. Though the Starlotus madra had gone down smoothly, his cores had still taken a few days to stop swirling like a pair of whirlpools. "They're calm, they've absorbed everything I can give them, and I'm ready."

His hands trembled on his knees, though he forced them to be still. Now that he was staring it in the face, he wondered if he was ready for Copper. He'd always thought that, by the time he reached this point, he would know more about the sacred arts and would be able to advance with confidence. Most people were following ancient instructions written in their Paths; the only Path he followed was the one he was making up as he went.

But those doubts were nothing next to the bone-deep hunger that gnawed at him. He didn't just want Copper, he *needed* it, and his momentary misgivings couldn't stop him.

And in front of him, he had a teacher more capable than anyone in Sacred Valley: a legendary Gold.

He exhaled carefully, inhaling again in accordance with his Foundation breathing technique. "I'm ready," he repeated. "What do I do now?"

"Well, you somewhat squeeze it on down. Like you're wringing water out of your clothes. Then you keep going until you're done."

He cracked one eye. "How do I do that?"

She spread her hands. "You somewhat, you know..." She made a fist. "*Squeeze* it."

He closed his eyes again and pictured one core being squeezed, as though in the grip of an imaginary hand. Nothing happened.

"That doesn't seem to have worked," he said, carefully keeping any accusation from his voice.

"Well, that's a rusty patch for you, then. You're in your own boat now."

He stared at her. "Is that all you can tell me?"

"First time I remember advancing, I was going from Copper to Iron. That puts me at about eight winters old. If I put this together when I was no bigger than a teacup, you ought to have it easy." She scowled at him. "And don't give me that look like you're trying to stab me with your eyeballs, it's not on my account that I never walked somebody through advancing to Copper before."

"Forgiveness, I was only concentrating." That wasn't *entirely* true—she was supposed to be the expert. If he knew how to advance, he'd have done it already.

Once again, he closed his eyes and pictured both his cores. Madra looped out of one like web from a spider, and he withdrew it all, drawing his power back into the core. Even with energy as faint as his, he felt it when it was gone; his limbs weakened, his aches intensified, and the cool wind gained just a little more of an edge.

He focused on his core, tightening his awareness on it, and exhaled. Breathing circulated madra, and when he had finally pushed all the air out of his lungs, his spirit stilled. He focused on that one core, shutting out physical sensations, *squeezing* with all the pressure of his will.

Nothing changed.

He took another breath, and both cores spun lazily once more. This time, he let a little power slide out from the core on the right...but instead of taking it into his madra channels, he held it around the core like a layer of cloud.

It was a simple hunch. He could control the madra freely, as long as it was outside the core. So he used that madra like a fist to clench down on the core itself.

Lindon felt the result as pressure more than pain, as though his heart were gripped in a vice. His first panicked reaction was to give up, take a deep breath, and try again. But if he breathed in, the madra would cycle, and he'd have to start over. So, ignoring the warning pressure, he squeezed harder.

A spike of pain shot through the right side of his stomach, leading to a tingling, freezing cold that danced over his skin. But now, when he visualized both cores, the one on the right seemed a little smaller...and a little brighter.

He took that breath now, letting the madra cycle through his body and calm his nerves, then he clenched down again. The pain was sharper now, the spasm longer, the cold on his skin lingering. Wind pressed even sharper against him thanks to his sweat, which flooded out as though he'd sprung a leak.

"Yeah, you've got ahold of it now," Yerin said, her excited voice close to his ear. He almost lost his concentration. "Keep ahold of it. I knew a man who stopped midway, and his organs—"

She cut off in a rustle of cloth and a whispering rasp that said she'd stood up and drawn her weapon, and Lindon's eyes *almost* opened before he forced them shut again. The core he'd compressed was fluctuating now, beating in an irregular rhythm, and it took all his concentration to wrap another layer of madra around it.

He could feel that she was right, though she'd cut off before the *important* part. He tried not to listen to her footsteps as she padded around him, facing some danger. If he left his core alone, it would go wild in his body. In the worst case, it could tear him apart from the inside.

He flexed his madra again, and the core reduced in size by another layer. He shivered as icy needles pricked him all over, this time even in the depths of his ears, under his fingernails, in the back of his eyes. He shuddered, but forced his breathing to stay steady. Though he had never followed a Path, he'd practiced his cycling technique for years. His madra didn't slip.

After the pain in his ears, he heard nothing but a high-pitched whine, though he felt the impact in the ground as something landed next to him. Once again, he focused completely on his core.

If it had been the size of his fist before, now it was only as big as Suriel's marble, and brighter. The larger core seemed hazier by comparison, less substantial, as though it were half a dream. The Copper core was brighter, more vivid. He hardly had to work at all to visualize it, floating inside him like a star.

Once he'd wrapped it more thoroughly in a tight fist of madra, he squeezed one final time. Yerin's voice came to him then, though she sounded so distant that he couldn't make out her words, and he couldn't be bothered to spare the attention anyway. His whole body stung and tingled, more painfully than before, until each of his muscles twitched. His core was resisting this time, like a nut unwilling to crack, and he had to bend all of his will and all his madra to *push*.

His core snapped down to a tiny pinprick of light, and he shuddered violently. An icy hand slapped the back of his skull, and he passed out.

He woke only an instant later, or so it seemed to him. The fire flickered with sullen red light, just as it had the last time he'd seen it, and its heat lay on him like an oppressive blanket. He began to move away, only to come to two startling discoveries.

First, as he lay sprawled out on the ground, his injuries should have been torturing him. He'd spent the last four nights snatching only the occasional handful of sleep because of the pain in his back, his ribs, his limbs. All that was gone, replaced with an unsteady weakness, as though he'd slipped into someone else's body. Despite the occasional cold tingle across his skin, just like the ones he'd sensed while advancing, he felt whole.

Second, there was something wrong with the fire. Spectral red lights drifted around the blaze in an orbit, like flames that had left their candles behind, growing in number at the center of the heat. He had to focus strangely to see the phantom campfire; it felt more like watching his core than something physical, as though he saw with his spirit instead of with his eyes.

Even when he moved his gaze away, the world was awash in color. The ground beneath him ran with veins of bright yellow as far down as he could see, each wriggling slowly like lightning trapped in jelly. He was seeing through the ground itself somehow, which gave him a dizzying impression like he was trapped on the outer membrane of an endless ocean, and he could fall through any second.

The logs in the fire sprouted phantom limbs of green that slowly blackened as they burned, and a furious red current ran beneath his own skin, as though his blood had started to glow.

He tried to sit up, but instead he curled like he'd pulled the wrong string on a puppet. After a few awkward attempts, he finally flopped one arm underneath him and pushed up, muscles trembling. He had to fight his way up to a seated position. He felt as though he'd wrung out each of his muscles like dishrags, but advancing usually left a sacred artist immobilized for a while. He'd recover soon.

Above all, the weakness was proof that he'd *made* it. He was Copper. By all reason, Copper should be the first, unremarkable step on anyone's journey, but he felt as though he'd been climbing a mountain for his entire life and only now had reached a ledge.

The thought of Copper sparked a memory, and he snapped his head up again, sparkling with excitement. If the biggest advantage of Copper was the ability to cycle vital aura from heaven and earth, that meant...

The bright ghosts of his surroundings had vanished. It was easy to lose sight of them if he wasn't focusing, as though they only existed when he held his eyes a certain way. As soon as he concentrated, looking beyond, the vivid phantoms returned.

The floating red flames in and around the campfire felt as though they *meant* heat, like they were symbols written in a language he had just learned how to read. When he realized what he was looking at, his heart leapt in pure joy.

This was fire *aura*. He'd always wondered what it looked like. This was the power that everyone absorbed and Rulers controlled.

He corrected himself before his thoughts had gone too far: out here, anyone could learn Ruler techniques. It had nothing to do with your birth. Everyone was a Ruler, and a Forger, and so on, but no one was Unsouled. The possibilities were dizzying.

He still didn't understand some basic mysteries—his family harvested light aura, not fire, but he didn't know how to spot the two, much less tell them apart—but the fact remained that he could see aura all around him. With training, he could draw the aura into his own madra, changing its nature and adding to its power.

The key to true strength lay all around him; he was awash in an infinite ocean of treasure.

He clawed for his pack, ready to write down his impressions before he forgot them. He pulled out a loosely bound bundle of yellowed papers that had once been nothing more than the technique manual for the *Heart of Twin Stars* technique. Now it was his instruction manual for the Path of Twin Stars.

As the founder of a Path, he had to make careful notes on every step. If he traveled as far down this Path as Suriel had suggested he could, his Path manuals could guide young sacred artists for generations.

When he'd finished scribbling down his thoughts—about squeezing his core, about how long it had taken him to cycle the Starlotus bud, about the fact that only one of his cores had reached Copper while the other felt the same as before—he realized the rest of the camp was absolutely quiet.

He didn't hear anything from Yerin.

In his excitement, he'd forgotten the sounds he'd heard while advancing: Yerin drawing her weapon, something landing heavily next to him.

Lindon glanced to the side, where a ragged spike of Forged green madra had been embedded into the dirt. It was longer than his finger, and judging from the noise he'd heard in addition to the shallow crater blasted in the ground, it must have impacted with significant force.

He scrambled to his feet, swaying with dizzy weakness and shivering from the cold. Something had attacked him, and he hadn't even known. In a moment, he was sure that fact would seize his heart with fear.

For now, he didn't have time to consider the fact that someone had been *inches* from killing him before he could react. There was a threat out there somewhere.

And Yerin was gone.

CHAPTER TWO

Yerin's unwelcome guest shifted around her waist, where she'd wrapped it as a belt and tied it into a great ribbon of a knot. Just as her master had shown her. The Remnant hissed, flickering with blood madra until its sullen red glow threatened to give her away.

It was responding to her anger, which had burned out of her control. She went into most fights cold—battle required focus, as her master had hammered into her, and she rarely had a problem with that. But these sniveling rats had attacked Lindon while he was advancing, showing that they had less honor than a crazed Remnant. Advancing to *Copper*, no less, which was something like attacking a sleeping baby. If she hadn't deflected that spike of Forged madra in time, she'd be alone now.

She'd walked her Path alone before. She'd shaken with fever in a cave, too weak to boil roots for soup. She'd slept in a dusty mausoleum for three days as a Remnant crouched outside, knowing that no one would save her. She'd marched through the ashes of a place that had once been her home, heading nowhere.

Her master always talked about solitude as though it was some great treasure, some tool that aided in focus and training. That was a pile of rot. He was the strongest sacred artist she'd ever met, but some things he just didn't understand.

She reached into a pocket of her robe, resting fingers on a disk of heavy gold. They wore badges in Sacred Valley, and her master had commissioned it for her in line with local customs, but she had no reason to wear it out here. No reason to keep it, either, except that her master had left it for her.

Yerin wasn't overly attached to Wei Shi Lindon; she'd only known him for a few days, and part of her still expected him to be playing some sort of twisty trick on her. She'd spent no small amount of time wondering if she should kill him and remove the danger.

But having Lindon around gave her someone to talk to, someone to help her with her bandages, someone to help keep the bloody memories and the acid-edged grief at bay. Plus, he kept a bunch of convenient odds and ends in that pack of his. And he was under her protection—like a helpless baby squirrel she'd adopted in the woods.

These cowards, whoever they were, had tried to leave her alone again. Unforgivable.

She knelt at the foot of a tree, watching Lindon stumble around next to the fire. She'd deflected the first attack aimed at him, but their ambushers hadn't tried a second. That meant they were creeping around, looking for a better angle. For an edge.

She didn't know how many of them there were—more than one, she was certain, or they wouldn't have attacked at all—but they would be trying to wrap her up in a circle.

So one of them would be walking around the wall-sized boulders that functioned as a windbreak for Yerin's camp. She gave them a slow count of a hundred, giving them plenty of time to move. The whole time, she kept her breath measured and her madra in a ready grip; if they launched another attack at Lindon, she'd deflect it with sword resonance. But no attack came.

At the count of ninety-nine, she felt something in her spirit: a brief whisper of corrosive, oily presence right where she'd expected it. Behind the largest boulder.

Madra flooded her legs as she kicked off, reaching the boulder in a blink. Her master's sword, a straight-edged plane of Forged white madra, hummed eagerly in her grip. Her guest hissed and twisted around her waist, sensing blood.

The woman behind the boulder looked even worse than Yerin had after weeks in the wilderness. She was only a few hungry days away from being a skeleton, her dark hair muddy and matted. A leather necklace of teeth hung down over dirty hide clothes that looked a size too big for her, like she'd dressed herself by robbing corpses. Her eyes widened as she saw Yerin, and she brought a shortbow up and pulled the string.

As the woman's arm straightened, she revealed a monster of green light clinging to her arm—some cross between a snake and a centipede, a tiny Remnant parasite sunk into the woman's limb. A Goldsign. So she was Lowgold, just like Yerin. No more easy battles, now that she'd left Sacred Valley behind.

A Forged green arrow materialized on the string even as the woman pulled it back, but the battle was over as soon as Yerin had drawn her sword.

Sword aura gathered around basically anything with an edge, so in her spiritual sight, Yerin's blade shone with a silver halo. She cycled madra according to the Flowing Sword technique, Enforcing the weapon like it was part of her own body.

A low hum, so deep that it was felt rather than heard, passed through the metal. Vital aura responded to the resonance, clustering around the weapon, so the silver glow grew brighter and brighter.

The blade of Yerin's master passed through bow and woman both, its madra infinitely sharp and cold, like a blade chipped from a glacier. The dirty woman's jaw dropped to her chest as she saw her bow break, and she had a second to look up like a startled rabbit. Then she recognized the pool of blood seeping from her stomach, and one hand reached up in disbelief.

Yerin snatched the green arrow from the air as it fell from the broken bow, jamming it into the woman's arm as she ran past. She'd bet her soul against a rat's tail that the woman used venomous madra. Those Paths always had ways to resist their own poison, but added to the blood loss and stomach wound...she'd die, but not so soon that Yerin had to deal with her Remnant.

She released the Flowing Sword technique, and the silver glow of the sword aura dimmed.

While the woman shrieked like a dying horse, Yerin passed like a flitting shadow from boulder to trees. The scream should beat her allies out of the bush, maybe make them stutter for a second—

Another fur-wrapped shadow unfolded from the underbrush, driving an awl straight at Yerin's chest. Before her eyes caught up, her spirit had already flared a warning, and she took the impact on the flat of her sword.

An awl was nothing better than a heavy nail set into a grip. It was meant to be driven with the full force of an Enforcement specialist to pierce armor—and, she'd suspect, to pump her full of poison.

Yerin was a skilled Enforcer, but this man had all the leverage and a better position. He'd struck a solid blow while she was running, turning momentum against her. It was a good hit.

But she had the better weapon.

Her white blade took the impact without a scratch, but the force pushed her back like the kick of an ox. She cycled her madra to her limbs, twisting in midair and landing on her feet.

For the first time, she got a clear look at her enemy. He'd done his best impression of a ragged bear, with his oily hair and beard, his hooded fur coat, and the musky stench that she smelled from ten feet away. Not a master of stealth, this one.

He held the awl in one hand, and in the other carried an axe that seemed to be half steel and half Forged madra. Its edge gleamed with a venomous green, just like the other woman's arrow, and veins of the same green penetrated the weapon's metal like a tree's roots through soil. He, too, had the same Goldsign: the centipede-snake creature bound to him, like a tiny green Remnant attached to his arm.

She gripped her sword in both hands and locked eyes with him, while he grimaced at her with black-and-yellow teeth.

She was wounded, blood trickling around her eyes and her body burning from a dozen reopened cuts. Bad as her wounds looked, her spirit was in even worse shape—every minute scrapping with this bear meant another day before she was back to peak form.

Quick fight's a good fight.

When the dying woman's scream tore the air again, Yerin swept her weapon down in an arc. She channeled madra into the Rippling Sword technique, and sword-madra blasted forward in a crescent, like a ripple of razor-thin glass.

It sliced branches off a tree, but the bandit ducked easily to the side, dodging the Striker move. He hurled his hatchet, approaching from behind with the awl. If she struck the hatchet down, she'd be exposed to his follow-up attack. He was trying to keep her on the back foot, where he'd keep her until he'd stabbed or poisoned her to death.

Which was all bright and shiny, as plans went, but she had skills beyond her advancement level. The Sword Sage wasn't known for coddling his disciple.

She slapped the hatchet back toward him, just as he'd expected. His eyes gleamed like a tiger spotting a fat pig as he brought the awl forward.

With a mental effort she'd trained every day for years, she extended her attention to the sword aura that clung to her sword. It sheathed her blade in infinite layers, dense and powerful around her master's weapon, and she struck it with her spirit like a gong.

This was the Ruler technique that had given her Path a name: the Endless Sword.

In her spiritual sight, the aura around her sword burst out in a silver storm. Everything sharp enough to cut within a dozen paces echoed the move, ringing and exploding in razor-sharp sword aura. The flying hatchet burst into dozens of unseen blades, smashing splinters of bark away from a nearby tree and cutting deep into the bandit's skin.

He stumbled and faltered, his awl dipping off-course, and she gathered sword-madra into the Goldsign that dangled over her own shoulder. The metallic sword carried her madra like a riverbank carried water, swift and smooth. It should pass through the bandit's chest and out again like the sharpest spear.

But her spirit cried a warning, and she aborted her attack to roll off to one side, whipping her blade in another Rippling Sword technique.

The wave cut a gouge into the nearest boulder, missing the *new* enemy, who had popped out of nowhere.

This man was smaller and thinner, a starving rat rather than a scavenging bear. He gripped a wooden spear in both hands, the spearhead a serpent's fang stained with what she could only assume was venom. The man had his own serpent on his arm, and the miniature Remnant snarled at her, revealing a pair of fangs in its mouth. Another Lowgold from the same Path.

Looked like somebody had sent half a sect out here to ruin her day.

She breathed deeply, cycling to hold back her anger, but that was trying to leash a dragon with a bowstring. This vermin had even less honor than she'd thought; they had the numbers and the power, and they *still* looked to murder a couple of sacred artists more than ten years their junior. In an *ambush*.

Her surroundings sharpened as she focused her anger and her spirit to a fine point. This fight was about to get bloody and rotten, and she knew it—she may have been the strongest being in Sacred Valley by a long margin, but in the real world, Lowgold practitioners like her were more common than flies on a dead dog. Skill only counted for so much against numbers.

She might even die here, in the woods on the back-end of nowhere, and her *guest* squirmed at the thought. If she did die, *it* would make sure that she took her enemies with her.

She didn't even waste a thought on getting help from Lindon. Putting him in a fight against these men would be pushing a spotted fawn to a couple of wolves.

Only a blink after he'd shown his face, the spearman lunged at her. She ran for the bear; he was still off-guard and under-armed, and letting two men catch her in a pincer attack was just begging to die.

The man dropped to avoid her stab, though her sword still bit the meat of his shoulder. But it wasn't free—his huge boot caught her on the outside of her leg.

She was using a basic Enforcement technique to strengthen her whole body with madra, but he hit hard enough to shake it. Pain flared in her thigh, and she stumbled off-balance.

If she hit the ground, she would die.

With that panicked thought, she triggered the aura in her sword. It exploded, detonating *inside* the man's shoulder, sending a spray of shredded meat into the air. He didn't even scream, collapsing on his back and writhing. His mouth flapped open and closed, as though all his air had leaked out through the hole in his shoulder.

Yerin caught herself before she joined him on the ground, but her leg moaned in red-hot pain...and her other wounds joined her in a chorus, dazing her for a critical second. She looked up to see the rat-like spearman coming at her just as blood dripped down into her eye, stinging and making her close it.

One-eyed, one-legged, all but crippled...and alone. Her rage blazed hotter, until she released a shout and staggered forward. A sacred artist lived and died on her feet.

For the first time, one of her opponents got to use a real technique.

The rat-like man grimaced and forced his spear forward. The strike was joined by half a dozen green reflections appearing out of nowhere. It was like he was striking with seven spears at once, and though six of them were made out of madra, she suspected any of them would kill her.

She filled her sword with madra, praying to the heavens that she could break all of her opponent's weapons in one hit. If she did, she lived. If she missed, she died.

Fitting that a sword artist's life would balance on a razor's edge.

Then her spirit flared in warning, and her eyes widened when she realized what it was telling her.

The fawn had thrown itself to the wolves.

●

With his pack on his back, Lindon lay belly-down on the Thousand-Mile Cloud. It sputtered and drifted, dragging him over the terrain on the pitiful trickle of madra he could muster. His Copper spirit had a noticeably greater effect, as he could move faster and farther than ever before, but he was exhausted after advancing.

He'd spent most of his madra in the last minute, drifting around the camp and planting six purple flags. He clutched the last one in his hand, urging the cloud toward Yerin and her opponent.

The screams of the dying woman still hung in the air, but Yerin and the filthy rodent with the spear were not distracted. As Lindon fed another drop of madra into the cloud and lunged toward them, they struck: the spear flashed forward, six acid-green mirror images blinking into existence around it, even as Yerin swept her white blade across.

Lindon tumbled off the cloud, resisting the urge to squeeze his eyes shut and desperately hoping that the impact from their attacks wouldn't kill him where he lay.

As a deadly cold sensation of pure terror passed over the back of his neck, he jammed the formation banner into the soil along with the last of his madra.

The White Fox boundary was kept in place by seven short banners woven from purple cloth and stitched with white script. When arranged in a circle and activated, the formation summoned aura of light and dreams in the immediate area, creating a cloud of illusions.

This was the first time he'd seen the boundary as a Copper, and it was much more impressive. With half an effort, he saw glowing aura roll in like a sunlit cloud, half-formed images shifting and twisting in its depths.

He'd placed the last banner between Yerin and her enemy, with the circle on the spearman's side. The rat-like man should be trapped at the edge of the boundary.

Lindon rolled into his back, propping himself up against his pack so he could see if his gamble had worked.

The spearman staggered back a step, his six madra-spears shattered by Yerin, his reptilian eyes flickering around. Lindon let out a relieved breath, and only then realized that he was panting—which would throw off his cycling until he restored his breathing rhythm—and covered in a light sheen of sweat. Sliding within a hair's breadth of death was more exhausting than hiking up a mountain.

Lindon turned to Yerin just in time to see her foot rushing at his face. It was gentle, as kicks went; instead of impacting with enough force to shatter his skull, her foot caught him on the side of the head and hooked him, scooping him to the side and sending him tumbling away from the Thousand-Mile Cloud.

He rolled over every root and stone on the way, sending extra spikes of pain through him, and landed with his pack digging into his spine. He stared up into scraggly leaves blowing in the wind, and it took him a long moment of disorientation to restore his breath and keep his madra cycling.

When he looked back at Yerin, she'd sent a scythe of sword-madra slicing out at waist height. The filthy man ducked so low it looked as though his bones had melted, ducking the attack, and his eyes gleamed as he swept his spear in a half-circle at the ground.

Spears of Forged green madra stabbed out wildly. One of them caught the White Fox banner, shredding the cloth. Another stabbed at Yerin, forcing her to one side, and the rat-like man coiled as though preparing to unleash his entire body's strength behind his spear.

A sick sensation hung heavy in Lindon's gut. He'd expected the boundary to do *something,* if only to slow the man down. It had been the lowest-risk move he had with a chance of working, but the most advanced sacred artist he'd ever trapped in the boundary had been an Iron. A Gold, even a "Lowgold" that Yerin mentioned, was obviously a different beast entirely. He'd tried to catch a wolf in a rabbit-snare.

Lindon ran his mind down the contents of his pack like he was running fingers along a bookshelf, trying to find the key to his situation. Yerin was wounded and visibly struggling; he needed to help somehow. His halfsilver dagger might be even more effective on a Gold than on a lesser practitioner, but he'd have to get close enough to use it. He had the feeling that the man's spear would end him before he got within ten yards. Maybe he could throw his parasite ring at the man, hoping that the halfsilver content of that device would throw the man off, but at that point he might as well be throwing rocks. Could the Thousand-Mile Cloud do anything?

As he was thinking, Yerin leaped on her one good leg. Despite her injuries and the blood dribbling past her eye, the move still looked graceful. The man brought his snake-fang spearhead up to point at Yerin, but she had already slashed out with another Striker technique.

Bright green madra gathered around his weapon, giving Lindon's Copper senses the impression of an infected wound. If Yerin was hit by one of those techniques, they wouldn't have the medicine to save her.

But he'd underestimated the Sword Sage's disciple.

Before the spearman had gathered his technique, Yerin lashed out in a wave of razor-sharp energy. It blasted down from her blade, crashing through the green power and into the ground...which was when the silver sword-arm on her back struck, sending a second identical attack into the man's skull. It sliced without resistance from his head down to his feet.

He crumpled into two halves. Lindon jerked his eyes away from the gory sight, turning to Yerin.

She didn't land so much as slam into the ground, crashing into a bush. He hurried over, heart tight with concern, slipping his pack over one arm. They were out of bandages, but he could cut his spare clothes into strips. That was assuming she only had surface wounds. If she'd broken a bone, he'd have to fashion a splint, and he had only a vague idea how to do that. And if she'd taken the man's toxic madra or an internal injury, there was nothing he could do. They'd have to risk the journey back to Sacred Valley for medical care, which would only be slightly safer than letting her die on the forest floor.

The thoughts flitted through his mind as he ran toward Yerin, fishing in his pack for a bundle of white outer robes and his halfsilver dagger. He'd found them both by the time he fell to his knees next to her, setting his tools aside to touch her with ginger hands.

Her back rose and fell, so at least she lived, but her white sword was an inch away from her outstretched hand. He couldn't help noticing how frost had already begun to gather on the nearby dried leaves, which steadily crumbled to frozen pieces. He was already a few feet away from the weapon, but he edged slightly backwards anyway.

Her skin was clammy but her pulse steady, and he could hear her breath gaining the familiar rhythm of a cycling technique. She stirred, trying to sit up, and he grabbed her shoulder to either help her or keep her from moving too much. He wasn't sure which.

"Where's the worst of it?" he asked, having decided that was the most pertinent question. If he could bandage the most severe injury, he could at least slow the rate at which she bled to death.

She grabbed him by the neck in a grip like a scorpion's claw, bringing her face close to his. Blood had matted her left eye closed, and the other was wavering and unfocused, but he stopped himself from jerking back in instinctive fear.

"Remnants," she grunted out, her other hand groping blindly in the dirt for the hilt of her sword. "Run."

The dying bandit woman's scream finally died out, leaving the clearing quiet for half a breath. Then a shrill screech cut through the silence like a snake's hiss and a teakettle's whistle at once. An acid green shape rose in the corner of his vision, from the center of the rat-like bandit's torn flesh.

Lindon didn't have a clear look at the Remnant, but he got the impression of a twisting serpentine body with insectoid claws running along the side, like a green Forged hybrid of an adder and a centipede. But he didn't waste time staring at it; he wrapped his spare robe around his hand in a few quick motions, grabbing the hilt of Yerin's sword with his newly gloved hand. He felt the cold even through three layers of cloth, but he slid it into the sheath at her side before the ice bit too sharply.

That accomplished, he shoved the robe and the half-silver dagger back into his pack, slipping one arm under Yerin's shoulder. She hissed in through gritted teeth as he lifted her, and under other circumstances he would have worried about making her internal injuries worse.

As he staggered over to the Thousand-Mile Cloud, Yerin's weight highlighting the exhaustion of advancing to Copper, he heard another of those sharp whistles rising up to the sky. A second Remnant was rising.

He glanced behind him to the first, which was even more horrible to look at than he'd imagined. Like all Remnants, it looked as though it had been painted onto the world in lines of color, though this one had a luminous yellow-green that no paint could imitate. Its head gave the impression of a snake, its body serpentine and propelled along the ground by rows of segmented insect legs. Worse, on the end of its pointed tail was a stinger.

It moved in a hideous slithering crawl in their general direction, but fortunately for them, Remnants were often disoriented as they were born. He'd seen some Remnants stand still after they were born, others drift aimlessly away into the distance, and still others go completely berserk. This one was so disoriented it looked drunk, weaving awkwardly around the dirt and leaves.

But it was still heading unmistakably toward them.

Lindon reached the rust-colored cloud in a few more steps, but each one felt as though he were walking beneath a headsman's blade. Both his cores were dim and guttering like candle-flames, but he squeezed the last bit of madra out of one as he collapsed onto the cloud, pack on his back and Yerin in his arms. They lurched down the hill, deeper into the black forest.

Yerin's breath was hot on his collar, her eyes closed and her voice shaky. "Things as...they are...I'd contend...we shouldn't stay here."

Through the trees, two bright green shapes scuttled after them.

CHAPTER THREE

Life in Sacred Valley hadn't been easy as an Unsouled, but it had at least been comfortable. He had his own home, all the food he could eat, a cozy bed...and a safe place to stay, which he'd once taken for granted. He was embarrassed by his own ignorance. If he had known how frightening the wilderness was, he'd have blessed the Shi family every night for the roof over his head.

After running from the venomous Remnants, he slid down a sloping hill on the Thousand-Mile Cloud until he'd run out of every drop of madra. Exhausting his spirit left him with a dull ache inside of him, an emptiness, as though he were made *less* by its absence. And no madra to circulate in his limbs meant that he ran out of strength quickly, hauling his pack over one shoulder and Yerin over the other.

Worse, the piping whistles of the Remnants followed them as they made it down the hill and into the black, blighted trees. Their constant presence pressed down on his mind, keeping him perched on the edge of terror. In hours, he felt as though a fire had passed through his spirit, leaving only a burnt-out husk.

When he could move no longer, he found a tree with a thick trunk and a gnarled hollow at its base. He dumped

Yerin into it, too tired to be gentle. She made no sound of complaint, only curled up among the roots with her eyes closed and breathing even. Probably cycling to improve her wounds.

Now that he thought of it, she had an Iron body. He might not have even hurt her by dumping her there. Her steel arm hung limp on her shoulder, blade dangling next to her cheek.

Lindon only wanted to collapse next to her, but the distant whistles continued. He forced his legs to carry him forward, scratching script into the dirt with the end of a stick. He extended the script all the way around the tree until Yerin was in the center of a warding circle at least fifteen feet across. Only then did he fall into the hollow next to her, digging into his pack for a stoppered clay bottle of water.

Yerin didn't open her eyes to take a drink, she simply plucked the bottle from his hand, guzzled half of its contents, and handed it back. By the time they had both drunk, only a few drops sloshed around at the bottom.

He'd resolved to find a source of fresh water when sleep took him. Even with Yerin's elbow shoving into his ribs on one side and a half-buried rock on the other, his body simply couldn't stay awake anymore.

When he woke, three rotten dogs snarled at the edge of his circle.

He jerked back against the tree, swallowing a scream. It took him a few breaths to realize that he wasn't trapped in a nightmare.

The skin of the dogs was raw, bloody red with spots of diseased black. It was stretched tight over a visible rack of ribs, and their stench soaked the air. Their eyes were scarlet as swollen blisters, and they bared shredded lips in snarls that revealed blood-caked teeth.

Like a child seeking the protection of his mother, Lindon shook Yerin's shoulder. One eye snapped open immediately, though she had to scrape dried blood away from the other with her fingernails.

Once she could fully see, she surveyed the dogs. "I called

Heaven's Glory a pack of rotten dogs, but I'd never con-
ceived they'd be quite that ugly."

As though they understood the insult, the dogs hissed
through teeth, lunging over the warding circle. Fear
stabbed Lindon's heart and he cycled madra on instinct, for
whatever good it would do them.

They stopped with only their front paws over the circle,
yowling and shuffling backwards. They lifted their claws
to avoid stepping on any of the symbols. They didn't make
the whimpering sounds of an injured dog; their howls
seemed to contain rage and resentment, as though the pain
infuriated them.

Lindon shivered, staring at the dirt just in front of their
paws. The script was written on nothing more solid than
loose forest soil, and though the dogs were avoiding direct
contact with the script, it wouldn't hold long. The dogs
didn't have to touch the symbols to scrape dirt over them,
and even the dirt might obscure the script before long.

Besides, the warding circle was meant to protect against
Remnants. Since the script had affected them more like a
screen than a fence, they must be sacred beasts...though
they looked hideous and diseased, unlike any sacred beasts
Lindon had ever heard of. Based on everything he'd been
taught, sacred beasts refined vital aura into madra inside
their bodies, and the advancement process perfected their
bodies. It made them stronger, smarter, more beautiful.

Whatever aura these beasts cultivated had corrupted
them, and he had no doubt that they would tear him to
pieces. Even if he could use his Empty Palm, he had no
idea where a canine's core was located.

"I don't want to rush you," Lindon said, eyeing the
spearheads these creatures had for teeth, "but have you
recovered at all?"

She cracked one eye. "Not gonna bleed out, but scrubbing out a couple of pups might get...sticky."

"Sticky? What makes it so *sticky?*" He was trying to stay
calm—the last thing he needed was to irritate the Gold at

his side—but these rotting dogs were prowling around the tree now, and he was sure they were looking for a weak point in the script. If he'd spaced one rune too far out, they'd rush in and pull him apart.

"You scowl when you're fearful," she observed. "Makes you look like you're gearing up for a fight."

He took deep breaths, trying to slow his heart and keep his voice from leaping up an octave. "I'd fight them if I could, but can *you?*" Despite his preparation, his voice still broke on the last word.

"Well, I'd observed that sacred beasts have been a little light on the ground the last handful of days. Spied a couple of Remnants, but nothing else. Weak and wounded as we were, we should have been hip-deep in predators before we took two steps out of the valley."

One of the dogs swept a claw at the air over the script as though scraping an invisible wall. Through his Copper sight, Lindon saw the aura the script had gathered: a circle formed from thin, tall rectangles that reminded him of paper doors. When he looked at the aura, he thought of force, impact, solidity...but rigid and thin, as though ready to break at any second. It was a pathetically thin protection against the beasts dripping blood-tinged saliva only a few feet away.

"Why weren't we, do you think?" Lindon asked, holding his tone steady.

"If we were with my master, I'd say they were scared off by his presence. But these things see me as prey for a pack. You're more like a bite they'd feed to their pups."

Lindon cleared his throat, unsure how to respond.

"Point is, they weren't scared off by us. Something drew them away."

Something impacted the tree behind them with a meaty thud, and the tree shook like a thick drum. A dog howled, but blackened leaves drifted down on top of them.

"They were drawn away," Lindon repeated, trying to focus on Yerin's words instead of the monstrous fangs. "Does that mean you can't kill them?"

She pointed with her finger and her sword-arm together. "It means they're all bunched up."

Lindon stared after her finger, where the gray pre-dawn haze was clustered thickly. He could see nothing but misty shadows beneath the trees.

But after watching for a second, he saw something move. It barely shifted, just giving him the impression of motion, but it was the size of a house.

He wasn't sure if the light finally improved enough or if his eyes finally picked out a pattern, but after a few more minutes of squinting into the haze, he saw it. Not one giant beast—an army.

The distance seethed with creatures, scurrying like ants in the grass. He could only make out their shapes; many of them looked like the rotten dogs, but others were the size of bears, or even trees. Leathery wings fluttered in the sky as something passed over the tree.

Black-stained teeth snapped shut two feet from his face, and the hound hissed out a putrid breath, but a cold weight had already settled into Lindon's gut. They weren't surrounded by three rotten beasts, but by hundreds.

After a moment of dizzy panic that felt like staring over the edge of an impossibly high cliff, Lindon's mind snapped into focus. They were safe here, at least for now. He had his pack and the treasures he'd stolen from the Heaven's Glory School, and he had a Gold on his side. There had to be some way to escape.

Yerin lifted an edge of her outer robe and scrubbed dried blood away from her scarred skin. "Don't fuss about it. Should be a way out, once I'm full up and ready to use the cloud. You should cycle too, it'll do you good."

The Thousand-Mile Cloud was actually outside the script-circle, a dense red cloud with wisps of essence drifting away from it. It would dissolve in a few days without maintenance; Lindon had been sustaining it on pure madra over the past week, just as he had with his mother's constructs back home.

He was grateful that the rotten dogs hadn't so much as glanced at the Thousand-Mile Cloud, but the unfortunate reality remained. They would have to breach the warding circle to get to the cloud, and they needed the cloud to leave.

"I'll rely on you, then," Lindon said. "If I may ask, how long will you need?"

Yerin closed her eyes again and steadied her breath before answering. "A day or thereabouts. My madra's in better shape than my body, but I should have everything stitched together come tomorrow's dawn." The loops of her red rope-belt squirmed away from the roots.

The dogs hissed again, just far enough away that he couldn't quite touch them if he extended his arm. One of them lay down on its paws, staring at him with fever-bright red eyes.

On a sudden impulse, Lindon looked past the dog to try and see its aura. It was easier the more he did it, but this time he didn't know what to make of the vital aura gathered around this monster. If identifying other types of aura was like reading simple characters, this was like trying to read a page that had been sliced to pieces and glued back together in a random order.

The aura gathered around the creature's shoulder swelled like a blister, slick and crawling black. This aura felt like death and decay, like a maggot's corpse. The deep purple aura around the dog's ribs was stringy and muscular, like roots or snakes, and it somehow gave off the impression of chains held in powerful tension. Deep red aura dripped from the hound's mouth, and Lindon could practically smell the coppery tang of blood.

He let the vision fade, thinking. He'd heard of blood madra, which supposedly held all sorts of sinister powers over living bodies, so he assumed that's what was running from the dog's jaws. But what was the rest? If he had to give a name to the bulb over the shoulder, he'd call it "death aura," but that was based solely on the feeling it gave him. He'd never heard of death madra or any aura of death, and he wasn't entirely sure what such a power would *do*. Likewise, he had no clue what his mother would call the tight aura chains. Connection aura? Binding aura?

There were more aspects of vital aura surrounding the dog than just those, and the unity of all those different powers in one body meant *something* significant. He just wasn't sure what.

But it might be the clue that let them out of here, so he meditated on it. Cycling didn't take much of his attention, as he didn't have to pull aura from the atmosphere and could focus solely on his own madra. He retrieved the parasite ring from his pocket, slipping the scripted circle of twisted halfsilver onto his finger.

Instantly, his madra turned sluggish, as though his madra channels had all halved in width. He had to force his madra to cycle, pushing it through the pattern described in his *Heart of Twin Stars* manual as though forcing syrup through a narrow tube.

It was twice as hard to cycle with the parasite ring on, but the exercise was supposed to strengthen his spirit twice as fast. He had just reached Copper, but that didn't mean he had time to rest. It was the opposite, as he saw it. He was years behind every sacred artist in his clan, so he had to work harder than anyone else to catch up.

Though it was harder now, cycling still didn't take much of his attention. It was a difficult task, but not a complicated one. His mind was free to ponder the mystery of the hideous sacred beasts with twisted auras.

As the day crept on, with dogs snapping and growling every few minutes, a new concern revealed itself: thirst. By late afternoon, he and Yerin had finished the last of the pathetic handful of water remaining in his bottle, and he had become painfully thirsty.

It was there that he missed his home so much that it hurt. He hadn't slept a full night since leaving Sacred Valley, he was only feet away from monsters held back by nothing more than a flimsy, invisible barrier, his entire body was cramped by a night crammed between rocks and roots, and the stress was wearing on his mind. Back home, no matter how badly the other members of his clan thought of him, at least he had all the water he could drink. And tea at every major meal. He could taste the flowery scent of his mother's tea, could even hear the whistle of the kettle...

His eyes snapped open at the same time as Yerin's, and this time the revolting appearance of the dogs didn't catch his attention. He craned his neck to the left, ignoring the dark shapes slithering through the bushes, until he saw it. A bright green shadow appeared under the afternoon sunlight, waving the claws of a centipede in the air and undulating like a snake.

The Remnants had found them.

Yerin braced herself on the trunk as she wobbled to her feet.

"It's nothing to worry about," Lindon said, trying to reassure them both. "The circle is intended to protect us from Remnants, so it should work even better against them than against the dogs."

Yerin limbered up her right shoulder, wincing as though it pained her. "Yep. They're not so strong as the dogs." She drew her pale white blade, and this time Lindon noticed the icy, razor-edged aura that clustered around the weapon so dense that he could barely see the sword itself. "But they're smarter."

He understood in an instant why she was concerned. The dogs hadn't left them alone because they *couldn't* break the circle, but because they didn't know how. These were the Remnants of a couple of Lowgolds—they would be stronger and smarter than any spirits Lindon had seen in Sacred Valley.

The circle might stop them for a while, but after enough time, the Remnants would toss some dirt over it. Lindon pushed himself, slipping off the parasite ring and gripping his halfsilver dagger instead. He'd withdrawn the weapon hours before, comforting himself with the thought that he could protect himself if the dogs managed to break through.

He looked past Yerin, deeper into the scene, trying to catch a glimpse of the vital aura around the Remnants. But he was sidetracked, staring at Yerin's waist. Or, more accurately, at her belt.

He'd known it was some sort of construct Forged from red madra, and had wondered if she wore it as some kind of fashion on the outside. Maybe sacred artists in the rest of the world distinguished themselves with clothes made of Forged madra, instead of the badges.

But looking at it now...it was a dense rope of congealed red power, identical to the aura dripping from the dog's mouth but a thousand times more potent. He could practically *taste* the blood coming off of it, and it made him want to vomit. Visions of slaughter, of an army's worth of corpses, filled his vision.

How could she wear that? It was like having a river of blood wrapped around yourself.

Lindon retched, as suddenly as though someone had punched him in the gut, but nothing came up. He was glad for that, not only because he didn't have the water to spare, but because the sudden impact of the motion knocked him out of his Copper vision.

Yerin watched him from beneath her straight black hair, eyes understanding. "Knew we'd come to this bridge eventually, but let's cross it later. Agree?"

Lindon refocused and steadied his knife and his breathing both. "No, that's not necessary. It's none of my concern, and I apologize if I've given offense."

She watched him for a second longer, then hefted her white sword and turned back to the advancing Remnants. "We'll talk," she said.

Then the acidic green Remnants were there, pulling themselves along on their centipede legs. The rotten dogs turned their tails to Lindon and hissed, lowering themselves as though preparing to leap and attack.

In response, the two Remnants made the motion of snapping their jaws open and shut, but there was no sound. They might as well have been the shadows of serpents biting at nothing. Afterwards, they did make a cry: the same whistling teakettle noise that had pursued Yerin and Lindon since their camp.

Lindon's spirits rose. *This* was something he hadn't considered; for some reason, he'd assumed the Remnants and the dogs would work together to breach the circle and devour the humans.

Only then did he realize how ridiculous that would be. One pack of predators didn't share prey with another. They would fight each other first, and in the chaos the humans might escape.

Some of the rotten beasts haunting the distant forest let out a chorus of growls. Another pair of corrupted dogs padded out of the underbrush, then another.

His optimism vanished, and Yerin's grip tightened on her sword. If the beasts joined together, it wouldn't be a fight with the Remnants so much as a brief extermination.

Turning from Yerin, he focused on aura again. "Allow me to break the circle," he said. "When I do, you can keep them off us, and I'll get to the cloud."

Her back was pressed against his, and he felt her nod. The area in front of him was clear, and he kept one eye on the impending battle between Remnants and rotten dogs. As he did, he slid closer to the script.

There was no reason they couldn't leap over the circle, leaving it intact—it wouldn't stop them. But it *would* affect any madra from Yerin used while it was active. If she tried to use a Striker technique from within the script, its power would be weakened. Maybe to the point of complete uselessness. And if she drew power into herself as an Enforcer, that power would be dispersed as she stepped over the circle.

In all, it was better to disperse the script before it became a trap for *them*. But he still felt like he was cutting a hole in his own boat as he slid even closer.

When the vital aura around the rotten beasts flared up like dark fire suddenly fed dry timber, he grew sick. Their auras swelled, growing twice as dense and two or three times as large. Somehow, they were growing more powerful.

Then he realized that *every* aura had inflated in the same way.

The world was awash in a chaos of color beneath his Copper vision, as the veins of yellow in the earth and the flows of green in the grass flared brighter...and then bent, like tree branches pressed down by a strong wind. The vital aura drained off in a phantom river, pouring away from its source, streaming deeper into the forest.

The flow looked like a rainbow river, and it left the world feeling dry and empty in its wake.

Every monster bolted. The Remnants left first, burbling and whistling as they followed the flow of the vital aura. The rotten dogs had an instant of confusion, in which they turned from their trapped prey to the rushing light, visibly torn. Finally, one of them gave a guttural bark, and all of them tore off. Even the dogs farther away from the warding circle followed, quickly overtaking the Remnants.

In the background, amidst the trees and undergrowth, the bigger rotten beasts left. They ran from the warded tree like they were fleeing a burning building, and in three breaths Lindon and Yerin were alone.

Lindon watched the physical world again, trading glances with Yerin. "You don't happen to know what that was, do you?" Lindon asked hesitantly.

"You're asking me, but who am I supposed to ask?" She stood with her white sword held forgotten in one hand, staring into the distance.

Now that the danger was over, Lindon's whole body went slack, and he leaned against the tree, panting. "Were they scared away? Is there something worse coming?"

Yerin gave him a look of surprise. "What? No, it's plain to see what happened to the beasts. They follow vital aura, so they followed it away. Stone simple. But I'm coming up

empty on what makes aura do *that*. Like it gathered together and then rushed off in a blink. Look; I don't know that
I've ever seen vital aura so thin on the ground."

Lindon looked and found that she was right, though that
came as no surprise. The world in his Copper vision was dim,
as though the scene had been painted in washed-out colors.
"How is that possible?" As he'd been taught, vital aura was like
the madra of the natural world. It took on different aspects
as it moved through the heavens and the earth, though it was
all connected. Even when you harvested aura and cycled it
into your madra, that was like taking a cup of water from the
ocean. Sooner or later, it would return to the source.

Lindon had never seen the ocean, but he'd read stories.
This struck him as though the tide had left *completely*, leaving the shore bare and dry.

Yerin sheathed her sword and walked casually across his
warding circle, not bothering to push the day's worth of
dirt away from her tattered outer robe. "Scripts can gather
up a bunch of vital aura, not considering aspects. Or push
it away, sometimes. But if a script is doing this...I'd contend
it's ten miles across, engraved in bedrock, and powered by
ten thousand Remnants."

Lindon didn't question it further. Whatever the event had
been, it had saved them from having to fight their way out of
an army of monsters. He seized his pack and hurried over to
the Thousand-Mile Cloud. There hadn't been time for him to
recover much madra, and he wasn't confident of his ability to
fly it for any length of time or at any great speed.

"How has your spirit recovered?" Lindon asked, hoping
she'd be able to feed power to the cloud.

She hopped up and straddled the front of the cloud as
though mounting a horse. "I'm not bursting at the seams,
but I'm well enough to ride this pony." She patted the cloud
behind her. "Come on up."

Lindon knelt first, running his hand along the side of the
cloud. As he'd expected, the cloud was slightly smaller than
it had been the previous day, its sides wispier. One day of

missed maintenance wouldn't affect its performance much, but one weed wouldn't overrun a garden either. It was better to take care of the problem while it was small than let it grow larger.

He let his pure madra flow into the construct, feeling it seized by the script at the cloud's center. Madra pulled from his weaker core, and there was a slight delay as the construct processed the pure madra and used it to nourish its Forged cloud madra.

Like a plant growing a thousand times faster, the cloud grew thicker and perhaps half an inch larger. He even thought it may have bobbed higher, though that could have been his imagination.

The effort drained that core dry, as it had been mostly exhausted already, but he switched to the other and climbed up behind Yerin.

"You're a fussy one," she noted.

"I've always found that a little work up front makes things easier later on," he said, climbing onto the cloud and securing his pack between them.

He hadn't quite finished when she kicked the cloud up to speed, sending him lurching back and grabbing onto her shoulders for support.

"I think you may have seen hard work sometime in the past," Yerin called back, "but you never came close enough to shake its hand."

She blasted through the forest, faster than they had usually gone on their way down from Mount Samara, black-leaved tree branches whipping by Lindon's ear. He leaned down behind Yerin so her Iron body could protect him, though her small back offered little shelter.

Only once he'd adapted to the speed did he recognize their direction. "Apologies, but...are we *chasing* the monsters?"

Branches whipped her as they passed by, but she ignored him as though they were nothing more than a gentle breeze. "Aura's heading this way for a reason. May as well find out where that is."

"We know one thing about where it's headed: there's an army of monsters there. That we know."

He felt her laugh. "Where did we leave the guy who spilled blood to leave the only home he'd ever known? You're weak, but I didn't suppose you were a coward."

That prickled his pride, and he straightened. A foolish move, as he immediately took a branch to the face.

Spitting out leaves that tasted of copper and rotten vegetables, he responded. "I'm not saying I won't go, I'm saying I'd like to be somewhat cautious."

"Oh, I'll be cautious." She steered the cloud to leap over a bush, rolling down a small hill as he clung to her arms for support. "Somewhat."

CHAPTER FOUR

In the first strike, she exterminated humanity.

Suriel's weapon activated as she whipped it down. It expanded in a microsecond, expanding from a meter-long bar of blue steel into a skeleton of blue metal containing a web of light. It looked like a bare tree, each of its branches arcing with power.

While it was sealed, Suriel called her weapon a sword. Now that it was released, the weapon regained its identity as Suriel's Razor.

It had been handed down to her from her predecessor, along with the identity of Suriel, the Sixth Judge of the Abidan Court. More than a tool for destruction, the Razor was meant as an instrument of healing. An infinitely complex, incalculably powerful scalpel.

Her mind ran along its familiar pathways even as she struck. First, she isolated the bloodline she intended to target. That feature was intended to remove pests in a home or a strain of virus in a body, but she could just as easily expand her focus.

To mankind. They were corrupted now, fused to and altered by the same chaos that destroyed their world.

Once her target was selected, she simply provided the energy, and the Razor did the rest. The Mantle of Suriel, a river of raging white flame that hung from her back like a cape, rolled with power as it drew on the Way. She funneled that power to her weapon, which flashed so brightly they would see it on the surface of the burning planet, kilometers beneath her.

Millions of lights blinked into existence all through the atmosphere, a blanket of tiny stars. Each light flashed, spearing down to the surface, and then was gone.

Her connection to the Way slackened immediately, like a sudden flicker of weightlessness in the center of her stomach. Humans anchored a world, their lives and their minds tying it to the Way, and when they were gone...chaos reigned. She had cut this world adrift.

[Targets eliminated,] her Presence informed her, the voice feminine and impersonal inside her mind. [Ninety-nine-point-eight percent population reduction. Proceed with manual elimination?]

In her vision, points of green ignited all over Harrow, indicating those that had survived her purge. These were the scraps that remained pure, even with their world corrupted. The last remnant of Harrow's population.

Abidan regulations stipulated that she complete the elimination, as the chaos could infect survivors at any time, but she was Suriel. She had fought her way to one of the highest positions in existence in order to save the lives that couldn't be saved.

She denied her Presence's request.

All told, there were two million, one hundred six thousand, three hundred and forty-four survivors scattered all over the dying planet. A huge number of lives, but only a speck of dust next to the number she'd just killed. Days ago, there had been five billion people on this planet. After the violent merge of Limit and Harrow, only twenty percent of the population had survived. Now? A scarce fraction, a handful of sand, easily swept away.

A weight settled onto her spirit, another slab of lead in a tower that was growing too high to manage. She knew the elimination was necessary, but she had still taken *so many* lives. How many had she killed now?

Her Presence could tell her, but she didn't ask.

The previous Suriel, her predecessor, had not died in the line of duty. He'd passed the Mantle and Razor on to her when they grew too heavy for him, and then he'd walked away. He lived the life of a mortal now, his power forcibly veiled. She hadn't heard from him in millennia.

The things he'd done in the name of his office had burdened him, broken him, and he was the Phoenix. His job was to *save* lives, not to take them. How much heavier was the weight borne by Razael, the Wolf?

Or Ozriel, the Reaper?

The world's problems had not ended with the destruction of mankind. If they had, the Reaper's job would not be necessary. Anyone with the power of an Abidan Judge were capable of eliminating a planet's worth of people, and most Iterations only had a single inhabited planet.

Beneath where she floated, high in the outer atmosphere, the planet rolled in visible turmoil. Seas appeared and disappeared, caught between Limit and Harrow, continents flickered and boiled as though trying to decide on a shape, cities crumbled to dust and were rebuilt in seconds. Clouds spun in rapid circles, taken by chaotic winds, and fire raged across such a vast territory that it was visible from space.

Now, the difficult and painstaking part of her task began.

Gadrael, a compact and muscular man with dusky blue skin and tight-packed horns instead of hair, hovered nearby. His arms were folded so that the black circle on his forearm, the Shield of Gadrael, was pointed out. He wore the same liquid-smooth white armor as she did, and a Judge's Mantle burned behind him as well.

He watched the world beneath him die without the slightest crack in expression. "Quarantine protocols will remain in effect for approximately six months Harrow time, after which my barriers will vent all fragments into the void and dissolve."

The role of the Reaper was to eliminate a world *without* leaving such fragments behind, which could give birth to the most dangerous elements in existence. The best she could do was a messy approximation.

"Acknowledged." She still didn't leave.

She had six months to save as many untainted lives as she could.

Of course, that was Harrow time, which was notoriously unstable. This world had drifted from the Way, which governed the proper flow of time. She felt as though she'd been here for minutes, but another world may have seen days pass.

Ozriel could have done this in moments, but he was gone. For the first time, she felt a hint of personal resentment for that.

"After this *reprieve*, Makiel expects you to throw your full effort into the search for Ozriel. He wants results within a standard decade."

Suriel turned to him, temper hot. Calling the power of the Way both demanded and produced inhuman self-control, but Gadrael was testing hers. Her Razor thrummed in her hand, sparking and hot.

"Do I have autonomy in this matter?" she asked coldly.

He had to see what she was doing, but he nodded once. "You do."

Everything about her blazed as she flexed her power—hair emerald, eyes purple, Mantle and armor white, Razor a flickering blue. She burned with the colors of a celestial glacier, until even Gadrael had to conjure barriers over his eyes.

"Then this falls under the purview of the Sixth Division, not the Second. If you interfere before I have finished my operation, I will consider you to have violated the Pact and take action accordingly. Let it be witnessed under the Way."

She couldn't kill him, as he may have been the hardest man in all existence to actually destroy, but there were any number of ways one Judge could make life difficult for another. Schisms among the Court of Seven were not common, but they were known to happen. Suriel would not risk the stability of the Abidan on a personal vendetta, but Gadrael—and by extension, Makiel—were threatening her authority.

If she allowed that to happen, she would not be worthy to remain Suriel.

A curtain of rich, layered blue tore open on the starry canvas behind Gadrael, and he stepped back into it, arms still crossed. "Six months," he said, "then you find the Reaper. We have set aside Iteration two-thirteen as a quarantine zone for your infected, so bypass Sector Control. A channel will be open for you."

Makiel. He had known she would never leave the survivors, and had planned accordingly. Even before she'd come here, he had known.

The Way zipped closed, and Gadrael vanished.

[Four hundred sixty-two Grade Six anomalies and counting,] her Presence said. [Pursuit recommended before expansion threshold is reached.]

Suriel set thoughts of Gadrael aside. He was a loyal dog, collared and leashed, and she would gain nothing from a conflict with him. Makiel was the one writing the script, and his plans could span eons. She had to meet him face-to-face.

But first, she had a job to do.

A world divorced from the Way gave birth to chaotic distortions. These were nightmarish monsters, entities that strained the rules of existence. If Harrow was allowed to fester over the next half a year, it could give birth to thousands of these abominations. Once they entered the void, they would drift, until even Makiel couldn't predict where they would emerge.

She had to destroy them now. At the same time, she had to reach as many of the two million survivors as she could, transporting them to a Pioneer world. It wouldn't be as stable or as nurturing as a full Iteration, but it should keep them alive.

On the north pole, a black spire shattered the ice, shooting thousands of kilometers into space until it stood out like a rigid hair against the surface of the planet. A featureless black tower, an obelisk standing so tall it shouldn't be able to physically support itself. An anomaly.

Suriel gripped her Razor and blasted forward.

Like a dying animal, a world was most vicious at its end.

⬢

As Lindon hurtled through the blackened forest on the Thousand-Mile Cloud, chasing after a legion of monsters, he contemplated their greatest danger: thirst.

They flew for the rest of the first day and past dawn of the second, and Yerin skirted every Remnant or rotten beast they encountered. But they had no more water, and the few times they stopped at a likely pond or creek, they found the surface stinking and corrupt.

Whatever blight produced the black, rotten trees and the twisted dogs, it extended to the water. They didn't need to taste it to know it was poison.

Before long, Lindon's head pounded and his throat burned so that he could hardly talk. It frightened him how quickly he'd weakened without water.

So when the trees parted to show a pyramid in the distance, Lindon's first feeling was not a call to adventure or a sense of danger, but a heavy relief. A structure meant people, and people would have water.

When Yerin slowed the cloud at the sight, Lindon wanted-ed to strangle her.

She choked out a word, swallowed, and tried again. Her words were simple and quiet, as though she meant to save water by speaking as little as possible. "That's it. Headed there."

Between the thirst, the lack of sleep, and the tension of the past few days, Lindon was having trouble thinking past the possibility of food, water, and shelter. He grunted something that sounded like "What?"

Yerin stabbed her finger at the pyramid. "*Aura.*"

With an effort that felt like crossing his eyes, Lindon focused on the aura around the pyramid. The edifice stood as high as Elder Whisper's tower back in Sacred Valley and a thousand times wider at the base, but it was assembled from layers of house-sized stone blocks. It was brown as mud, its first few layers obscured by black trees, but the visible portion was enough to dominate the landscape like a mountain jutting out of a field.

A rainbow of vital aura rose over it, spiraling down into the structure like a narrow cyclone. The aura from miles around had been drawn here, which meant...

He finally caught up with Yerin's observation. If the aura was drawn here, then those trees at the foot of the pyramid would be swarming with Remnants and twisted beasts.

He nodded to show that he understood, even as she took the cloud a little higher. The cloud was meant to skim over the ground rather than fly, and it started to struggle at about ten feet above the earth. At fifteen, it stopped entirely, and Yerin's face tightened in focus as she held them there.

From their new vantage point, they surveyed the land ahead of them. Two things stood out immediately.

First, while they couldn't see any sacred beasts through the canopy, there *was* something swarming around the pyramid: people. Lindon glimpsed a distant crowd, the peak of a few tents, and even a wagon rumbling across a clearing. These people must hold the structure against the Remnants and sacred beasts. Maybe the pyramid was their home, and they were drawing in aura for some purpose.

But Lindon couldn't consider that for long, because the second feature of the landscape had snared his attention: a wide lake, bright as sapphires, just south of the pyramid. He could only see the corner of it through the trees, but it was obviously not as tainted as the rest of the water around. His throat convulsed involuntarily at the sight.

"We have to get there," Lindon croaked.

Yerin didn't say anything to agree, she just pushed the cloud to its highest speed and slammed back into the ground, dashing through the trees at reckless speed. For once, Lindon didn't mind that he was almost sent hurtling off the back of the construct. He added his own trickle of madra to the cloud, hoping that it might coax a little extra speed out of their mount.

It wasn't entirely a surprise when they crested a hill and ran straight into a slaughter.

Lindon had long expected to catch up to the host of twisted beasts, and he'd smelled the heavy scent of blood even before they'd reached this hill. But he still wasn't prepared for the field of torn, dismembered, and disassembled creatures strewn over the ground.

For what must have been a mile across and many miles wide, the black forest had been cleared. Stumpy logs dotted the ground here and there, and the grass must have been lush before some battle mulched the soil. The people camped at the base of the pyramid would have wanted a clear perimeter, so they cleared the trees so that anything advancing on them would be visible. They posted guards, obviously waiting for any Remnants and sacred beasts to attack.

And when that horde of creatures had rushed at them, the guards had turned this field into a butcher's shed.

Half of a corrupted bear-sized beast hung from a slowly dissipating Forged spear. A pack of six rotten dogs had been blown apart, bodies strewn in pieces around a fresh crater. A pile of glowing green debris marked the death-place of one of those insectoid snakes that had been stalking Lindon and Yerin; one centipede leg was still scratching at the bloody mud even as motes of green essence drifted away from it. Similar scenes of destruction marred every step for a mile.

Across the clearing, a line of sacred artists stood in front of a low wall of spiked wooden logs. Even at a distance, Lindon could tell they were powerful.

There was a unique confidence, almost arrogance, in highly advanced sacred artists. The Patriarch of the Wei clan had carried himself like a lion among cats, and Yerin spoke as though she was destined to win and her enemies had already lost.

The warriors against the wall moved with the same awareness of their own superiority. One figure, carrying a huge hammer on its back, knelt to rifle through corpses as though sacred beasts may have held something valuable. A group of people carrying hook-curved sickles took turns kicking a rotten dog to each other. It was the size of a full-grown wolf, but the sacred artists kept it in the air as though it weighed no more than a leather ball. The twisted hound turned in midair, trying to bite each new human, but a foot always caught it in the side and sent it sailing away.

Someone in blue-and-white robes hung tucked between the wooden spikes, lounging at his ease, with something that appeared to be a bottle clutched in one hand. Yellow hair—possibly a wig—hung down over the wall. A figure in darker blue casually spun a spear in elaborate loops, the spearhead catching the light more brightly than steel should account for.

Lindon almost missed the movement, as it appeared just as relaxed and natural as the ones that preceded it. One second the blue-clad sacred artist was spinning the spear, and the next second he whipped the spear in Lindon's direction.

The spear didn't actually go flying through the air, but the *light* did. A Striker technique, Lindon realized instantly, but too late for him to do anything about it. Silver-white light the width of a finger screamed through the air, blasting for their Thousand-Mile Cloud.

Even Yerin was caught off-guard, judging by the way she jerked backward, but she still responded as befit a Gold. The bladed arm that hung over her shoulder flickered forward, catching the light. It slammed into the flat of her sword, deflecting slightly to the side as he'd seen her do with beams of Heaven's Glory madra.

With Heaven's Glory, though, there had been heat as a byproduct. It would have scorched him. This time, he felt no warmth from the light passing nearby...but a slit appeared in the sleeve of his outer robe, as though someone had sliced a razor across his arm and narrowly missed skin.

"Die and rot!" Yerin shouted, and driven by her Iron lungs, the sheer volume of it pounded Lindon's skull. He winced and stuck fingers in his ears before the next words. "You got a grudge with me, you come out and draw swords like a sacred artist."

The spear-spinning figure froze, then vanished. When it reappeared, it had moved close enough that Lindon could make out some detail: the spear artist in blue robes was a tall man with an even taller spear. His hair stood straight up as though he'd frozen it in sharp waves, and he rubbed the back of his neck with his free hand.

"You have my apologies, new friend. We've seen no one but monsters come from the west." He paused, then added. "From a distance, anyone would mistake your cloud for a Remnant. Take that into consideration and forgive me, would you?"

He clapped his hands together in what Lindon took as an apology, though he was still holding his spear between his palms.

Yerin hopped off the cloud, gesturing to Lindon. "I'm hauling a Copper," she said. Her voice was still hoarse from thirst, but anger lent her words strength. "You nick me with your spear and I'll survive, but how'd you apologize if you gutted a junior?"

The spearman had walked closer, and now Lindon could make out the evident surprise on his face. "Never seen a Copper so big." The stranger surveyed Lindon frankly, then turned back to Yerin. "Is he, eh…" He tapped the side of his skull.

Yerin stood absolutely straight, steel arm poised over her head like a scorpion's tail, one hand on her sword and her tattered robe blowing in the gentle wind. "What do they call you?" she asked.

The man in blue tucked his spear under one arm in a practiced motion, bending at the waist. "I am Jai Sen, of the Jai clan whose honor echoes in every corner of the Blackflame Empire. To repay the insult I have caused you and your junior, I would take responsibility for guiding you through the camp of our Five Factions Alliance."

"Five Factions?" Yerin asked, but Lindon had joined her by then, with pack on his back and Thousand-Mile Cloud drifting behind him.

"Water," he said, and Yerin pointed to him.

"He's right," she said. "Water."

Jai Sen patted at the cloth wrap that belted his waist. "Ah, forgive me. There's no drinkable water for a dozen miles outside the Purelake. I should have considered that you'd be thirsty." He pulled a stoppered waterskin out of his wrap and laughed. "Half a minute into our acquaintance, and I'm already a bad host. Forgive—"

Yerin had already snatched the skin from his hand. She guzzled it down, spilling water over her chin, and Lindon suddenly had the crazed, suicidal idea to jump for her and try to wrestle the water away.

But she tossed the half-full skin to him, breathing heavily, and he had scarcely caught it before squeezing it into his mouth. It tasted stale and musty, as though the water had been wrung from the fur of a wet dog, but he didn't care. The relief as water cut through the desert of his throat was like shade on a hot day.

He had only taken one swallow before he choked, doubled over coughing, and had to wait until he recovered his breath to continue drinking. He finished the contents in seconds and bowed, presenting the empty skin back to Jai Sen. He would have thanked the man, but he didn't trust his own speech.

Jai Sen eyed him with interest. "Clearly, you have been away a long time. Where did you come from, I wonder?"

"Our home lies to the west," Lindon began, his voice still rough, but Yerin cut him off.

"We're from beyond the Wilds," she said. "We have no blood with you or your enemies."

Jai Sen waved that away as though it hadn't been what he meant at all, but he also looked relieved. "There's no concern of that, none at all. The only enemies of the Jai clan are monsters and tyrants, and even the blind can see that you are an innocent and intrepid adventurer." His smile included both of them, but Lindon noticed that his words did not.

"Gratitude, honored Jai Sen, for your generosity," Lindon said, to improve his image in the eyes of this stranger. "The Jai clan must be great indeed, to defend their home from such an army of beasts."

Sen smiled proudly, straightening up and planting his spear in the ground. "You have a good eye, little brother. The Jai clan is not the only faction in the Alliance camp, but we have defended this land as though it was our own for hundreds of years. Since the Ruins rose and the dread-beasts crash every day like the waves of the sea, the Jai clan has slain more than any other."

Yerin shifted her blood-red belt. "We're fresh across the border, Sen. Heard no whispers or mentions of these Ruins, though I think we've met your dreadbeasts." She kicked the severed head of a dog so far that it arced through the air and over a hill. Lindon winced and looked away, though Sen didn't seem to notice.

"*Jai Sen*, if you please," he said. "I'm a blood member of the clan. It would be my honor to explain the history of the Transcendent Ruins to you, sister."

"Yerin," she said simply.

"And you, little brother?"

"This one is Wei Shi Lindon," he said, bowing with both fists pressed together. "Jai Sen's kindness to humble strangers is an honor to his family and a credit to his clan."

The blue-clad spearman laughed out loud and clapped Lindon on the back. "If you keep talking like that, Wei Shi Lindon, I'll have to keep you around."

"If it pleases you, you may call this one Lindon, as his family does."

Jai Sen looked surprised for a moment, then sympathetic. He squeezed Lindon's shoulder with one hand. "They'll take you back someday, little brother."

It seemed the older man had come to some awkward conclusion, but before Lindon could clarify, a hand on his back shoved him forward.

"Trot," Yerin said, including Jai Sen with a glance. "This isn't where we want to rest."

The smell of blood and worse was beginning to choke Lindon, underscored by the stranger scents of decaying Remnants. He turned to give her a grateful look, but she wasn't watching him. Her eyes had landed on the other sacred artists.

Most of the strangers were looking in their direction with interest, and a few began to drift toward them.

Remembering how powerful they were, a chill rippled down Lindon's spine, but he reminded himself not to be a coward. He couldn't let people of this level intimidate him; his goal was much farther away. These shouldn't be frightening enough to discourage him.

But judging by Yerin's gaze, she wanted to avoid a meeting even more than he did.

Jai Sen strode forward, oblivious to her wariness or pretending to be so. "Please don't be offended if I assume you know nothing about the Desolate Ruins."

The blocky pyramid loomed over them, blocking out light, and it looked even more ominous in his Copper sight.

"That would not offend us," Lindon said.

"Only a week ago, this was nothing but a minor outpost of the Purelake Temple. Don't trust your eyes," he said, sweeping an arm out to include the wooden walls and the crowds of people Lindon could see inside. "All that you see before you was constructed on the spot by valiant sacred artists of the Wilds. It's amazing what we can accomplish when we unite, as the Grand Patriarch of our clan once believed."

Yerin stabbed a finger at the pyramid. "You built *that?*"

Jai Sen gave a sheepish laugh. "No, naturally not. Those are the Transcendent Ruins, built by masters ancient beyond memory. No living sacred artists could construct something like that these days. But as impressive as it is to the naked eye, the truth will set your minds *ablaze*."

He turned to walk backwards, bending over so that he was on an eye level with Yerin. Lindon had to skip a step so the man's spiked hair didn't take him in the eye, and that close he could see that the hair actually seemed metallic; it must be the physical change that came upon artists as they rose to Gold, like Yerin's extra limb.

"Seven or eight days ago, a team of Fishers were working the Purelake in the gray light of early morning. As dawn broke, the lake began to tremble like a bowl in unsteady hands. The waves grew until they tossed the Fisher boat about, and it took all the strength of a Lowgold and a Highgold working together to bring the craft ashore.

"Only, when their feet touched the ground, they learned that their troubles were not over. The earth shook and the land pitched more violently than the water! They ran for help, as Fishers tend to do, when the trees split apart and the Ruins burst into the sky!" He spun and presented the top of the structure as proudly as if he were personally responsible for its appearance. "Last week, the horizon was clear. Now, the power and reputation of the Transcendent Ruins calls sacred artists from all over the Wilds."

Now that Lindon looked for it, he could make out chunks of soil clinging to the tiered pyramid. Many of them still had grass attached, and he thought he saw the base of an uprooted tree.

If he could tell what they were at this distance, those patches must be enormous. Either someone had driven carts full of earth up to deceive gullible newcomers, or Jai Sen might be telling the truth.

Their guide was still watching Yerin for signs of a reaction, and his smile widened as she skipped a step, her eyes locked on the Ruins. Lindon was impressed by her resistance; he was afraid his own eyes had grown wider than teacups.

Before he could say something admiring the tale, Yerin spoke. "Seven days before now, did you say?"

He laughed and turned back around to face forward as he walked, holding his spear casually across his shoulders. "Some say seven, some say eight. I myself only arrived three dawns ago, so I can't stake my honor on the time. But I've heard the story from enough trustworthy sources that it must be true."

By this time, they had reached the wall of sharpened wooden logs. This close, Lindon could appreciate how large each trunk really was; it would take two men his size linking hands to wrap arms around one log. And these had been cut, measured, sharpened, and placed in the last week.

He couldn't help but admire what an army of Golds could accomplish. If Sacred Valley had such a force of workers, what might they have built?

In the front of the wall was a wide opening with wagon-tracks worn in the dirt. Lindon supposed it must function as the main gate, as the loose group of young sacred artists clustered around it must serve as guards.

The youngest looked around Lindon's age, about fifteen or sixteen, while the oldest must have been a peer with Jai Sen in his second decade. There were six in total, three men and three women, and they looked like the types of rough brawlers Lindon imagined just *might* attack complete strangers.

They each wore a hide cloak with the head still on, and from the diseased-looking skins, Lindon recognized more of those rotting creatures that Jai Sen had called dread-beasts. Each man and woman had the same disturbing sign of their Gold status: a miniature green snake-insect, like a lesser copy of the ones that had chased Lindon and Yerin here, clung to one arm on each of them.

The serpents varied in size, but they all gripped their host's arm with their centipede legs and coiled serpentine tails around the human's flesh. They were Forged from acid-green madra, and Lindon would have taken them for constructs except for the way their legs and tails sunk into flesh. They were bonded to the bodies of these men and women, but the snake heads were alive and curious, surveying Lindon with alien gazes.

The guards gripped long and gleaming weapons, and they eyed Lindon and Yerin like hungry dogs.

Lindon tried to stop his breathing from quickening, because he knew they would hear it. These sacred artists were the same as the ones who had attacked them in the wilderness, the ones whose Remnants had chased them here. If these six knew somehow that he and Yerin had been responsible for the death of their comrades...

Jai Sen slapped the shortest woman on the shoulder, and Lindon noted that her serpent was the largest, stretching from the back of her right hand halfway to the elbow. "Wei Shi Lindon, Yerin, it is my honor to introduce the best of the young generation among the honored Sandvipers. They have a long history of friendship with our Jai clan, and are our allies in exploration of the Ruins."

The young woman looked Lindon up and down as though she couldn't believe her eyes, the Forged insect-oid arms of her serpent parasite clacking as its tiny claws opened and closed. "I am Sandviper Resh," she said. "Are you as weak as you seem?"

The question pricked him like a needle, but he was the weakest one present by miles. He readied an ingratiating smile, prepared to humble himself as far as needed.

Yerin drew her sword and slapped the woman across the face with the flat of its blade.

Among the Wei clan, there would have been a moment of stunned silence before people erupted into action. Here, in the midst of such highly trained sacred artists, everyone but Lindon and the wounded Resh had drawn weapons and shifted into a combat stance in an instant. The parasites on the Sandvipers' arms raised their heads and let out tiny whistles like teakettles. Spearheads, halberds, and tridents pointed at Yerin. Many of the weapons had venomous green madra rolling around their shafts.

Yerin was matted with dirt, wearing a tattered robe, and half-wrapped in dirty bandages. But she still managed to look even more dangerous than the Sandvipers, as she stood with back straight and icy mist rolling from her master's sword. "This is a new spot on the map for me, Lindon," she said, rolling her shoulders. "But I've laid eyes on dogs like this a thousand times. They'll bark and bark, they'll push us around, and then they'll make us fight so they can prove they're above us. Forgive me if I cut ahead a bit."

Resh was doubled over on her knees, one hand raised to her head. When she moved it, Lindon saw an angry red welt on her cheek in the shape of Yerin's white blade. It looked as though it had been burned into the skin.

She gripped a long-hafted axe in the ground and unfolded. "You—" she began, but before she got halfway to her feet, Yerin's sword had already met her on the other cheek. Resh doubled over again.

"Heard this song before," Yerin said to the woman on the ground. "There's eyes all around, so the only way you get out of this is by beating me face to face, but it's too late for that." Nearby, the group with the hook-weapons had dropped the dreadbeast they'd been tormenting, looking to the Sandvipers with interest. The young man draped over the wall blinked bleary eyes and focused on them. A lone, distant figure with a black cloud over its head actually rose a few feet in the air to get a better look.

Yerin rapped her knuckles on one Sandviper man's forehead, and he actually recoiled. His green serpent, a tiny thing tightly wrapped around his wrist, whistled a warning. "See, now they've got a tiger on one side and some rocky cliffs on the other. They could rush me together and beat me bloody, but then they're the weaklings who joined hands to beat a wounded stranger."

Resh rolled to the side, gripping a spear, but Yerin had expected it. She whipped her sword up, leaving an all-but-invisible scar hanging in the air. Lindon had seen one of these before: a razor-sharp blade Forged in midair and left there as a trap. Resh froze, the edge of madra half an inch from her nose.

"You're strong, you get respect. You're weak, and you better know someone strong." Yerin slowly laid the flat of her blade down, resting it on the top of Resh's head. The Sandviper woman flinched, and frost began to form in her hair.

Yerin looked down, staring until Resh reluctantly met her eyes.

"The Copper's with me," Yerin said.

Lindon stood like a statue, too wary to show any sign of pleasure at the humiliation. If the Sandvipers decided to take their embarrassment out on anyone, it wouldn't be Yerin.

But Resh only nodded.

CHAPTER FIVE

From his perch on the pointed wooden logs that served the encampment as a wall, Eithan saw the girl with the steel arm over her shoulder arrive with an over-aged Copper looming over her. Invisible webs of his power filled the field before him, carrying information back to him in delicate strands, so he'd heard every word of their conversation. As such, he'd learned their names.

"Well, this is a lucky day," he said, hopping down from the wall. His blond hair flowed behind him like a banner, and a simple Enforcer technique made him drift slowly to the muddy ground. His shoes were cheap and simple, but he couldn't land and splash mud on his clothes; they were expensive shadesilk imported from the west sewn by a team of artisans in the east with a preservative script stitched into the hem. And they were white, so the stains would never come out.

People in a million fascinating variations swirled and eddied around him, and even with his mind fixed elsewhere, he felt them all. "Yerin," he said thoughtfully, trying out the name. To his left, a ladder tilted fractionally; it would tip over in a moment, and the man balanced on it would have to use sacred arts to right himself. Eithan pressed one finger against it, pushing it back into balance.

"Wei Shi Lindon." He liked that name better. Yerin was clearly the disciple of a Sage—her spirit was so pure and clean that only someone at the end of a Path could have helped her create it. He couldn't afford to offend a Sage without losing his position or worse, and if Yerin's master was still alive, Eithan would never be able to recruit her.

Fortunately for him, the Sage of the Endless Sword had vanished in this region a few months before. Now here was his disciple, in ragged clothes that had seen a month of wear, her wounds aching, belly tight with hunger, and expression tight with buried grief. His webs of madra brought him all that information and more, and it was a simple deduction from there: her master was dead.

A sad loss for the world, to be sure, but potentially to Eithan's gain.

A girl hurried by, arms full of flowers, and one was about to fall. He plucked it from the air as it did so, catching its long stem between his fingers. He lifted the nest of yellow petals, inhaling the delicate scent, and then pressed it into the hands of a pretty young woman. She hadn't been sleeping well lately, her training taking up much of her time, and her master was cruel to her. She was on the frayed edge of breaking.

He read that story in her worn shoes, in the welts on her back, in the slump of her shoulders. When a flower appeared seemingly out of nowhere, she spun around, searching in vain for its source. That easily, her burdens lightened just a fraction.

Only a hair's worth of difference, but enough hairs could tip the scale. Or something. He was sure he'd heard an idiom like that, at some point.

He returned his attention to the pair of newcomers. If Yerin was a prize, Lindon was a puzzle. *Two* cores, one even weaker than the other, in an otherwise healthy body. The quantity of his madra was severely lacking, but in terms of density and quality, he'd almost caught up with others his age. He must have had a lucky encounter with an elixir or spiritual herb of some kind. His wooden badge was etched with an ancient symbol: 'empty.'

That was enough to tell Eithan the story of a boy growing up in an isolated region with no ability in the sacred arts. But there were a thousand stories in the crowd around him, many equally intriguing.

What piqued his interest were the little things: the way Lindon stared around as though to devour every new detail with his eyes, the way he seemed to subconsciously bow to everyone around him with a Goldsign, the pack full of knickknacks he carried on his back.

He liked to be prepared, this Lindon. He planned ahead. He was looking for opportunity even here, in what would be—to someone like him—an ocean of sharks.

And he kept his tools neatly separated, packed efficiently into his pack. He carried very little on his person, just a halfsilver dagger, the badge, a few coins, and a—

Eithan stumbled over his own feet, catching himself on the edge of a stone building.

What was that in Lindon's pocket?

A transparent bead less than an inch in diameter. Not glass, but a barrier of...Forged madra? If so, it was so stable it wouldn't dissipate for a thousand years. And seamless enough that even *his* senses couldn't penetrate. It had to be a product of someone at least on Eithan's own level.

Where had a little Copper gotten something like that?

Eithan had only come this far west to find Yerin, or at least someone like her. If he returned to his clan with her in tow, he could consider this trip worthwhile.

But now, it seemed, he may have found a truly unexpected prize.

●

The encampment surrounding the Transcendent Ruins, which Jai Sen called the Five Factions Alliance, remained a marvel even though it looked as though it had been tossed together in an hour. Shacks and shops were cobbled together from fresh planks, many in a half-constructed state. The one road was nothing more than a wide track of hastily packed dirt, carrying wagons pulled by bulls, oxen, or Remnants of a dozen descriptions. Children dashed between ramshackle huts, tossing fistfuls of mud at one another.

But the mundane details could not hide the impossible, which surrounded Lindon from every angle. Yerin and Jai Sen walked casually along, unimpressed, but he felt as though he couldn't turn his head fast enough.

A girl that couldn't have been more than twelve years old hauled a boulder as tall as Lindon's shoulders over to the side of the road. When she slammed it down, the ground shook. She paused a moment, glancing over the irregular lump of stone that rose higher than her head, and then drove stiffened fingers straight into the rock. The top of the boulder slid away, crashing into the ground, and leaving the stone smooth and clean on top. A pile of enormous stone blocks waited nearby, and Lindon knew she'd carved those with her fingertips as well. Probably in the same morning.

A group of older men and women dressed in gray strode by, their outer robes sewn with images of dragons and birds in flight. A small cloud hung inches over each of their heads, and when they passed Lindon and his group, their gazes turned to Jai Sen. The clouds darkened, a few even flashing with lightning, and Lindon stared at the reaction in fascination even though the spearman seemed not to notice. After they'd passed, Lindon craned his neck back to continue looking, and the clouds had faded back to pale gray.

In front of a newly erected wooden shop front, a man hovered in midair, examining the second floor with a focused frown. He stroked his black beard, then reached for a strange weapon on his back: a hilt with a blade bent into a wide crescent, so that it looked like a sharpened hook. He leveled his weapon at the building as Lindon passed beneath him, seemingly unconcerned that people were flowing underneath his feet.

And the *people*. Outside of the Seven-Year Festival, Lindon had never seen so many different people packed into such a tight space. Sacred artists carried swords, spears, whips, hooks, axes, awls, halberds, and weapons for which Lindon had no name. They were dressed in everything from intricate formal robes that burned like a phoenix's flames to shoddy brown castoffs. The crowd came in tides, so that one second they were packed tight as a river, the next scattered like puddles after a rain.

Above it all, the titanic layers of the Transcendent Ruins loomed like a mountain carved of brown stone.

It was so strange compared to Sacred Valley that Lindon wasn't quite sure what to make of it. He was surrounded by Golds, which made him feel even more fragile than an autumn leaf in this crowd. One instinct urged him to dash into a corner and hide.

But another emotion held sway: the dizzying relief of absolute freedom. In the Wei clan, everyone knew him. They knew how useless he was. Here, he would start over from the beginning.

And reaching Gold was nothing, here. Even a child could do it. Even him. Every time he saw someone younger with a venom-green Remnant wrapped around their wrist or a cloud over their head, he couldn't suppress his smile. Those were Goldsigns, and if these people could raise their children to that level, he could make it too.

Ahead, Jai Sen's compliments to Yerin had flowed even thicker than the crowd around them. "It's rare that a sacred artist your age has such keen insight. You must surely be close to Highgold, which is worth bragging about. I myself have only reached the threshold of Highgold; when you're my age, you will surely have surpassed me. As for those Sandvipers, they're not even worth mentioning."

Yerin had spent the rest of the conversation putting him off with mutters and half-statements, which Lindon was certain had as much to do with her thirst as her disinterest. She'd kept one hand on the hilt of her sword and the other on the blood-red rope she had wrapped around her waist like a belt, as though trying to decide which she should draw. This time, she glanced back and saw Lindon listening.

"That was nothing special," Yerin said, as much to Lindon as to Jai Sen. "They wanted to back me into a corner, but they'd caught themselves in the same trap. They could have stepped up one at a time, and they'd have worn me down steady and true. But the first one to step up is the first to get slapped down, and that one would lose face. They could group up, and then they'd have beaten me sure as sunrise, but then what kind of standing would they have? Even dogs can win a fight as a pack."

She glanced back at Lindon again, emphasizing her point. "Sacred artists care more about their reputation than about their lives. You cut one, she'll heal and laugh about it. You embarrass her, and then you'd best be willing to draw swords on her, her mother, and her entire clan."

Lindon nodded to show her that he'd taken the message, but in truth it wasn't terribly strange. The notion of honor in Sacred Valley was similar, if perhaps a little less aggressive. As the saying went, *"A man holds grudges for a day, a family for a year, and a clan for a lifetime."*

Jai Sen chuckled even as he nudged a passerby aside with the butt of his spear. "Well said. It becomes a delicate dance, walking among people with such fragile pride. You and your family must make sure that you stand as tall as possible, so your enemies are too wary of you to bother you. But a tree that grows too tall, too quickly, is liable to be cut down." He turned enough to include Lindon in his grin. "The wisest course is to join a clan with such a firm foundation that it can never be shaken, with an unassailable reputation and untarnished honor."

Lindon might have been new to the area, but he could take obvious hints. "Would the Jai clan welcome strangers?"

Jai Sen stabbed a finger at him. "*This* one is almost as wise as you are, though perhaps he has...lagged a bit on his Path. Indeed, there is no faction in the Wilds as strong or as proud as the Jai clan. Our branch here is comparable to the Purelake Temple in influence, and it is but a fraction the size of our main branch in the Blackflame Empire. As an honored guest under the banner of Jai, none of the Sandvipers would dare to disrespect you again. We would give you the treatment of an outer disciple, which you surely deserve, and any honors or merits you render to the clan will be exchanged fairly for scales or treasures of your choosing. And when we recover the spear, as it was ours to begin with, every member of the clan and our respected guests will all receive a hundred scales as a bonus. We would even feed and house Wei Shi Lindon, as a courtesy to you."

Lindon was full to bursting with questions, in contrast to Yerin, who looked as though Jai Sen had offered her a pile of mud and a filthy stick. He had intended to ask about the factions of the Wilds, then about 'scales,' which he assumed were some sort of currency, but all his other concerns were pushed from his mind at the mention of the spear.

He stepped between Yerin and Jai Sen, catching the man's attention. "Your pardon, Jai Sen, but we have traveled from far away." He hadn't planned to keep Sacred Valley a secret, but Yerin had stopped him from revealing it earlier, so he steered toward caution. "We came upon this land by chance, so we know nothing of the spear."

Jai Sen, who at first had seemed irritated at Lindon's interruption, brightened. He waited until a cart had rattled by, deafening with a sound like clattering pottery, before he spoke. "The spear is the prize of the Transcendent Ruins. The Ruins are a treasure in themselves, drawing vital aura from hundreds of miles around, and filled with ancient secrets of great power. But the one everyone seeks, the weapon that could elevate one faction to the heavens, is the spear."

He was warming up now, gesturing with his hands so that his own spear bobbed wildly and caused several bystanders to duck and curse him. He continued as though he hadn't heard them. "Almost a thousand years ago, the Desolate Wilds were totally lawless, plagued by beasts and by wild sacred artists no better than animals themselves. Each man considered himself an Emperor, each woman an Empress, and they ruled whatever they could take at the end of a blade. But one day," and here Jai Sen drew himself up proudly, "a woman emerged from nowhere with a shining spear in her hands. She united these rogue sacred artists under one name, killing those who resisted, and spreading law and civilization across the Wilds. No one could stand against them, because no one could oppose her...or rather, no one could oppose her spear."

He smiled wider, because even Yerin was listening with obvious interest. "You see, her weapon was said to devour spirits. When she destroyed a Remnant, she consumed its power, until she grew so strong that she could slay entire armies at a stroke. For the next two centuries, while she lived, all the Wilds remained peaceful under her rule."

He waved a hand as though brushing aside two hundred years.

"The story of her death is a long one, but it's enough to say that the Ruins rose on the day of her death. She entered, taking the spear, and never emerged. Some say that she received the spear from the Ruins in the beginning, and she was only returning the power she had borrowed. I believe that it was a test, that she locked her strongest weapon into a secure vault to safeguard her legacy until a descendant could claim it once again."

"Will you retrieve it yourself?" Lindon asked. Though it was clear that Jai Sen wasn't the most powerful young sacred artist in the Jai clan—no matter how different the outside world was from Sacred Valley, he wouldn't believe that any clan would send its elites out to guard the gate from dogs—but a little flattery could only help him.

Jai Sen clapped Lindon on the back so hard that Lindon thought he would bruise. "You sure know how to speak. I should keep you around just for that. But I know my place; I'm only here to bring some small glory to my clan, as much as I am capable." He smiled over at Yerin, and Lindon wondered how much glory an esteemed visitor was worth to the Jai clan.

The tall spearman drew up short next to a cube of gray stone blocks very similar to the ones he'd seen the girl cutting barehanded. They were stacked one on top of the other, bound without mortar until they formed a square house bigger than the entire Shi family complex. Horses and stranger animals filled a fenced area nearby, and men and women with the spears and robes of the Jai clan entered and exited freely.

"This is the Inn of the Drifting Light, an establishment that sprouts up whenever and wherever promising members of the Jai clan need a place to stay." Jai Sen presented the enormous stone cube with a proud flourish. "As my friend, you are welcome to a room inside. Humble as it may be, I guarantee you won't find better anywhere in the Alliance."

Yerin gave Jai Sen a shallow bow. "I regret that my exhaustion prevents me from thanking you properly," she said, in the most formal sentence Lindon had ever heard from her. "I owe you a debt for every favor you've done on my behalf."

"Not at all, Yerin, not at all. There is no need for such formality between us, not when we will soon work side by side." He ushered them into the wide, doorless entrance, where a matronly woman had taken up a seat behind a wooden table.

She raised eyebrows when she saw him. "Jai Sen, have they closed the gates already?"

He cleared his throat. "Honored aunt, this is Yerin of no clan. I greeted her arriving at the gate, and she expressed an interest in working alongside our clan during her stay here. She is a guest of mine, and her friend is under her protection."

The woman appraised Yerin for a moment before giving her a broad smile. "I hope that my nephew hasn't worn out your ears on the way. Finding you shows more insight than I would have expected from him, and it's a credit to your wisdom that you accepted. You have a bright future here, with you so young."

To Lindon, she said nothing.

Clearly pleased with himself, Jai Sen swept his spear out to the side as he bowed to the room in general. "Aunt, honored guest, I am sorry to be so rude as to leave, but they need my presence at the wall. Sister Yerin, I hope that we might share a meal at sunset tonight, once you have a chance to refresh yourself and to rest."

Yerin bowed to him in response. "I'm sure I'll have a mouthful of questions once I've wet my throat a little more."

Jai Sen laughed. "More water for the thirsty travelers!" he said to his aunt. "And a bath, if I may be so indelicate as to suggest it." The woman nodded firmly and scribbled some words on a tablet.

"Then I'm off!" Jai Sen announced, spinning on his heel—almost catching Lindon in the head with the shaft of the spear—and walking out the door.

As Lindon had expected, a room in the inn was a hollowed-out stone block the size of a closet. A bed stood against one wall and a pile of blankets against the other—Lindon assumed that was for him—with a tiny table crammed into the corner balancing an unlit lamp, a paper covering what he guessed was a bowl of food, and four bottles of water beaded with condensation. As soon as they opened the door, Lindon and Yerin didn't even bother dropping their belongings before they darted for the water. The Thousand-Mile Cloud hovered in the hallway like a lonely puppy.

The woman at the entrance had told them baths would be heated within the hour, so once Lindon had finally slaked his thirst and devoured a bowl of rice, he started flipping through his pack for a clean change of clothing. The ones he was wearing were more appropriate for the fireplace than the wardrobe, after so many days in the wilderness, and in the tight confines of the room he was starting to notice the smell. His longing for the bath sharpened, until it was almost as powerful as his thirst had been earlier.

Yerin, meanwhile, was looking at the square hole in the wall that served as their window. "Think you could squeeze through this?" she asked.

Lindon looked up with his hands full of clean clothes. "The window?"

"If we get caught because your shoulders are stuck and you're dangling half out of the wall, I can tell you I won't be smiling."

"You want to *leave?*"

She lifted her sheathed sword, placing it across his shoulders as though taking a measurement. "I'm not staying here, you can take that for true."

Just when he'd been looking forward to a bath and a bed, even curled up on a stone floor. "May I ask why?"

"If Jai Sen mistook us for Remnant, he's dumber than a sack full of hammers. He wanted to know if I had a sharp enough edge on me to take his attack, and if I didn't, he planned on looting our corpses clean."

Slowly, Lindon replaced his clothes into the pack. "How do you know?"

"See something enough times, and you start looking for it. Unspoken rule of the world: you kill the last person to own something, it's yours, and nobody asks too many questions. That's not where it ends, either. He insulted you to see if I'd take it, because the farther I'll bend, the farther he can push me. Those Sandvipers at the gate were supposed to be his friends, his allies, however you want to say it. But he didn't stop them when they were going to make trouble, or stop me from beating on them. That sound friendly to you?"

Lindon had noticed that, but he'd taken it in stride. That was how many in the Wei clan had treated an Unsouled, after all.

"Now he's taken us to a place where we're stoppered up like flies in a wine bottle. Don't know if he still wants to rob us, or kill us, or maybe just what he said: get us working for the Jai clan. But I'll dance to his tune when he makes a puppet out of my corpse, and not a second before. We're leaving."

She held up her sword to the window horizontally, considered a moment, then nodded. "You first. I'll push."

CHAPTER SIX

The Sandvipers had their own corner of the Five Factions Alliance territory. The space wasn't assigned to them according to some plan or design, as would have been rational, but instead consisted of all the ground they could seize and hold. Typical of sacred artists, in Jai Long's opinion: so consumed with gaining strength that they never considered how they should use it.

Most of the Sandviper territory was taken up by a single, garishly red tent of many peaks. While the lesser minions settled for huts made of twigs and scavenged boards, their future chief reveled in luxury. Sounds floated out of the tent on a warm wind—mingled laughter, the clink of glasses, splashing of water.

Jai Long could have joined them. He had the status, and he'd contributed more merits than the Sandviper heir. But if he was honest with himself, he preferred it out in the cold night.

He sat at a rough table arranged on the mud, a stretch of fabric above him guarding from rain and providing shade. It was hot here when the sun was high, and cold when it wasn't, but his personal comfort was secondary. This position allowed him to focus on his duties, placed him in the way of any attack on the tent, and kept him close enough to respond to any of Kral's whims.

No sooner had Jai Long thought of the name when his master stuck his head out from the tent. Kral was twenty-two years old, and fit from years of martial training. He always gave the impression of an imposing leader, standing tall and confident as though to inspire those around him, gaze fixed on some distant vision of victory...until he smiled. Then, he looked like a rogue trying to charm his way out of trouble.

He was smiling now.

Water ran down his body, and black hair plastered to his face and neck. Even the towel wrapped around his waist was soaked.

"Send for some more water, would you?" Kral asked. The Sandvipers called Kral the young chief, though he hadn't ascended to his father's title yet, because of the great influence he had among the sect. He was issuing a command, but he respected Jai Long enough to at least pretend it was a request. "Somehow we keep losing it." A chorus of laughter followed that statement from within the tent, and his grin broadened.

Jai Long nodded to a pair of nearby servants, young boys born into the Sandviper sect, and they ran off at his signal to find the jars of water he'd ordered filled earlier. There were constructs in the tent to heat what water they brought, but if there existed any constructs that could create water out of madra, only the Purelake might have Soulsmiths skilled enough to build them. Maybe the Fishers, but he couldn't have any dealings with the Sandvipers' ancestral enemy. Not openly, anyway.

Request fulfilled, Jai Long turned back to his work, expecting that Kral would leave. Instead, the heir sighed.

"You're not a slave," he said.

Jai Long turned back, somewhat surprised at the statement. "If I thought I was, I wouldn't stay." He and Kral had reached the same stage of advancement in the sacred arts, but the future chief wouldn't be able to stop him by force. Jai Long wasn't arrogant enough to assume that he was the strongest Highgold in the Five Factions Alliance, but he was certainly the best among the Sandvipers.

If he'd thought the sect was treating him unfairly, he would have cut his way through them, and Kral knew it. The only one that could have overpowered him was the current chief, a Truegold, and Kral's father was out hunting.

Kral nodded to the paperwork. "Then why are you working like one? Come join us." He peeled the tent flap back a little, and another humid gust bloomed in the night air.

No laughter accompanied this statement from inside the tent, but none of them argued. Kral's friends were afraid of seeming too displeased, but they certainly weren't eager to have Jai Long join them.

He resisted lifting a hand to feel the strips of cloth wrapped around his head. The cloth was red, wrapped so tightly around him that not a hair or scrap of skin was visible from the neck up. Only his eyes peeked out of the middle, and if he could have covered those up without losing his vision, he would have.

"Let's not inflict my company upon them," Jai Long said dryly. "They're having fun."

If Kral's companions could have cheered that statement without losing face, Jai Long was sure they would have.

Kral's smile sharpened. "They won't say a word about it, that I can promise you. They know the hand that feeds them."

They wouldn't need words to express their displeasure, Jai Long knew. No one did, really. When he'd returned to his family with his sister's bloody and broken body in his arms, his parents were more horrified by his face than by the fate of their daughter. *What have you done to yourself?* they didn't ask him. *Was it worth it?* they didn't say.

When the Jai Patriarch banished him to the Wilds, the words were hollow and empty, forms without substance.

The old man's disappointment oozed across the room, so tangible that it might as well have been vital aura taken form. The star that would have guided the clan into the future had stepped off the Path, ruining his future advancement. And he was hideous...how could he represent the Jai like *that?*

Nothing truly important needed to be said. When he returned to the clan, unseated the Patriarch, and forced the rest of the family to bow before him, he wouldn't need any speeches either. Above all else, sacred artists respected strength.

Jai Long intended to use his.

"Can you imagine me saying yes?" he asked Kral, and the young chief gave a bitter laugh.

"In truth, no. But what sort of host would I be if I didn't ask?"

Kral had his faults. He pursued sacred arts with admirable dedication, but at every other sort of work he balked. He was lazy, irritable, quick to anger, slow to apologize, arrogant, and even occasionally cruel.

But he'd treated Jai Long well, and it would not be forgotten.

Jai Long said none of this, because he didn't need to. He waved his hand. "You're letting out the heat. Call for me when you need more wine."

Kral sighed again, but headed back inside. The laughs started up again almost immediately.

Jai Long looked down at the papers beneath him, conjuring a tiny star on the tip of one finger so that he had enough light to see. Four piles of papers sat on the desk, divided roughly into quadrants. Each page was a map. The maps were rough, sketched by many different hands, and incomplete. Jai Long was making notes of his own on the many blank spaces, filling in from other maps and from his own inferences, slowly and steadily building a complete diagram.

There were still many riddles to solve, but he could feel the information gathering into a whole. In another week, maybe two, he'd have an advantage beyond any of the other Five Factions: a map of the Transcendent Ruins.

The stories passed down about the ancient Jai spear were more myth than fact, but two things remained true to a reasonable degree of certainty. For one thing, it was almost absolutely true that the spear remained somewhere in the Ruins. There were hundreds of eyewitnesses to the Jai Matriarch's entrance, and while popular stories said she'd died within, her closest advisors recorded that she emerged from the Ruins weak and battered. She told those advisors that she'd left the spear within, and died days afterward.

He had enough information to consider that story true. But there was a second fact he'd verified, and it was equally important: the spear really had devoured the strength of Remnants and added their strength to that of the Matriarch's. One of her advisors had observed the process, even noting down possible methods and some runes on the spear's shaft that might have been some form of script. The early Jai clan had tried to reproduce the spear, but had ultimately failed.

No one else had considered the nature of that ability, except that it was a powerful way to advance quickly. The others, he was sure, sought the spear for one reason alone: with it, they might be able to break through the bonds of Truegold. There was only one Underlord in the Desolate Wilds, and only a handful in the Blackflame Empire. Advancing past Truegold meant advancing beyond the realms of common sense, to rise from the earth to the heavens in one leap.

They all thought so small.

More accurately, their vision was narrow. Jai Long's competitors, including the Sandviper sect, were so focused on advancement that they neglected to consider what it *meant* to consume someone else's power.

No one could gather madra that was too different from their own. That was a fundamental law, and one that Jai Long had no reason to believe the spear could break. If he, whose madra carried aspects of light and the sword, tried to absorb a Sandviper Remnant, the spear might allow him to do it. His madra would gain a toxic aspect, and he would have a harder time finding the right aura to cycle, but he should be able to do it.

But then, if he took a Fisher's Remnant, what would happen?

There was a point beyond which the absorption would fail. Even if it didn't, the different types of madra could mix in violent or chaotic ways. It might even damage his core, or the madra could rebound on him and tear his body apart.

No, though everyone envisioned taking the spear and gathering the powers of their enemies into one body, that was just a childish fantasy. It would never work.

The spear would be at its best when devouring compatible madra. In other words, madra from sacred artists on the same Path.

If Jai Long held the spear, he could advance by doing nothing more than cutting down others on the Path of the Stellar Spear—blood members of the Jai clan—and gutting their Remnants.

The spear's nature aligned so closely with his own desires that he almost considered it the will of the heavens.

Even better, the other Factions were considering this a contest of strength. Which was how they considered most things, now that he thought of it. They pushed into the Ruins, fighting the dreadbeasts sealed within as well as the other competitors, with the understanding that the most powerful would come out on top.

Jai Long didn't think of himself as an arrogant man, but sometimes it seemed that he was the only one with eyes in a crowd of the blind.

Couldn't they see that the strongest weren't always the victors?

So he worked on his map even as the young servants returned, carrying jars of water bigger than their whole bodies. As they ran back out, one of them stopped at Jai Long's table and bowed with fists pressed together.

He stayed that way until Jai Long noticed and raised his head. "What is it?"

"I ran into Grenn on the way back," the boy said. "His mother called him in to cycle, so he couldn't deliver messages to you tonight, so he passed them on to me."

Jai Long held back a sigh. He'd wondered what was taking his usual messenger so long, and once again he lamented the lack of discipline among the Sandvipers. There was so much he despised about the Jai family, but there was a reason they were a first-class clan in the Blackflame Empire while the Sandvipers remained nothing more than a second-rate sect in the Wilds. Without organization and control, strength meant nothing.

He gestured impatiently, and the boy's spine straightened like a broomstick. "Sir. Grenn said that the foreman said that the miners can't go into the southwest corner of the fourth floor. Too many beasts."

Jai Long scribbled a note. In the four floors closest to the entrance of the Transcendent Ruins, he had accurate maps of virtually the entire area. Only a few spots remained blank, so he'd ordered the mining crews to move their operations.

"Tell the foreman he can expect three more Lowgold guards by sundown tomorrow," Jai Long said. A single guard would be a great help in protecting the mining crew from dreadbeasts; three was perhaps too many. But this was a race, and he intended to win.

Kral might balk at committing so many of his Sandvipers to what he saw as a slave duty, but Jai Long would talk him around.

The messenger boy stood there mouthing words, awkwardly committing Jai Long's message to memory. When he'd finished, he straightened again.

"There was a message from the Jai clan too, sir. A Lowgold stranger showed up at the gates today, and she had a Copper with her."

"Her son?"

The boy shook his head, and his smile had a bit of a

sneer to it. "Grenn saw the Copper himself. Said he looked even older than the Lowgold."

That happened sometimes—a child was born with a tragically weak spirit, or had it crippled in some accident before he could advance further. Those unfortunates deserved pity, not ridicule.

But whatever they deserved, this one had earned not a whit of Jai Long's attention. "If you deliver me a message every time an outsider shows up at the gates, you'll walk your feet off."

"No, that's not...the Copper's just strange, sir. Not important. The *important* thing is that she beat Sandviper Resh in the middle of her squad, and then walked away with one of the Jai clan."

"Ah." Now Jai Long understood why the message had mentioned the Copper. If he, as a representative of the Sandviper sect, wanted to avenge Resh's humiliation, he couldn't punish a Lowgold under Jai protection. He'd have to target the Copper instead.

"Where are they now?" Jai Long asked, dipping his brush to write a letter to his former clan.

"Uh, they were taken to a Jai clan inn, but it looks like they snuck out. Grenn said he was supposed to tell you that nobody could find them."

Jai Long's suffering had begun when he first advanced to Gold. In the heat of battle, he'd been forced to adopt a strange Remnant instead of the one his family had planned for him. Instead of the Goldsign borne by most on the Path of the Stellar Spear—hair as sturdy as a helmet, and rigid as iron—he was cursed with a face that...a face that he didn't like to think about.

There had been a few other consequences of that Goldsign. His voice hadn't changed, but his laugh...

It rang out of him, wild and crazy, like the cackling of a deranged murderer. His usual voice was cool and composed, but when he laughed, he sounded like a blood-drunk killer. The messenger boy paled and took a step backwards.

Jai Long swallowed the last chuckles, but a smile still stretched the edges of his cloth mask. "They lost her. The Jai clan can't find their new recruit, so they turn to *me.*"

Technically they had turned to the Sandvipers to help, but there was no real difference. He handled most of the day-to-day workings of the sect, and whichever of his relatives had sent this message must have known where it would end up.

Surely, that knowledge had burned them.

"I think so, sir..." the boy said hesitantly.

"I'm amending my previous message. Tell the foreman he will have to wait for his three Lowgold guards. Then go to Sandviper Tern, get three of his best, and tell him the story you just told me. They're to retrieve the Copper for the mines. Do *not* kill his protector, but don't retrieve her for the Jai clan either."

His clan had handed him a razor-sharp opportunity. In one move, he could regain the standing the Sandvipers had lost at the hands of this stranger, show her that she couldn't treat their sect lightly, and reinforce to the clan that Jai Long was their servant no longer. And he would gain a miner. Only a Copper, but enough single scales could eventually pile up into a fortune.

The messenger boy was standing in place with brows furrowed, repeating words silently to himself.

"What will you say to the foreman?" Jai Long snapped, and he forced the boy to repeat each message until they were all perfect. One day, he was going to have to train better messengers. Maybe he could purchase a few speaking constructs from the Fishers. Through a proxy, of course.

When the boy finally finished, Jai Long picked his brush back up and dipped it into the inkwell. "Is there anything else?" he asked, by way of dismissal.

"Nothing special," the boy said, fidgeting in place. Clearly there was something he wanted to say, but not an official message.

"Did you hear something?" Jai Long asked, his attention on the paper in front of him.

"It's just a rumor. Some of the Cloud Hammers were talking about it, and I only heard them because I was sitting behind a fence and they didn't know I was there, because one of them asked the other one if he was sure, and then *he* said..."

Jai Long let the boy ramble on excitedly as he worked. Eventually, a point would emerge.

"...after he'd stopped, he said—I mean not him, the first one—said they'd have to speed up, because Arelius would take everything when he got here. So the second one kind of laughed, but not a *funny* laugh—"

When the boy's words registered, Jai Long stood up so quickly that he upended his inkwell, sending it splattering off the edge of the table. Part of his mind noticed with relief that it hadn't ruined any of his maps, but the majority of his consciousness was taken up by sheer panic. He seized the boy by the shoulders, and it was only a last-minute awareness that prevented him from accidentally ripping the boy's arms off.

"The Arelius family is coming *here?*"

The boy's eyes were so wide that they seemed to take up most of his head, and he looked too scared even to struggle. "I don't know, brother Jai Long. Please, brother, they just said Arelius. I don't know what it means, I don't know..."

That same calm part of his mind noted that the Sandvipers only called him "brother" when they wanted something from him.

Meanwhile, his panic was quickly transforming into fury. After all his work, all his meticulous effort, *now* a faction from the Empire was just going to step in and take the rewards.

Jai Long didn't tend to raise his voice. It showed a lack of discipline. Instead, he lowered his tone until he was very quiet indeed. Quiet like the slow rasp of a drawn blade.

"Why," he said, "didn't you tell me this earlier?"

Tears had come to the boy's eyes, and he blubbered incoherently. Jai Long released him, disgusted with himself.

He wasn't the sort of weakling who took his frustrations out on children. This boy couldn't be older than twelve; he was even younger than Jai Long's own sister.

Jai Long bowed deeply to the messenger, fists pressed together, as he would bow to a superior. "My deepest regrets," he said, and the fear on the boy's face almost instantly transformed to shock. "Now. Deliver your messages as instructed, but on your way, grab every messenger the Sandvipers have. Send them all to me."

The boy bowed and bolted.

Within the tent, the splashing and laughter had stopped. "Kral," Jai Long said, and the young chief's head poked out.

"I didn't hear much of that, but I will *die* if you don't tell me the details," Kral said.

"The Arelius family may be coming here."

It took the future Sandviper chief a moment before the gravity of that statement sunk in. "From the empire?"

Jai Long didn't nod. His silence would be answer enough.

"When?"

"That's what we need to know."

Kral vanished for a moment, and when he reappeared, he was tying a loose emerald robe around his waist. He shouted orders, every inch the commanding chief, and Sandvipers boiled out of the camp in droves.

Jai Long snatched up his spear from beside the table, marching off into the darkness. He had his own tasks to perform. He'd already forgotten about the other orders he'd sent tonight; compared to confirming this rumor, other matters were unimportant.

The second the Arelius family showed up, his part in this game was over.

●

INFORMATION REQUESTED: JAI LONG.

BEGINNING REPORT...

The Jai clan began as one of many barbaric factions in the stretch of blighted wilderness known as the Desolate Wilds. The light-aspected combat techniques on their Path of the Stellar Spear made them the most formidable family of sacred artists in the area, and they unified the region more than once over the centuries. Each time, their rule proved violent and brief.

It wasn't until they produced an Underlord that their family rose to prominence, moving their main branch from the Desolate Wilds to the civilization of the Blackflame Empire. They have flourished under the guidance of that Underlord for over a century, never forgetting that their good fortune is held together by a single linchpin.

If their Patriarch is ever unseated, the clan will crumble. And now, despite his great advancement along his Path, he is starting to age. Within one more decade, maybe two, age will claim the leader of the Jai clan.

As such, they train their disciples with unusual rigor. The safety of the next generation will only be secure if they can produce a second Underlord, an heir to their Patriarch's glory.

Thus far, they have failed. No genius of the clan has climbed past the peak of Gold and reached the heights of the Underlords.

But one showed promise.

Jai Long's affinity with the Path of the Stellar Spear was second only to the Patriarch's. At twelve years old, he sparred with disciples five years his senior. By thirteen, he had reached the peak of Jade, and could have broken through to Lowgold if not for the decree of the clan's elders.

To advance from Jade to Gold, one must take on the power of a Remnant. Sacred artists always prefer to receive Remnants from the same Path, to ensure compatibility and prevent deviation, so the elders waited for a Remnant worthy of Jai Long. They waited for a clan elder to die.

When Jai Long turned fourteen, he still had not been granted permission to advance to Lowgold, for the elders remained stubbornly attached to life.

It was during this time that a group of rebels, a disen-franchised branch family of the Jai clan, staged an uprising against the head family.

They practiced their own warped version of the Path of the Stellar Spear, and had been exiled for it. Marginal-ized and mistreated, as they saw it, their frustration finally boiled over in an attack on the main branch of the clan. Among their targets was the famous golden child of the head family: Jai Long.

As Jai Long was still stuck at Jade, he should have been easy pickings for older warriors. One Lowgold boy of sev-enteen, seeking to make a name for himself, isolated and challenged his rival in a duel to the death.

Jai Long pinned him to the wall with his spear.

This was a mistake that an older sacred artist would not have made. Killing his rival released a Remnant, a twisted twin to the normal spirit of the Stellar Spear. If the Rem-nant had attacked, Jai Long—depleted as he was from the fight—would have died.

But Remnants are unpredictable, and this one crawled through the house in search of easier prey.

It found Jai Long's sister, six years old, still asleep. It dragged her from her bed, away from the home, to con-sume her madra in private.

Jai Long raced after it, catching the spirit in minutes. But the damage was already done: her core was cracked and damaged, her madra channels ravaged, the Remnant stron-ger than ever. And his Jade senses told him that the rebels were closing in.

He had no chance of escaping safely with his sister. Not unless he grew stronger.

Jai Long trapped the Remnant with a simple script and began the process of drawing it into his core. He had long since reached the limits of Jade and prepared for this step, so he reached Lowgold easily.

Though not as smoothly as he'd hoped.

Though compatible with his madra, this spirit was not

quite from the Path of the Stellar Spear. It left him with a Goldsign unlike that of his family: a face scarred and twisted, disgusting to look upon.

When he fought his way free of the rebels and returned to his home, carrying his sister, he did not find the welcome he'd expected. They provided shelter and medical care, but nothing further. Even his parents began to distance themselves from Jai Long, as they found their future in the family jeopardized by his presence.

The next Patriarch of the Jai clan could not have deviated from the Path of the Stellar Spear. His face could not be monstrous.

Even his sister, though cared for out of pity, had nothing for her in the clan any longer. The elixirs and training resources she had once received to bolster her sacred arts were withdrawn, for the family could not place all their bets on a lame horse. She was tucked away to fade, forgotten.

And Jai Long, once the bright star guiding the clan to glory, was quietly shipped away to the Desolate Wilds. His talent could not be ignored, so he was given the task of supporting one of the Jai clan's oldest allies: the Sandviper sect. There, he could benefit his family without bringing them shame.

Here in the Wilds, he has languished all this time. Training. And waiting.

SUGGESTED TOPIC: THE FATED FUTURE OF JAI LONG. CONTINUE?
DENIED, REPORT COMPLETE.

CHAPTER SEVEN

By moonlight, Lindon could barely make out the words painted on the board: "Bathhouses for rent."

They looked more like outhouses than bathhouses, rickety sheds of wood only large enough for a single person. They were packed like grave markers in a cemetery, and customers emerging after their bath had to pick their way out through a maze of boxes.

Like the rest of the Five Factions Alliance encampment, these facilities had clearly been tossed together. One young man sat at an uncovered table, chin in one hand. He yawned as Lindon and Yerin approached.

"Two scales each," he said, not so much as glancing at either of them.

The sun had fallen long ago, and one lantern dangling from a nearby tree's branch provided the only light. Lindon and Yerin had wandered for hours, trying to find another place that would take them for the night, but most were packed full. The rest demanded scales, obviously the currency of the region, and refused to listen further when Lindon said they didn't have any.

"A good evening to you," Lindon said, bowing over a sacred artist's salute. The man didn't acknowledge him.

"We're from far away, so perhaps elder brother could help us."

Some of the innkeepers had addressed him as "little brother" before they realized he didn't have any money, so Lindon reasoned that it must be polite around here.

The man snorted, still not looking at them. "Who's your brother? If you have no money, then shoo. Shoo." He waved them away with one hand.

Lindon could actually hear Yerin's hand tightening on her sword hilt.

"We don't have *much* money, I'll grant you, but I'm sure we can come to an agreement," Lindon said pleasantly. He withdrew a shadesilk bag with a portion of his leftover chips in it; he kept most of his chips inside his pack, but he typically carried twenty or thirty for small transactions. He spilled a few of the rectangular halfsilver tokens onto the man's table.

"We'd be happy to trade, if you think these are worth a few scales." If they weren't, he still had the halfsilver dagger to trade. Or if halfsilver was worth nothing more than rocks here, he was sure he could find some treasure they could trade for the local currency. Even the Thousand-Mile Cloud that drifted behind them would be worth selling, if they could get a good enough price.

The man sighed. "Scales or nothing," he said, raising his hand to brush the chips away from him.

He froze at the sight of the speckled metal, like stars stuck in silver.

His eyes bulged.

And Lindon sensed vulnerable prey.

"I think I can do you a favor, little brother," the man said, voice straining to stay casual. "I'm sure I can lend you some scales of my own, if you're in that much need. How about...two of your coins per a scale?"

"True and clear," Yerin said impatiently, slapping her palm down on the table. "So that's eight for the both of us?"

The man looked like he'd just seen gold rain from the heavens, but before he could grab the chips, Lindon had already swept them back into his bag.

"I'm sorry, elder brother, but as I said...we're only poor travelers. I'm not sure we can part with eight of these chips. I'm certain four would be asking you to take a loss, but would five do?"

The man pointed at Yerin. "She said eight was fine! She said it!"

Lindon tightened the strings on his purse and sighed. "She did. So I'm afraid I'll have to find another—"

The man cut him off by grabbing his arm. "Five is good enough! Five is fine!"

Lindon focused on him like a hawk sighting a rabbit. "How about three?"

This time, the man obviously realized that Lindon had caught on, because a blush ran from his cheeks down his neck. He didn't back down, though; the value of halfsilver must be higher than Lindon had thought. "It's hard on me, but three is fine."

Yerin leaned her elbows on the table. "Is it, now? And you were going to let me drop eight?"

She obviously hadn't cared before, but now the man was getting Yerin's full attention. He shifted under that weight.

"It's a negotiation, little sister, not worth getting upset about."

Lindon kept his smile from growing. Now that Yerin was involved, her intimidation could only help him.

"Of course you're right," Lindon said, "just a negotiation." He reached two fingers into the purse and withdrew a single halfsilver rectangle. "How about one of these, and you give us each a room?"

"Two keys," the man said, snatching the chip from Lindon's hand. Swiftly, he produced a wooden circle with a script engraved into it. Lindon recognized it as rough work, but it was probably enough to engage and disengage a basic scripted lock.

"Feel free to come back and see us later," he said cheerily.

Lindon bowed in response, wondering by how much he'd overpaid. If he found out a single chip was worth a thousand scales, he'd weep blood.

He turned to go to his bathhouse, but Yerin rapped her knuckles on the table before she did. "There's a good chance we won't cross ways again," she said. "Our School's High Elder needs us in the Ruins at dawn. Not a man you want to ignore, hear me? Not unless you want to bleed a river."

She laughed cheerfully, and he tried to join her. Only then did Yerin turn and follow Lindon.

"Could you explain that to me?" he asked.

"Halfsilver's rare," she said, "but it's not *that* rare. He was looking like you were carrying phoenix feathers soaked in dragon tears."

Finally the reality dawned on Lindon, and he shivered. "Forgive me. I was shortsighted." If he hadn't been so tired, and so focused on making a profit, he would have seen it immediately.

In Sacred Valley, an Unsouled carrying a fortune was begging to be robbed. Out here, a Copper was the same. He'd be lucky if they only beat him.

"Nah, it's all settled now. His bones are rattling so hard he wouldn't dare pick up a coin if we tossed it to him. But possibly don't flash any more halfsilver around until we get away from here."

Which killed his newborn plan to trade all his halfsilver for elixirs and training resources. He'd only been rich for a few seconds, and now he couldn't even spend it.

They found a pair of shacks back-to-back. Even though Lindon could barely squeeze inside with his pack, he finally managed it, and he could hear Yerin as she stepped into her own.

He paused, looking at the center of the bathhouse, and he heard her do the same. He'd expected a tub full of cold water, maybe a simple construct for heating if they were really luxurious. Instead, a crystalline pool of water sat in the center of the ground, deep enough that it would be up to his shoulders. The ground surrounding the pool was just dirt, but the water was protected by walls of rugged white rock. It was like they'd grown a hot spring in the middle of an ordinary field.

"Is this natural?" Lindon asked, his voice carrying easily through the slats of the wood.

"No hope of that. Brought the water up somehow, I'd guess."

Their stalls stood back-to-back, each made of boards loosely slapped together. They did nothing to stop the sounds from her side: the rattle of her sword as she set it aside, and the steady rustle of cloth as she slipped out of her clothing.

He lowered his eyes to the ground though there was nothing to see, his cheeks heating. Most of the girls in Sacred Valley were promised to someone from an early age, so it would have been inappropriate for any besides his sister to spend time with Lindon. Once he was known as Unsouled, none even wanted to.

Now that he was hearing a girl undress, he was irrationally afraid that she would read his thoughts. He intentionally rattled his pack as he set it down to the side, unlacing his robe in determination to act normal. He shouldn't be flustered by something this petty; he was almost sixteen years old.

He froze with his outer robe down to his waist as he realized *she* could hear *him* even more clearly. She had an Iron body; from this distance, she could probably hear him blink. His blush became a fire in his cheeks, and he snuck out of the rest of his clothes like a thief picking his way through a field of traps.

Mercifully, Yerin remained quiet even when he tried to lower himself into the water and gasped at the heat. It wasn't hot enough to burn him, or so he hoped, but it felt strange and hot against his skin. He wondered how long it had been since he'd had a hot bath, and that thought was enough to get him to slide into the stone-edged pool.

It was deeper than it was wide, so he was practically standing up to his shoulders in warm water, but he still let out a deep sigh of relief. As layers of dirt floated away, the heat sunk deep into tired muscles. He leaned his head against the grass behind him, letting his eyes close.

Yerin's voice came almost as soon as he had closed his eyes. "Sorry we're not getting beds."

"Hm?" He was so tired, the words almost didn't make sense.

"Beds. You miss your house, true? I get it. We could have stayed with the Jai, it just scrapes me raw to bend to their tricks."

Lindon couldn't deny *some* regret that he hadn't been able to sleep indoors for once, but letting the Jai clan do whatever they wanted seemed like the worse option. Even if they had nothing but good intentions, Yerin had been right that their actions weren't honorable.

"You have no reason to apologize to me," Lindon said. "Without you, I'd be a raw meat in the middle of a wolf pack. If you told me to sleep outside for the rest of my life, I'd do it without a complaint."

She was silent for a minute or two after that, so he had no idea how she'd taken those words. Maybe she didn't believe him.

When she spoke again, she sounded flustered, though that could have been his imagination. "Well, if you can recall, the Jai clan guy mentioned a Blackflame Empire. I don't know it, but the world's big. There's bound to be some regular villages around here. People who *haven't* flocked to the strange and deadly ruins. Tomorrow we can skip it, move on, find some friendlier places."

"Where will we find somewhere better than *this?*" Jai Sen's story of the spear had caught him up in its mystery, and being surrounded by Gold martial artists was inspiring. Even the Transcendent Ruins fascinated him; they were a dark and deadly labyrinth left behind by powerhouses of an ancient world. Who knew what treasures lay inside?

If they left, he'd be giving up any chance of finding something for himself.

"It's not comfortable here," Lindon continued, "I certainly agree with you on that, but why would we leave? Sacred artists from all over are gathered; maybe one of them knows some pure madra techniques. Maybe they could teach me a second Path, or even take me inside the Ruins..." His imagination was spinning at full speed, showing him images of the endless benefits he could gather inside the pyramid.

"You think it's so easy to learn a Path, do you? You even want to try for *two,* like you're the first person with that idea."

Lindon was trying not to feel too embarrassed about his Sacred Valley education, but Yerin didn't make it easy. "I know I could be wrong, but it was my understanding that most people don't have two cores."

"Sure, you have an advantage in that respect. Same way somebody with no legs has the advantage of saving on shoes. But I've got one core packed full of sword madra; why don't I learn a second sword Path? I'd learn twice as much."

Lindon hadn't considered that, but now that he thought of it, he wondered why she didn't.

"First step, I'd have to find somebody to teach me, and they wouldn't. They know I'm on another Path; they won't teach me their secrets. That's handing a sword to your enemy's son. He won't thank you for it, and he might turn it against you someday."

"But if you *could* find someone to teach you—"

"Still wouldn't do it. Say I have a job that takes all my time. Just because I want some more money doesn't mean I'm going to go out and find a *second* job. Sure I'll make more, but that doesn't leave much room for sleeping." Water splashed around on her side of the dividing wall. "Besides, one Path is enough danger for my taste. I didn't get my scars because I'm so bad at needlepoint, if you hear my meaning."

He had wondered about her scars in the past. They were too regular, too smooth, so that they looked as though they'd been left by razors. He assumed she'd gotten them from training her Endless Sword technique, and it seemed he'd been right.

"I'm not afraid of a little more pain," he said. That wasn't entirely true, but he was prepared to endure whatever he had to in order to travel farther down the path of the sacred arts.

"You've had one taste at Copper, and you're thirsty for the whole bottle? Let me tell you, I had the same thoughts as you when I heard about the spear. You know how many sword artists there are in the world? There's enough Path manuals to pave the streets from here to Phoenix Height. If I could take their power by beating them, drain sword Remnants and stealing their power with that spear...I might even reach my master, someday. It draws me. But I don't chase prey I know I'll never catch."

It somewhat hurt, having his dreams punctured one by one, but he gave her words the full consideration they deserved. She wasn't one to give up lightly—Yerin was the person who stood against the entire Heaven's Glory School and prepared to die rather than retreat from battle. If she wanted to skirt this one, it meant she really believed there was nothing to gain here.

But something about that stuck in him like a needle beneath the skin. He reached over, grabbing a smooth wooden medallion next to his pack: his badge. The character in the center glared at him, as it had every single day for the last eight years. *Empty.*

"I need something, Yerin, and this is where I can get it. I can finally feel the aura all around me, even now, like I'm lost in endless power...and I can't touch *any* of it. I need a Path to teach me how. It's like I'm dying of poison, and I'm drowning in a sea of the antidote."

"You think people just accept any disciple that asks?" Yerin sounded angry now. "You think they teach Paths to anybody? No one will take you, no one will teach you, not until you're worth something. That's the steel truth of it, and you'd best swallow it now."

The bath was starting to feel uncomfortably hot.

"I can get a faction to accept me," Lindon said. Yerin's doubt cut him, but he knew his own abilities. There were enough different Paths represented here that he had to be able to find a way in somewhere.

"Are your ears just for decoration? If I say it's hard, it's *hard*. If a School does take you, they'll nail your feet to the ground. They don't want their precious disciples wandering out, taking their secrets with them. That's years, *years,* stuck in one place by yourself, because you can bet they won't take me in."

"Then you can leave!" Lindon said, and he regretted saying it even before the words emerged. He tried to control the damage immediately. "Of course, I wish you wouldn't. It's not...I would like you to stay with me, but I wouldn't want to burden you. You're already finished with your promise to me, so there's nothing..."

It was at that point that he realized he was digging himself a deeper grave, and decided to put the shovel down.

She was silent for so long that Lindon started to overheat. He reached for the paper-wrapped bar of gritty soap that he'd brought with him from home. While he scrubbed himself down, he kept one ear open for Yerin's response.

She remained quiet.

Finally, when he'd rinsed himself and begun putting his clothes on—slowly, to give her as much time as possible to respond—Yerin spoke.

"Let's not go charting any courses yet. We'll find somewhere to spend the night first." The words sounded dead, so Lindon responded with forced cheer.

"Of course! I wasn't planning on making any decisions tonight."

At that moment a shadow passed in front of his stall, and footsteps came to a halt in the grass.

"Little sister, little brother," came the voice of the bathhouse attendant, "it would be best if the two of you finished soon. You're welcome to return any time you like, of course, but it seems as though there will be some trouble..."

A smack echoed around the bathhouse grounds, like the slap of wood on wood, and the attendant sighed.

"...very soon. If you don't have ties to either the Fishers or the Sandvipers, I'd recommend you hurry."

Lindon tugged on the rest of his clothes, slipped the pack onto his back, and pulled on his badge. When he pushed his way out of the bathhouse, Yerin stood in front of him. Her hair hung limp and wet as well, and she was still tightening the thick red rope that served her in place of a belt.

She tied it into a wide bow, then twisted the whole mass around so that the bow hung behind her. All the while, she kept her eyes off her hands and on Lindon.

The silence was painful. He felt as though he should say something, but what he settled on was, "Shall we go see what's happening?"

"I can't recommend that," the attendant said. "It's a hornet's nest over there." He scratched at the back of his right hand, and Lindon saw a bright red circle there. A Goldsign. So even the servants in a place like this were stronger than anyone in Sacred Valley.

Yerin met Lindon's gaze and nodded. "Won't be hard to find them, at least." She turned and walked off without acknowledging the attendant again.

For his part, Lindon bowed to the man with his fists pressed together before he followed Yerin. The Thousand-Mile Cloud trailed after him, dragged along on an invisible leash of thin madra.

The loud noises had been joined by raised voices, with two groups arranged on the road outside of the bathhouse. One group was wearing furs, and each had a bright green lizard-creature attached to one arm. These Remnants, or parasites, or Goldsigns—whatever they were—acted independently from their host, hissing and spitting at the enemies opposite them, though they never left. Maybe they were attached somehow.

The other group must have been the Fishers, based on the attendant's words. Most of them were dressed in clothes that would have been considered poor even in Sacred Valley: threadbare brown robes, sandals on the edge of breaking, woven reed hats with wide brims that would protect against harsh sunlight. Some of them wore them even now, after dark, though a few more had strapped the hats to their backs. Each of them carried the same weapon, which Lindon had noticed before—a wide crescent blade on a hilt, like a sword that had been bent into the shape of a hook.

One of the Sandvipers reached up and pulled another board away from a building. Like most construction in the Five Factions Alliance, this place was slipshod and half-finished, and it looked like it was only one or two boards away from collapsing. Clearly, the man had done this before, judging by the pile of wood next to the half-disassembled building.

"...we're just passing the time as we wait here," the Sandviper said casually, peeling another board away from the structure. The whole hut groaned. "If we don't have anything to call us away, we might as well stay a while longer."

A tall woman stepped up as the representative of the Fishers. Unlike the others, she carried two of those bladed hooks, one in her hand and the other on her back. A sneer gave her a twisted, malicious cast. "While you're waiting here, maybe I'll go back home. I made some new friends today, and they have all sorts of *interesting* stories to tell us about you."

The lead Sandviper's face contorted until it looked like hers, and he stepped forward himself. In a flicker of motion so fast that Lindon almost didn't catch it, a pair of long knives appeared in each of his hand. Vivid green madra coiled around each blade. "Give me my miners back, and we can let this go here."

"If you want to give me my brother's *eye* back, then we can—"

A new voice, quiet and even, sliced through the argument like a razor. "What is this?"

The Sandvipers parted like a crowd of puppies before a wolf. The first detail Lindon could see of this new figure was a spearhead, which gleamed bright even in the light from the smoky torches. The shaft was red, worked with detail that looked like it may have been script, but the weapon hardly attracted attention compared to the man who carried it.

He was roughly as tall as Lindon, but thinner, so that his build matched that of his spear. He wore ordinary dark robes, like more than half the sacred artists Lindon had seen that day, but he wore something they did not: long strips of red cloth, wrapped tightly around his head. It looked as though he'd tried to bandage himself for grievous injuries to the skull, but his wounds had bled through.

Every one of the strips of cloth was covered, without exception, in what was unmistakably script. Even if Lindon had been close enough to make out the script in detail, he likely still wouldn't have been able to tell what it did.

Perhaps it had some intimidating effect on onlookers, because everyone grew quiet at the masked stranger's approach. The Sandvipers shut their mouths like children before a parent, and the Fishers had all reached for their weapons. Even the few handful of bystanders who had stuck by to watch the confrontation, like Lindon, did not dare to utter a word.

Except Yerin. "He's strong," she said to Lindon, though even she kept her comment to barely above a whisper.

The stranger stopped at the lead Sandviper, who drew himself and saluted over his fists. "Brother Jai Long," the Sandviper said, "these Fishers captured some of our miners on their return from the Ruins. We wanted to at least recover the scales, in order to save face for the Sandviper sect."

Another member of the Jai clan, Lindon noted. And once again in the company of Sandvipers. Those men and women at the gate hadn't just been Jai Sen's friends, then; their factions were close allies. He wasn't sure if that fact would be worth anything, but he tucked it away nonetheless.

"For the Sandviper sect," Jai Long repeated softly. "Who was responsible for the missing mining team?"

"Ah, that is...I was responsible for guarding them, but the Fishers sent too many for me to handle on my own."

"Then you were both careless and weak. You have lost respect for yourself and for the sect, and the young chief will punish you accordingly."

The Sandviper man's hands curled into fists. He straightened his back, glaring. "Then I will hear as much from Kral's own mouth. He does not need an outsider speaking for him."

Despite Lindon's expectations, Jai Long did not grow angry. He tilted his head back, looking up at thick, black branch hanging over the street. "I suppose he doesn't."

A man jumped from the branch, landing with knees slightly bent as though he'd hopped off of a curb. It looked so easy. So natural.

The Sandvipers backed away at the sudden appearance of this man, who wore fine black furs and held his chin so high it looked as though he were about to issue a royal decree. He stared at the lead Sandviper like a emperor looking down upon a criminal.

Here was yet another sacred artist who could casually do the impossible, whose very presence overwhelmed lesser Golds.

"Young chief Kral," the Sandviper greeted him, stuttering a little and bowing even more deeply than he had for Jai Long. "I intended no disrespect to you."

"When you disrespect my friend, Jai Long, you dirty my honor," Kral pronounced. Like Jai Long, he seemed to have no need to raise his voice to transfix the whole street. "How will you make amends?"

The Sandviper man dropped to his knees before Jai Long, bowing until his head hit the dirt. "My eyes were blind, honored Jai Long. I will never—"

Jai Long kicked him in the shoulder. The sound rang out in the night, even louder than the wood-on-wood impacts earlier, but the man wasn't visibly affected. He raised his head, confused.

"My pride is not worth our time," Jai Long said. "Stand up."

The man staggered to his feet, and abruptly Kral grinned. The smile transformed him, turning him from a haughty prince into a mischievous boy. He threw one arm around the man's shoulders.

"He says all's well, so it's well," Kral said, patting the man on the back. "Now, *what* exactly are our friends the Fishers doing out here?"

He looked to the other camp as he said that, friendly grin still in place, but the green serpent on his arm hissed loudly.

The woman in charge of the Fishers held a hook in each hand now. She took an aggressive step forward, brandishing a weapon, but neither Jai Long nor Kral reacted. "This is our territory. What's strange is your presence."

"Territory?" Without removing his arm from the Sandviper man's shoulders, Kral turned to Jai Long. "Is the camp divided into territories?"

"Not officially."

"See?" Kral said to the woman. "Nothing official. So what I choose to believe is that my subordinates were walking back to the mines, tired after a hard day's work, and they were ambushed by some thieves looking for easy pickings."

The Fisher woman turned red. "You *dare* to—"

"And these thieves," Kral continued, riding over her words, "were courageously captured by you Fishers, who are now eager to return our stolen property to us. Like the young heroes that you are."

The woman stopped, uncertain.

"How many scales did they take?" Kral asked the man under his arm.

"Sixty-two, young chief," the man said nervously.

Kral leaned a little closer. "How many?"

"...sixty-two?"

Kral sighed. "How many stolen scales are these Fishers going to return to you?"

At last, the young man caught the point. "At least one hundred scales, young chief."

Releasing him, Kral spread both hands. "See what an opportunity for goodwill we have here? Return the stolen one hundred scales to us now, and we'll trust your honor that the miners will be back in our camp come dawn."

The Fisher woman gave a crooked smile that had no humor in it. "It's the law of the Wilds, Sandviper. You take whatever you can keep. If you were too weak to keep it..."

Kral's smiled faded as though it had never been, and he drew an awl from beneath his furs with each hand. The heavy spikes gleamed with green light. "I have a sudden urge for some exercise. Will you oblige me, sister Fisher?"

Jai Long clapped a hand on his shoulder. "We've spent too long on this, young chief. Sister Fisher, we have other work to be about, as do you. Let our stolen property serve as a down payment for you to deliver this message, because our other messengers have yet to reach your sect: the Arelius family is coming. In no more than a month, their Underlord will take all prizes from us, and we will be left with only scraps."

The Fisher turned, exchanging glances with someone in the crowd behind her. "We'd heard rumors," she said.

"They are more than rumors," Jai Long said. He produced a blue-and-white banner, which unfurled as he held it out in front of him. In the center loomed a single black crescent moon. "A Cloud Hammer sect long-runner returned bearing this, only a day gone. If Arelius hurries, they could be here in two weeks. At most, a month. Send word to your Fisher Ragahn that if we do not share the meal now, none of us will see a crumb."

The man turned, red-wrapped face expressionless, though Lindon did catch a glimpse of gleaming eyes between the strips of cloth. At least he didn't have the power to see through his mask; that would have been too inhuman.

The Fisher woman's next words were less welcome than a stone through a pane of glass. "Carry the message of a Sandviper worm?" She spat on the ground. "I'd rather cut out my own tongue."

Jai Long froze with his back to her. Slowly, he lifted his spear from his shoulder and grasped it in both hands. Beside him, Kral took a step to one side, chuckling.

"Is this your official response as a representative of the Fisher sect?" Jai Long asked, voice colder than steel in winter.

"This is my response," she said with a sneer, and whipped her hook forward.

Lindon didn't see how it happened, but the blade detached from the hilt as she swung, but it didn't fly out wildly. The curved blade flew in a wide arc as though it were on the end of a whip—or a fisherman's line—but there was nothing visible connecting the handle to the blade. It descended toward Jai Long's neck like a headsman's axe.

The red spear spun in a blurring circle, the spearhead tracing a bright line like the tail of a falling star. His move caught the Fisher's hook, taking it out of the air and sweeping it to the ground.

When the curved blade started flying back toward the Fisher woman as though she were retracting it, Jai Long turned. He kept both hands on the haft of his spear, but now his whole air had changed. He crouched like a tiger about to pounce, and his shining spearhead was a deadly claw.

"If the Fishers will not listen to reason," he said, "then they are not needed."

CHAPTER EIGHT

As Jai Long tensed and readied his spear to attack, shadows slid like dark water down the surface of the nearby buildings. Lindon wondered for an instant what technique Jai Long had used to summon them—maybe he had cultivated shadow madra, which sounded exciting to watch—but the shadows unfolded into eight-legged silhouettes.

A dozen spiders the size of small dogs sunk from the branches above. They hung from threads that were all but invisible in the darkness, and with each fraction of a second they were closer to landing on the back of the spearman's head.

Jai Long must have sensed something wrong, because he leaped back instead of forward, his gleaming spearhead held at high guard.

The spiders stopped about head-height, dangling from their delicate strings. Yerin kept her hand on the hilt of her sword, but they were far enough away that she didn't draw it.

All of the sacred artists in the street reacted differently to the sudden appearance of the creatures, but Lindon's eyes were stuck on the spiders themselves. They were made of dim color, a gray-purple that was the next best thing to black, so at first he'd taken them for Remnants. But he could see through the joints on each of their legs, like they were puppets assembled from Remnant pieces.

More people had gathered along the roadside by this point, and now Lindon scanned from face to face, looking for a drudge. A Soulsmith might have sold this many constructs to someone else, but controlling so many at once took skill and practice. The spiders' creator was probably here, among the crowd.

Most of the witnesses looked disgusted, confused, or alarmed, save for the man with the long yellow hair that Lindon had seen before. At least, he assumed it was the same man; in a camp this size, perhaps there were many disciples of this strange Path that lightened hair color. He was wearing intricate robes of blue and white, so that the cape on his shoulders was raised and separated to resemble wings. It looked as though he'd prepared for a parade.

He met Lindon's glance with eyes of pale blue, no doubt another consequence of his Goldsign. He gave a cheery wave.

Lindon focused on him as the only individual that stood out, but he didn't see a drudge. In fact, the yellow-haired man casually scanned the crowd himself, as though waiting for the one responsible for the spiders to come out.

Only a breath or two had passed since the constructs had descended from overhead, but Lindon had already started to push his way through the crowd to look for the Soulsmith.

He stopped when an old woman drifted down the road from behind the Fishers, her body remaining perfectly still as though she rolled on wheels. He craned his neck to see why, and saw eight legs moving beneath her sacred artist's robes.

What kind of mad experiments were they up to in this Five Factions Alliance? Did Soulsmiths graft construct legs onto human beings? His mother would have called it a horrifying violation of conscience, and she would have hunted down anyone who dared to break such a taboo.

This woman was old, perhaps older than anyone he'd ever seen in his life, with gray hair tied up into a tight bun. Her face was little more than a mass of wrinkles, her body so shrunken that he might have been able to tuck her comfortably into his pack. She held her hands behind the small of her back as she drifted forward on spider's legs, and never reached for the huge bladed goldsteel hook that gleamed on her back.

When she reached the fight, she hopped down and continued on her own two feet, leaving a spider construct behind. Of course she hadn't grafted a spider's legs onto her own, that would have been crazy. That much, at least, was the same here as in Sacred Valley.

The spider she'd left behind was different than the others. It was bigger than the others, its main body lower to the ground, its legs proportionately longer. It was duller than the others, a flat gray, and it didn't seem to have a head; it looked almost like a mechanical disk with spider's legs attached to it.

This one wasn't floating, but Lindon had seen variations of his mother's own segmented brown fish often enough. Drudges didn't look like other constructs—they were duller, usually, more mechanical looking, as though they were made out of real physical parts rather than manifest madra.

This tiny woman wasn't wearing the hammer badge of a Forger, nor the crossed hammers of a Soulsmith, but even so...she was everything that Lindon had ever wanted to be. And no matter how powerful those sacred artists were, she had stopped them with nothing more than the presence of her constructs.

She scurried up to Jai Long, peering at him through eyes almost fused shut with wrinkles. "What is this? Hm? You think Fishers are your mining slaves, that you can beat us whenever you like?"

The young Fisher woman stepped forward, a hook in each hand. "Fisher Gesha, this—"

That was as far as she got before the Soulsmith, Fisher

Gesha, turned and made a beckoning gesture. The young woman jerked forward as though pulled on an invisible string, pulled forward into Gesha's waiting slap.

"If I want the words of a silly girl, I will reach back a hundred years and ask myself."

"Can she really do that?" Lindon asked Yerin, voice low. She gave him such a look that he swallowed the question.

The old woman had turned back to Jai Long, hands clasped behind her back again. "The silly girl called me for help. And I come here, expecting to see dreadbeasts by the thousand, and instead here is a boy with a bag on his head threatening my sect. Do you think that I am not needed? Hm? Do you wish to test yourself against Fisher Gesha?"

Jai Long loomed over the tiny Fisher, but Lindon was impressed when the man didn't take a fearful step back. Instead, he ground his red spear. "I was trying to send a message to the leadership of your sect. It appears I have succeeded."

Fisher Gesha growled and gave the young man's shins a kick. She might as well have kicked a tree, for all the reaction that provoked. "Prattle prattle prattle. You have a message, tell me the message! Do I have to pull it out of your throat? Hm?"

"The Arelius family is on their way," Jai Long said.

The Fisher froze, the statue of a thoughtful grand-mother. "You have confirmed this?"

"To our satisfaction. I can have the evidence delivered to you tomorrow."

Fisher Gesha thought for a moment longer, then turned to the tall young woman again. She was still rubbing her cheek, but Gesha leaped two feet into the air and slapped her on the other side. Then once more.

"Stupid girl! Selfish girl! Your pride is more important than the sect, is it? You think that your honor will matter when Arelius gets here? You think the Underlord will let your eyes touch his spear?"

Underlord, Lindon thought. Was that a title of respect,

like 'Patriarch'? Or was that the rank beyond Truegold?

The young Fisher woman looked as though she were teetering on the edge of tears, but her voice was clear. "I assumed their words were Sandviper lies."

"How can a blind girl see the difference between truth and lies? You pass the words on to me, and I will tell you whether or not they are speaking wind."

Shakily, the young woman buckled her bladed hooks onto straps on her back, then bowed over a salute to Fisher Gesha. "Your unworthy servant understands."

"Hmph." Gesha turned back to Jai Long. "The young are stupid. This was nothing more than an argument between children."

Kral stepped forward before the spearman could respond. His expression was grave again, a prince negotiating with a respected enemy. "One moment, Fisher Gesha. The young woman and her friends have disrespected us gravely. They have a mining team that belongs to us, along with all the hundred scales they harvested from the Ruins today. If we do not recover our property, it will be a slap delivered to all Sandvipers."

The young Fisher woman started to speak up, her voice indignant, but the old Soulsmith cut her off. "Was I wrong? Was this a battle between our great sects, hm? Not a childish spat? If that is so…"

From overhead, all of the spiders hissed in chorus, working their legs furiously on their strings.

"…then this old woman will keep you all company for a while." Her face molded itself into a sketch of a smile.

This time, Jai Long was the one to reply. "We were unwise and unworthy, honored Fisher. The message is delivered, along with our respects. The Alliance will not be divided before the arrival of outsiders."

He bowed himself back, melding into the crowd of Sandvipers. Kral waved them all away, and they seemed only too eager to leave.

The old woman grunted. "You get too strong too early,

and it inflates your head," she muttered. Then she turned back to the Fishers, leaping into the air once again to grab the leader woman's ear. "I shouldn't have to drag a married girl back to her mother once again, but we'll see what she has to say about you."

In the trees, shadowy shapes were scuttling down branches to meld with the darkness. The Soulsmith's drudge walked after her on its eight legs until she hopped backwards on it without looking, instantly gaining over a foot in height.

Lindon followed as though pulled, absently tugging the Thousand-Mile Cloud along behind him. Yerin seized his sleeve. "Where is it you're going?"

"I'm going to see if she needs a...well, 'disciple' is a strong word. So is 'apprentice.' Maybe she needs someone to sweep up her foundry."

"Be careful," Yerin said, heavy with irony. "You aim that arrow too high, it'll fall back down and catch you in the eye.

Lindon faced her, holding her lightly by the shoulders and speaking as he would to his own sister. "I need someone to guide me. *Need.* I can't wait for Iron, because without a proper cycling technique, I don't know when I'll get there. I know you don't want to join up, but I have to."

Something dark passed through Yerin's eyes, like the look his father got after spending too long in drink and old stories, and Lindon hurried to get his next words out. "If it's not too much for me to ask, I'd like you to come with me."

The cloud left her, leaving confusion. "To the Fishers?"

"If I can convince Fisher Gesha, yes. If not, I'm sure there are other Soulsmiths somewhere around. You won't be a part of their sect, and I respect that. But can you at least...stay for a while?"

He felt as though everyone around could hear every word he spoke, and he imagined their gazes boring into him from every direction. Still, he bowed deeply in supplication. "Forgiveness; this one has no right to ask it of you, but he asks still."

Every second that passed was another bead of sweat down his neck, but he remained stuck in that position. The witnesses were beginning to whisper, but he closed them out.

It was truly selfish to tie Yerin down with him, but his chances were infinitely better with her than without. And if he was honest with himself, the thought of being on his own in such a massive collection of Gold sacred artists was terrifying. They could kill him by accident, and no one would ever know what happened to him.

She pushed on his shoulder. "Straighten up. Don't beg me like that, it draws attention. When he straightened, she shifted in place and didn't meet his gaze.

"Follow the Fisher first," she said finally. "One step before the other. Can't tell you I'm going with you if I don't know where, can I?"

That was all Lindon needed to hear. He bolted down the road toward Fisher Gesha, pack bouncing on his back. Yerin didn't run after him, but he didn't think much of that. She was the one with the Iron body; she could catch up whenever she wanted.

●

Following Lindon and Yerin had been even more rewarding than Eithan had hoped; he'd gotten to see an entertaining little show as well. A few sips of rice wine from an untended store shelf, and he had actually enjoyed himself. When the spider woman showed up, it was the perfect twist.

He'd sensed her coming a mile away, so he hadn't been surprised, but then he never was. He had learned to enjoy the reactions of others.

On which topic, he'd been especially delighted with the reactions of his two prospective recruits. Yerin had kept her hand on her sword and her eyes on the biggest threats—Kral, Jai Long, the young Fisher woman whose name no one had mentioned. When the spiders appeared, she had started gathering sword madra from all over the street, so subtly that no one but Eithan had noticed. He was now absolutely certain that she was the Sage of the Endless Sword's disciple, and as such he felt a brief flash of gratitude toward the Sage in the afterlife.

It must be difficult knowing that you had cut and polished a diamond only to have it decorate someone else's crown, but such were the twisting vagaries of life.

Lindon was another pleasant surprise. He had watched the proceedings with undisguised fascination, a hunger burning so hot that Eithan was somewhat tempted to warm his palms against him. He would have been treated badly for his madra deficiency, that wasn't a difficult inference to make, but such mistreatment could have any number of disastrous effects on a young man. It seemed as though Lindon hungered for self-improvement rather than revenge, and he wasn't cringing or sniveling. Eithan could certainly work with that.

Such drive could and probably would get the boy into trouble, but it was also the most indispensible ingredient in taking him past Gold. No one walked far on any Path without both resolve and desire.

Coupled with his pure madra, twin cores, and broad frame, Eithan was wondering if he could have *designed* a better recruit. The boy was simply a blank canvas, waiting for the brush of a master.

Well, there weren't any masters around, but Eithan would do his best anyway.

He didn't follow Lindon as the boy hurried after the Soulsmith, Gesha. She wouldn't want to take him in as her apprentice, but she had a soft heart, and Lindon would—in his own, innocent way—squeeze that until he got what he wanted. Nor did he follow Yerin as she came to her own decision, though either of those paths promised certain entertainment for him.

Instead, he let a whim lead him and followed the Sandvipers.

Kral and Jai Long were locked in a conversation, and none of their subordinates were eager to interrupt. Eithan skipped along behind, touching down with one foot and using an Enforcer binding to launch himself far enough that he almost appeared to be drifting through the air. When he landed, he simply kicked off on the other foot.

Every eye turned to him, which was to be expected with his bright blond hair, flashy movement technique, and stunning good looks. He was better at stealth than anyone expected, but it had never been his strongest approach. He preferred walking in the front door, preferably with a parade behind him and trumpets in front.

One old man gaped at him, jaw dropping foolishly until his lit pipe was ready to fall out. Eithan snatched it from him as he passed, wiping the pipe carefully on his own sleeve—no need to expose himself to infection, even if only the bravest disease would dare to invade his body—and taking a puff himself.

It was a locally grown leaf, and somehow it tasted to Eithan of autumn shadows. He couldn't entirely explain that. What did autumn shadows taste like? He wasn't sure, but that was the first thought that popped into his head, so he went with it.

Finally, his last leap took him close to the Sandvipers, so he settled to a normal stride and walked alongside them, puffing at the pipe.

"...won't work with us," Kral was saying. He was appreciably strong for his age, though flaws in his technique and character meant that he would never make it past Truegold without a truly heaven-defying run of good fortune.

"They might not," Jai Long allowed. This one, on the other hand, had a much better foundation. He could make it to Underlord someday, or beyond. If he did it fast enough, even Eithan might have to bow to him. He smiled at the thought, keeping the pipe clenched in his teeth.

"We don't need their assistance," the Jai exile continued. "We need them to stay out of our way. Even if the Fishers do work against us, they will at least stay quiet about it for the sake of appearance. That's all the space we need."

"We're finished with the maps, then?"

"Within the week, but we'll need more miners."

"You'll have them," Kral said.

Eithan found their whole way of mining fascinating. They gathered these ingenious little scripted constructs at points of heavy vital aura, then operated the script while waiting for the devices to print scales. Where he'd grown up, the process was much more artistic, but perhaps less efficient. Maybe he could bring one of these devices back, have it copied.

It was an impressive and resourceful process, even if it left the operator vulnerable.

Any aura convergence drew Remnants and sacred beasts like flies to rotting meat, and anyone operating the mining construct was helpless. Hence the guards.

So the Sandvipers had come to the conclusion that using captured prisoners was the most expedient way to gather large numbers of scales in a short period of time. The operators would die, but replacing them was cheaper than sending strong sacred artists to guard them. It wouldn't last as a long-term operation, but in the short term it was a ruthlessly efficient strategy. Eithan wondered if it had been Jai Long's idea.

Jai Long started moving casually in Eithan's direction, and Eithan saw through the young man's intentions immediately. He puffed away at his pipe as though oblivious.

When you saw everything, you usually had to pretend you didn't. It was more polite that way.

"The most we can hope for is a temporary truce," Jai Long said from behind his scripted mask. "This is a game we can win alone, but not if we allow enemy agents to do as they like."

The spear strike had quite a powerful technique behind it. If Eithan let it land, it might even split through his chest and skewer him on the rough wooden wall at his back.

But he felt the technique build in the accelerated cycle of Jai Long's madra, in the quick breathing as the young man ramped up his spirit. The muscles in his arm tightened, as his whole body moved in concert like a finely tuned instrument. Eithan saw the move before it was born, felt it in the thousand webs of invisible power that passed through everything around him.

Jai Long was very powerful, Eithan couldn't deny that. But he'd found that people tended to overrate raw power.

The spear passed over Eithan's head, trailing light, as Eithan sank casually to a crouch. A ribbon of smoke traced his descent, even as the smoldering leaf in the pipe's bowl went dark.

He used his finger to tamp it down, taking a half-step to the left. The spear passed to his right. Then, before Jai Long could execute a technique with more madra behind it, Eithan walked into the crowd of Sandvipers.

One of them had a light.

"Forgive me," he said to the young woman with the scripted bit of wire in her pocket. He held out his pipe. "Would you mind?"

The Sandvipers scattered as Jai Long swept his spear in an arc, glowing with light to rival the moon and enough force to split a tree's trunk. Eithan followed the young woman's motion as she threw herself out of the way of the technique, dipping a hand into the pocket of her fur coat and withdrawing the metal wire.

Jai Long's deadly madra passed over his back. He gave a flick of his spirit, and the end of the wire sparked to life.

He straightened as he used the tiny device to light his pipe, sighing as the leaf caught. Eithan blew a ring of smoke in Jai Long's direction and then tossed the scripted wire back to its owner.

"Thank you." To Jai Long, he spoke out of genuine admiration. "Your spear is everything I'd heard it would be. The Jai clan must have been blinded when it came to you, that's my honest opinion. Casting you out because of your

Remnant. Give them a chance, and I'm sure they'll take you back."

Eithan had a general policy of being encouraging whenever possible, though he'd found that it wasn't always taken in the spirit he'd meant it.

Kral, for example, had darkened as though he was prepared to pass a death sentence. He cradled a pair of awls that crawled with corrosive green madra, brandishing them like a couple of stingers. The Sandvipers spread out, entrapping Eithan in a formation they'd obviously practiced. The pale blue aura of the air began to crawl with toxic green; they were calling up some kind of poison aura, probably to trap him in a deadly fog.

They'd reacted quickly. He favored them with a half-bow of respect.

But the poison fog would ruin the flavor of his pipe, so he would have to decline.

Eithan turned to Jai Long, who—unlike the members of the Sandviper sect—had no special body to protect him from the incoming poison. The man with the red-wrapped features had paused with spear cocked in one hand, regarding Eithan.

"Who are you?" he asked.

"Ordinarily, you would ask that question *before* trying to stab me with your spear," Eithan said, blowing out another mouthful of smoke.

"You've been following us."

"You're more interesting than most of the people I follow," Eithan pointed out. "And there is a purpose to this, despite what you may think."

Jai Long readied his spear. "I am Jai Long, attendant of the Sandviper sect."

Kral stepped out. "Kral, heir to the Sandvipers."

The spearman looked at his friend, ready to protest—it wasn't entirely honorable for a sacred artist to fight two against one, but that was the only way this would hold any interest for Eithan.

He spread a hand in a generous gesture. "You're welcome to come at me both at once. I don't have anything else to do for the evening."

Kral gripped his awls tighter, and Eithan could practically hear him refusing out of general stubbornness. He sighed.

"Fine then. I spit on the honor of the Sandvipers, that pathetic collection of cowards and cripples. You don't have a spine between you, you only use poison because it takes courage to face an enemy in battle, and I could improve on a Sandviper warrior by stapling a snake to a scarecrow's arm. Also your mothers were dogs and your fathers were blind, and so on. Fight me."

Some of the less mature among them were actually angry. Kral in particular was growing hot around the collar; he wouldn't be used to people challenging him to his face. The majority of them were either confused or looking for a trap. Jai Long glanced around the road as though to find Eithan's companions.

"I'm alone," Eithan said. "No need to soil yourselves."

That was enough to make Jai Long level his spear again, if only in reservation. "If you wanted to kill yourself, you didn't have to bother me."

Eithan blew smoke in his eyes.

There were eight enemies. Three women, five men. Of those, only Kral and Jai Long were at the Highgold level; the rest were Lowgold, though that didn't mean he could entirely discount them. A Sandviper's venom would do to flesh what a live coal did to a sheet of thin paper, and he was surrounded by toxic aura now; a quick scan of the area with his spirit showed him an ocean of malicious green. All the Sandviper Goldsigns hissed at him, green madra rolling quickly through seven sets of madra channels.

And though he toyed with them, Highgold was actually a fairly impressive stage of advancement. He reminded himself of this even as he enjoyed the smoky taste of autumn shadows.

A power like the one he'd inherited from his father's line tended to make one careless. Superior awareness made him difficult to hit, but did nothing to protect him otherwise. He had to remind himself that there was a reason why people usually felt fear.

But ultimately, even his own reminder did nothing to make him more alert. Why should it? He was born careless, after all.

And this was fun.

A twisting line of starlight represented the Jai clan's spear techniques, and he stepped forward in between one thrust and another. Needles of green fell from above him as a Sandviper tried to drop Forged spikes on top of him, but he brushed into the crowd and the sacred artist had to cancel his attack or risk impaling his friends.

Smoke trailed behind him as Eithan waded deeper into the crowd, hands in his outer pockets. An awl pierced where one Sandviper expected his head would be, but it passed harmlessly through yellow hair as Eithan sped that step up a fraction. A sword slashed at his ribs, but his next stride carried him slightly to the right, and the sword caught another Sandviper in the ribs.

Venomous aura swelled and burst, leaving a cloud of poisonous green fog around him, but he'd already slid to one side, letting that cloud stop Jai Long in his tracks, preventing him from thrusting a spear through Eithan's back.

Though Eithan walked evenly through the pack, puffing contentedly on his pipe, every move the Sandvipers made either struck an ally or blocked another's approach. He moved no faster than they did, simply slid into gaps that his web of madra showed him would be there.

To them, he must have looked like a ghost drifting through.

To him, it was as simple as a child following his father's footsteps in the mud. While enjoying a nice pipe.

Eithan emerged from the other side of his eight opponents. The two Highgolds looked more astonished than the rest of them, as though they'd grasped truths the others hadn't, although that could be because the Lowgolds were mostly groaning in pain at wounds inflicted by the others.

Pulling the pipe from his mouth, Eithan waved. "My apologies, ladies and gentlemen. If it's any consolation to you, I will repay you for this."

Kral shouted and gathered his madra, preparing to use a broader technique, perhaps the best one of which he was currently capable. Eithan turned to him with interest.

Jai Long stopped his friend with a hand. "What is your name, elder brother?"

'Elder' brother might have been a bit much, in Eithan's opinion. Surely he didn't look much older than Jai Long himself did. But it was an expression of respect around here, so he smiled. "They call me Eithan."

"Eithan. If for whatever reason we have offended you, I will take responsibility. Don't let petty issues come between you and the Sandviper sect, not when we could work together for mutual benefit."

Eithan watched Jai Long's dark eyes through the gap in the man's wrappings. He was shrewd, for his age. He'd go far.

"I have nothing but respect for the honorable Sandviper sect," Eithan said, which wasn't entirely truthful. "I sought a diversion, and you diverted me, for which I thank you." He bowed with a flourish of his stolen pipe.

Kral pointed an awl at him. "My father returns soon, and he will tolerate no disrespect to our name."

"I'm sure he won't," Eithan said, already casting his mind out to the rest of the camp. Surely there must be some other opportunity for amusement somewhere. "Until we meet again, gentlemen."

He didn't turn around, but Jai Long bowed to his retreating back. There was a wise man.

Kral glowered and prepared a Striker technique that hissed and spat with green fury on the edge of his hand before he growled in frustration and let it die.

So there was a little wisdom in him too.

CHAPTER NINE

The Fishers led Lindon back to a tall building that looked like more of a permanent structure than anything around it. He thought of it as a barn, wide and tall with broad doors, and Gesha's spiders scuttled up its walls and inside through holes in the roof.

"I'll deal with you tomorrow, girl," she said to the young woman as they reached the barn doors. "Be here at dawn, or I'll come root you out with my hook." The razor edge of her curved goldsteel blade gleamed. The tall woman paled and babbled something, then took the slightest excuse to hurry off. Her friends joined her, casting fearful glances back at the Soulsmith.

Gesha stood there, hands behind her back, like a pocket-sized elder. The spider legs of her drudge worked impatiently against the dirt, but she didn't so much as shift.

Lindon glanced around, looking for some reason why she was just staring at the barn doors. Did she expect them to open themselves? Was she waiting for her spiders to open them for her? Or was she waiting for someone?

With his height, the pack on his back, and the rust-red cloud following him around, Lindon knew he cut a recognizable figure in the darkness. He backed up a step, though he was far enough away that he shouldn't have bothered the Soulsmith. He watched, waiting for some clue, as five minutes turned into ten.

Finally, the old woman barked out, "Do you know what happened to the last man who kept me waiting? Hm? I married him. That's a threat."

Lindon kept looking around, waiting for someone else to step out of the darkness, before she turned and speared him with a glare over one shoulder. "Well? Do they only teach manners to short Coppers, and not tall ones?"

He rushed a bow over fists pressed together. "This one apologizes for his lack of manners, honored elder. This one was ignorant, and did not realize he was being observed."

A snort ripped out of the tiny woman. "'This one,' is it? Hurry up, get closer. I may have eyes everywhere, but this pair doesn't work like they used to."

Lindon hurried over, steadying his pack as he ran. He'd planned on doing something drastic to attract the Fisher's attention, but she was inviting him over on her own. She'd noticed him, and that could only be a good thing.

He bowed again when he reached her, both to show respect and to give him an excuse to lean down so she could get a close look at his face. She squinted at him for a moment through a mask of wrinkles, then patted her bun.

"Are you the tallest five-year-old in the world?" she asked suddenly.

"No, honored elder. This one's training was somewhat delayed."

"*This* one, *that* one. If you say that again, I'll spin your Copper head around on your neck. Now, tell me your name."

"Wei Shi Lindon, honored elder."

She grunted. "Does the Wei clan teach you to skulk around as you make requests of an elder? Hm? Are you from a clan of skulkers, Shi Lindon?"

Honestly, he was. The Wei specialized in illusions, and as a result typically hid and waited until they could take advantage of the battle. They fought like snowfoxes, not like tigers, but he doubted that answer would satisfy her.

"Apologies, honored elder. This...*I* would like to offer my humble services to you, in any way I can."

She glared at him, her spider's legs clacking against stones hidden in the dirt. "Humble? Humble is an apprentice who can't make a levitation plate out of cloud madra. If a Copper could offer me *humble* services, he'd be a genius. Are you a genius, Copper?"

He wished she would stop calling him that, but he wasn't about to say so. "My mother was a Soulsmith, and I worked as her assistant since the day I learned to cycle. I know my knowledge is deficient and paltry, but I know many of the basic scripts, I can dissect a Remnant into its functional components, I can perform basic maintenance—"

Gesha made a 'tsst' sound and threw up her hands. "You don't think I have enough to worry about? Go. Go! If you bother me again, I'll set the spiders on you."

Lindon bowed to her, projecting compliance. "Of course, honored elder. You're tired, and I'm keeping you from your rest."

In an uncanny display of mind-reading, Gesha said, "I'd best not see you here in the morning, waiting for me to wake up!"

That had been his plan, in fact. A bead of sweat rolled across his forehead. "I would not disrespect the honored elder's wishes that way. But if I may be so rude as to offer one last explanation—"

She flicked fingers at him, and a spider ran down the barn door toward him. Not her drudge, on which she still stood, but an ordinary construct that was probably intended to do nothing but observe and report as commanded.

It was made of jointed purple madra, and it ran on the door as easily as on the ground. Its head was featureless except for a couple of mandibles, which opened as it chirped at him. It sounded more like a bird than a snake, which he hadn't expected. Hadn't it hissed earlier, or was that his imagination?

He dropped his pack to free his shoulders and drew the halfsilver dagger. The constructs back in Sacred Valley had been deadly if directed, but predictable enough if unguarded. But this was the product of a Gold Soulsmith at the head of a sect full of Golds. It might drill its legs through his flesh, leaving little spurting holes, or tear into him with its mandibles, or leave him spun up into a cocoon to decorate the ceiling of the nearby barn...

One of its legs hitched and it almost stumbled, its gait uneven, before it righted itself and continued on. A stumble meant a defect. It must be old, in need of maintenance. That was a weakness he could exploit.

But it was close now, so close that he could hear its sharp feet pricking into the dirt, and that one stumble no longer looked like a weakness at all. Sometimes constructs didn't perform as they should. Maybe the ground had been more treacherous than it looked. It was a slim chance to gamble on.

Then it had reached his feet, and Lindon moved.

He seized the pack from the ground beside him with one hand, holding it like a shield as he flopped belly-first on top of the spider-construct.

The spider tried to scuttle out of the way, but he caught it on the edge, imprisoning it beneath his pack. Its legs flailed, and it gave an angry chirp, but it was pinned. He had it.

His body surged down suddenly, as though he'd grown twice as heavy or someone was standing on his back. His head was pulled down until his nose was all but pressed against its slick gray-purple back, and he realized the truth: the spider was pulling him in.

He didn't know how—undoubtedly it was some function of its madra, or some kind of script—but the spider was using an invisible force to pull him closer.

The halfsilver dagger was in his hand, burning to be used, but he kept it gripped in a tight fist. He'd need that option available, but he had something else to try first.

With a good deal of writhing, he squirmed forward enough to get his left hand onto the spider's back.

Then, adjusting his breathing from panic to a measured cycling technique, he fed pure madra into the construct.

Something like the Thousand-Mile Cloud was relatively simple in its construction. It was made of densely packed cloud madra, which floated. You could activate a single script-circle buried at its core in order to get it to move. It followed the direction of the operator's spirit, not any directions in its actual script, so it was a flexible but simple tool. It would never be able to fly off without active guidance.

The spider, by contrast, was an intricate clockwork of branching scripts, interlocking plates of madra, and delicate organs that must have been extracted from Remnants. His madra flowed through it, giving him a vague picture of its functions, and of the scripts that had to remain active to keep it following orders.

A spark of madra came from a crystal flask, a tiny speck of a vessel that must power this construct's operation. Using his own madra, Lindon forced the flow from that flask aside.

It didn't take much power to do so; there was no will behind that madra, so it was easily directed. He simply blocked the flow into the script, keeping it bound inside the crystal.

The spider shivered once, then collapsed. The invisible force on him vanished, leaving him panting in gulps of air.

Irregular, spiky footsteps scraped along the dirt as Gesha slid closer on her drudge, and she would arrive to find him limply hanging on her deactivated construct. He pushed himself up, running shaking fingers along the edge of the spider's leg.

He might have noticed a defect before, a place where the construct was in need of maintenance. If that was the case...

One plate of the leg made a harsh noise as his hand moved over it, crackling like thin ice. He pushed madra into it desperately, fueling it with all the force his rapidly cycling spirit could churn out.

The *best* way to maintain a construct's parts was to infuse it with madra of the same Path, which would keep that part fresh and new for as long as you wanted. The second best way was to purify madra through a device like a crystal flask or a specially designed script and use that instead. It took much longer, was less efficient, and resulted in less accuracy for some cases that required delicate craftsmanship. But it worked.

In fact, Lindon had only recently understood that the purity of his madra was why his mother let him work with her on her projects at all.

The leg-plate strengthened a little. Enough that it wouldn't collapse under the construct's own weight, at least, which should demonstrate his value somewhat.

He looked up to see Fisher Gesha an inch away from him, her gray bun even with his head, peering into the construct. After a second, she slapped his hand away, feeling the spider with her own fingers.

"Did you steal the Path of the Fisherman? Hm?"

"No, honored elder," he said, though it was just a formality. If the Path of the Fisherman was what the Fishers followed—and he had a good feeling that it was—she would be able to sense that power on him if he had it. She'd only asked out of irritation.

"Then come here." She grabbed him by the back of the neck, and he remained perfectly still. In his experience, those with Iron bodies tended to forget the fragility of those without.

She pushed him back a second later, eyes wide. The expression looked comical in her heavily wrinkled face. "You have no training?"

"No, elder."

"No Path at all?"

"No, elder."

"You're Copper, but you've never taken a *taste* of aura?"

"I was never given a Path, honored elder. I don't know how."

Something like pity sparked in her eyes, and she patted him roughly on the back of the head. "You come from a clan of fools."

He hesitated before protesting. "They are my family, honored elder..."

"Bah." She made a spitting noise at that. "No family of yours. But you can make scales for me, so I'll take you."

He searched her quickly for signs of mockery, disappointment, irritation. Anything that might indicate she was lying. "You'll teach me?"

She slapped him in the back of the head. "I'll work you until your bones are nubs, that's what I'll do for you. You won't get the secrets of the sect until you've brought enough value to us, which you'll do slowly and obediently. Is that clear enough?"

Lindon dropped to his knees, pushing his head into the dirt, blinking back sudden tears. "The disciple greets his master."

"Stop that. I'm not your master."

"Your disciple understands."

"I'm going to make you do what my servants can't do, because they've advanced too far. You understand? Hm? You're lower than my servants." She waved a hand aside, and the barn door rumbled open.

He understood that he was going to be working inside a Soulsmith's foundry. Even if he did nothing but sweep the floors, it was an opportunity for him. He'd take it. He'd take anything.

"Get in there," she said. "Maintenance on all constructs by dawn, and don't think you'll get any sleep. If you look like you're going to finish early, I'll make another one."

"Yes, master," Lindon said, hurrying inside.

At last, he was going to be a Soulsmith.

As dawn's first light filtered through the blackened trees surrounding the Five Factions Alliance, Yerin returned, dragging a bright blue corpse behind her. It looked something like a crab painted onto the world in the colors of the sky, and it leaked azure light as she trudged through the outer gates and down the main street.

At her peak condition, she should have been able to run carrying something as light as this, but she felt like her bones had been filled with lead. Now that she settled down and thought, she hadn't had a real rest in...months, probably.

Even now that she'd crossed the threshold to Gold, gaining a shiny metal arm with a sword stuck on it, her body had limits. She was starting to feel them.

Didn't help that every rotten set of eyes on the way in was looking at her like she was dragging a bloody sack of dead dogs behind her. This was a camp of sacred artists, wasn't it? Couldn't be that unusual, seeing someone dragging in a Remnant's corpse.

Or maybe it was the cargo she'd slung over her shoulder that they were staring at.

It took her a handful of wrong turns to find the Fisher section of camp again, by which time she wondered if she could learn to sleepwalk on the fly. The crowd could just wash around her like a river around a boulder, and rot take them all.

Finally, she passed down a street she recognized, dragging the blue-leaking Remnant under trees that had been decorated with spider constructs the night before. It looked different in the light, like it had been dyed a different color.

She grabbed some Fisher pup about ten years old, demanding directions to Fisher Gesha. He looked like she'd popped out an extra eye—worse than that, to be true, since there were more than a few Goldsigns that gave you an extra eyeball—but he gave her rough directions.

When she followed them to a huge barn that had been slapped down in the middle of camp, she almost turned back to show the kid the flat edge of her sword. Soulsmiths required a lot of space for their work, that was true, but it was her observation that they liked to do their business in as flashy a place as possible. Last Soulsmith she visited had built a glowing palace out of shining pillars and sat on a throne of burning inhuman skulls.

But the Desolate Wilds *were* the back-end of nowhere, where even Sacred Valley looked civilized. Weak, but civilized. Maybe working in a barn was showing off.

She could have rapped on the door, but that would have taken energy. Instead, she simply hauled the door open.

It slid on a track, spilling sunlight into the barn.

The floor was actually covered in hay, but this was clearly the foundry of an active Soulsmith. A rainbow of severed limbs hung from hooks in the ceiling, drizzling colored sparks. Spiders hung from the rafters like bats in a cave, and stalls that should have held animals instead contained massive constructs—duller than Remnants and mysterious in construction. She didn't want to think what constructs that size had been built to do, so she didn't bother.

Lindon was sitting at a long workbench arranged down the center of the room like a feeding trough, broad shoulders bent over a half-assembled spider. He looked older than he was, until she happened to reach out and scan his spirit. Then she'd sense the pathetic strength of a Copper, which she always associated with children. It gave her a queasy feeling, like seeing a grown man with a baby's head on his shoulders.

It was a relief to see him, though she still hadn't fully shaken her irritation. He'd *insisted* on joining a faction, like he knew up from down out here without her. He did need some real training, and she couldn't give it to him, but this was still an inconvenience.

Now that she had eyes on him, her previous worries seemed simpleminded. Foolish. Of course he wasn't going to run off, leaving her alone in a sea of strangers without a single friendly soul. No reason he should.

Fisher Gesha hopped down from an upper floor that Yerin hadn't noticed, caught by the legs of the spider-construct that jutted out from under her robes. She held her hands behind her back, wrinkled face stuck in a mask of irritation. "What is this? Hm? You think we take customers now?"

"Rumor says you take in strangers for a price," Yerin said. She hauled on the rope binding the Remnant, bringing the blue crab forward. "This is supposed to be worth something." She'd found it by following a team of Fishers who had skirted around this Remnant as too dangerous. Not so dangerous when she dismembered it from two hundred feet away, it turned out. Now its limbs were bundled up on its carapace, and she pulled it along on its belly.

Fisher Gesha rubbed her chin with two fingers. "What do you want?"

"Shelter in the Fishers for me," Yerin said. Then she pointed to Lindon. "Training for him. Real stuff, not this sweep-and-gather rot."

Lindon raised one sheepish hand. "Gratitude, Yerin. I will repay you for this, but she already agreed—"

The Fisher cut him off with a gesture, eyeing the pack on Yerin's shoulder. "You have something else for me, don't you?"

Yerin slapped the bundle down on the floor, unrolling it with one foot. It was a trio of blood-spattered furs that, until a few hours ago, had been worn by Sandvipers.

"Dead?" Gesha asked, eyes sharp.

"Not quite," Yerin said, because she had known better than to unleash three hostile Remnants in the middle of a crowd. "But I can tell you they're not happy."

A smile creased Gesha's face. "I think we can find a space for you."

CHAPTER TEN

The space they'd found for Yerin was among the main sect, in rooms reserved for the women of the Fishers. They'd given Lindon a spot up among the rafters, in a pile of hay only accessible by a creaking ladder. He had to sleep motionless on his back for fear of rolling off the edge, which meant he spent his nights staring up at the spider constructs dangling over his head.

But he wasn't concerned about sleep. Not when there was so much to learn.

The first day, Gesha had her drudge run over the blue crab Remnant that Yerin had brought, the construct's eight legs moving at blurring speeds to dismantle the spirit and separate it into usable parts. She handed him first a claw bigger than his whole upper body, then a pile of tubes that looked something like intestines, then a Forged blue beak. The whole mess didn't act quite right; it smelled of lightning storms and salty water rather than rotten guts, and it felt more like oiled glass than anything natural.

After he'd separated the parts into buckets, a task he'd often performed for his mother, he sealed them with scripts to prevent them from decaying and 'sent them to storage.' Which meant that he shoved the boxes into the giant closet at the back of the barn, labeled only with a code that he hoped Fisher Gesha could read.

Most of the crab would go back there, to serve as what Gesha called 'dead matter.' These would be the most mundane parts of a construct—maybe the shell of a spider, maybe the hilt of a sword—and were needed only for their physical properties.

The parts she *didn't* send into storage, the parts she kept out on her workbench, those were more interesting.

Lindon's mother had never allowed him to help with this part, though he'd caught glimpses through cracked doors and around corners. This was the part of being a Soulsmith that required delicacy and skill, but Fisher Gesha hacked away at these treasures like a butcher working on a slab of meat.

She started with a cluster of blue rocky madra about the size of a fist, but after a few strokes of her bladed goldsteel hook, she was left with a...

He wanted to call it a 'heart,' because that was the nearest analogy in a living being, but it didn't look like that mass of muscle that was left over after his father cleaned a deer. It was a tightly wound tangle of tubes, so that Lindon thought it might actually be *one* tube, so folded and looped in so many different directions that it became a knotted mass.

Gesha held it up in one hand. "We call this a *binding*, you see? We work with these like a blacksmith works with iron."

"And the rest of the material? Do you still use it for constructs?" he asked, gesturing back toward the closet door. Even the dead matter of an unusual Remnant would have supplied his mother for months.

She snorted. "We fold it into different shapes, use it to build the skeletons, but the heart and soul of every construct is a binding. If we could work with bindings completely, we would. You think the rest of the Remnant is expensive? No. This is the gemstone inside the mountain."

She tossed it to him, and he caught it in both his hands. It smelled like a rainy day.

"Put your hand over the tube at the top," she said. "Point the other end—no, not at me! You want me to toss you out? At the floor! Now, funnel a trickle of madra into it. Just a little, do you hear me?"

Lindon did, careful not to put in too much. The binding made a tiny whining sound.

"Well, more than *that*," she said.

He took deeper breaths in rhythm, cycling his madra and forcing more power into the binding. It squealed louder.

Gesha muttered to herself.

He forced all the madra he could into the twisted organ, and finally it spurted out a spray of water.

"Finally," she said, snatching it back. She shook the binding in her hand, drawing his attention to it. "This was a Purelake Remnant, you hear me? Primary aspect of water. When this sacred artist was alive, she made water from the aura in the air, you see? This was a technique she'd mastered, and it becomes part of her spirit. Her Remnant uses this binding, does the same thing."

Lindon's jaw almost cracked under the force of his questions.

"Her technique becomes a part of the Remnant? How? Why?"

"Patterns," Gesha said shortly, tucking the binding away in a drawer. "You've seen scripts, haven't you? What are they, if not shapes that guide madra? What is a technique, if not weaving madra in a certain pattern?" She held out a hand. "You move the right madra, in the right way, with the right rhythm, and you get..." A pair of pliers smacked into her open hand, drawn by some technique she'd used. "You move it any other way, and you get..." She waved her hand. "...nothing. Hm? You see?"

"I believe I do, but please forgive another question. A binding is like a script *inside* your soul?"

"You think it's that simple? No. A script is a drawing, a

binding is a statue. Bindings are pearls, and Remnants are the clams around them. You see?"

On some level, he did. Bindings had weight, depth. A script-circle was nothing but a carved circle of letters. But they seemed to do the same things, so he wasn't entirely sure what advantages a binding had.

He pointed to the drawer containing the binding. "How did you know which end took madra in, and which end spat water out?"

"Experience," she replied, prying at the shell of what he guessed was another concealed binding.

"How did you know it would create water, instead of something else?"

"Drudge told me." She ran a hand down the smooth carapace of her large spider-construct, which rested on the desk next to her. "It tastes the aspects of madra for me, you see? It tells me which madra touches on water, which touches on ice, and which is simply blue."

"And now that you have the binding, you can use it in a construct? One that will automatically produce water? Is that all you can use it for, or can you do something else with it?"

She pointed at him with the pliers. "*That* is the question worthy of a Soulsmith." He tried to restrain his smile to polite levels, but he couldn't hold it back. She glowered at him.

"Don't smile. A smile doesn't go with those eyes. You look like you want to eat me for breakfast." She smacked herself in the forehead with the back of her hand. "Tsst. What am I doing? You are not my student. Sweep! Sweep the floors!"

During the days of sweeping, he watched customers come and go. They usually met Gesha or other Fishers elsewhere, and only the most determined tracked her to her foundry. That was when Lindon found the answer to his question.

More than once, Gesha would take a binding and encase it in dead matter, using her drudge to seal it up so that it looked like a sword, or a shield, a shovel, or whatever the customer ordered. Once, when she'd encased a crystalline binding into a hammer that looked like it was hacked from glacial ice, a burly man in thick furs came to pick it up only seconds after she'd finished.

He had no sandviper Remnant on his arm, and he was dressed in much thicker clothing. The dark furs of his outfit were even dusted with snow, though autumn was only beginning and the days were still warm.

He took the hammer from her without a word, caressing it in gloved hands. Before Gesha could say a word, without warning, he turned and slammed the icy head into the planks of the barn.

Ice bloomed from the center of the impact, blasting away like waves that froze instantly. Lindon jumped at the sound, but a moment later he stopped in awe. A flower of ice had bloomed in the barn.

It could have been the man's own sacred arts that had created the ice, but he suspected that wasn't the case. The man could have tested his own technique anywhere, without the hammer. No, he was trying out this weapon...with the binding inside. He'd seen one produce water, so why not ice?

The sword Yerin had inherited from her master was white and unnaturally cold, and her techniques seemed more deadly with it than without it. Did it have a binding in it too?

Gesha beat the stranger around the shoulders for ruining her barn floor, and made him pay extra scales to fix it. Lindon had heard of other transactions before, but this was the first time he'd seen one, and therefore the first time he'd actually seen a scale.

It was a little disappointing. It was nothing more than a coin, though one Forged of madra to be sure, translucent and threaded with blue. Fifty scales for the hammer, twenty more for her floor, and five because he'd made her get up early. He paid gladly, whistling as he carried his new weapon out over his shoulder.

When Gesha noticed Lindon's interest in the scales, she nodded to him. "You're curious? Hm? Good, because this will be your job now. Once you clean up that ice."

●

Sandviper Tern was a thin man, not tall, with a tendency to avoid Jai Long's gaze. He shifted his weight nervously with every word, and even the serpent Goldsign on his arm was smaller than usual. He gave the impression of a frightened child even when he was perfectly confident.

Which, today, he was not.

"The Copper is with one of the Fisher Soulsmiths," Tern said to Jai Long's boots. "We had him observed in shifts, but he didn't leave her foundry. She must have taken him in."

Jai Long looked over Tern's head to the cages full of captured miners. There were two rows of scripted cages, framing a strip of grass that led directly into the cavernous entrance of the Transcendent Ruins. He didn't open his spiritual senses, but the signs of gathered vital aura were everywhere: each blade of grass blew in different directions, a patch of frost clustered like mold onto the edge of one cage while the inhabitants of another sweated, and the clouds over the Ruins churned like they were being stirred by a giant hand.

The heavens and the earth overflowed with power. And here were his miners, shaking the bars of their cages in fear and anger.

Not mining.

"She likely wants him to sweep the foundry, clean up after botched constructs, sort boxes, that kind of thing," Tern continued, raising his voice to be heard over the racket behind him and shifting his gaze to Jai Long's shoulder. "If she throws him out in the next few days, we'll see it. No need to worry about that. His companion might be more of a problem, considering she—"

"What is happening here?"

Tern straightened and very nearly looked Jai Long in the eyes. "Just a bit of trouble, nothing to concern you, High-gold. A little dissent in the ranks, that's all."

One of the cages shook forward under the weight of its occupants, threatening to tip over.

"Where did this trouble *come* from, Sandviper Tern?"

Tern winced, shifting from foot to foot on the grass. "The dreadbeasts, they're...getting worse. We don't know where they're coming from, but there's no end to them. And the Remnants...at the start, they acted like Remnants. A good few of them attacked, but some of them just climbed back into the tunnels, or sat down, or started counting clouds, or what have you. Now, they all want blood."

Jai Long stared him down, waiting for a further explanation. His masked face disturbed some people—it disturbed everyone, in reality—but it was nothing compared to how they'd react if he walked around with face bare. He was considering giving Tern a nice big grin.

"...the miners won't go back in," Tern said finally. "The Remnants cut into them last night, and we lost more than one team. Now they won't listen to us. We picked the one that was screaming the loudest, speared him up in front of them, made them watch as he died. Still didn't get them into the tunnel."

Jai Long hefted his spear. "I see."

"We could shove them in, but I don't know how we'd get them to work."

"No," Jai Long said, "you don't." He stalked forward, weapon in one hand, gathering Stellar Spear madra into the steel head as he walked. More eyes turned to him with every step, agitated miners and overwhelmed Sandviper guards alike.

By the time he reached the middle of the row, the noise had settled into what—in this crowded camp—passed for silence.

"Take whatever you can keep," Jai Long announced, and though his voice was even, it carried to every cage. "It's the law of the Wilds. The Sandvipers took you because you could not repay a debt, because you lost a duel, because you challenged us and failed. One and all, it was because you were too weak. Would any among you dispute that truth?"

A few angry voices shouted out in response.

"If you are dissatisfied, if you believe that bad fortune is to blame rather than your own weakness, I will give you a chance to prove it." Jai Long ground the butt of his spear into the earth and let his spearhead glow like a beacon next to his eyes. "Step forward, and I will have your collar removed. You will face me with honor, like a sacred artist, and show me your strength."

This silenced most of the voices, but one bulky man stepped up. He was twice as wide across the shoulders as Jai Long, with his muscular neck straining against his restrictive collar. "I have confidence in facing any Lowgold," he rumbled. "Send one as your champion, and I will face him. There is no sense in fighting a Highgold."

Only duels between those of the same stage could possibly prove anything, otherwise Jai Long may as well be slaughtering sheep. He looked to Tern.

"Sandviper Tern, remove this man's collar."

The Sandviper did so, with a glare and unnecessary shove to the prisoner. For his part, the big man gave a deep breath and flexed his hands, no doubt feeling the madra passing through his body unobstructed for the first time since his capture.

"Now place it on me," Jai Long said, eyes on his opponent.

Every Sandviper stared at him. So did the bulky miner.

Sandviper Tern's mouth gaped. "Highgold, don't you think it would be better for me to face him?"

Jai Long did not move his gaze or adjust his inflection as he said, "You are one mistake away from filling a cage yourself. Your safest path forward is to do what I tell you, precisely when I tell you to do it. Starting now."

Tern tripped over himself to snap the collar around Jai Long's neck.

The light of his spear dimmed dramatically, and the flow of madra within his core squeezed tight. The restriction of the collar wasn't anything so straightforward as reducing his power to the levels of a Lowgold; it hobbled him in every way, leaving him with nothing more than the physical strength of his Iron body, his combat skills, and the most basic of techniques.

"If this man wins, he goes free of whatever debts he owes to the Sandviper sect," Jai Long said. "If he does not, his life is mine to do with as I will."

The big man nodded, signaling his own agreement, and a Sandviper handed him a spear of his own. He ran a hand down the shaft and took the weapon in both hands, feeling its balance, holding it ready.

When the opponent was prepared, Jai Long moved.

It was a simple thrust, honed from millions of repetitions and glowing with the last embers of a weak Stellar Spear technique. The bulky man's dodge was a hair out of place, his counterstrike a beat too slow.

The glowing spearhead passed through his heart and emerged from the other side.

Jai Long withdrew his weapon even as a Remnant—creamy off-white, like fresh butter—peeled itself out of the man's body with a couple of shovel-shaped hands.

It cocked a head like a bucket, staring at the Ruins, and then lumbered away from Jai Long. It followed the flow of aura in the air until it disappeared into the darkness of the entrance.

In the cages, the miners were quiet.

"Your lives belong to me," Jai Long said, without raising his voice. "When the Five Factions Alliance disperses, I have no more use for them. You will be set free, safe, your debts clear, and encouraged to return home. At that time, you may consider your time in the Ruins little more than a dream."

He tapped his collar, and Tern removed it with shaking hands. "That is my will. To you, it is law. There is no alternative. There is no escape. If you die in the Ruins, it will be for the same flaw that brought you here in the first place: your own weakness."

Jai Long turned and walked away, gesturing for Tern to follow him.

Behind him, the cages began to murmur.

"They'll go into the Ruins with you now, but watch for runaways. Have guards return any that escape, don't kill them."

Tern nodded frantically.

"And what did *you* learn today, Tern?"

The man stumbled, then hustled to catch up. "How impressive you are, Highgold. Your reputation does not do you justice."

"So when I tell you to capture a Copper..."

Tern swallowed loudly.

"You wait for an opportunity," Jai Long said, fixing Tern with his gaze. "If you die of old age, you will do so at your post. The second the Copper leaves, or the Fisher leaves him, you will be there with a sack ready to pull over his head. And, Tern?"

The Sandviper quivered with the effort of looking him in the eye.

"This is not important to me. This is the *least* of my priorities. But it should be very, very important to you."

Sandviper Tern dropped to his knees and bowed until his head reached the ground.

●

Lindon lost his appreciation for that beautiful, wild ice sculpture after he scraped every inch of it away from the floor with a shovel. When he'd finished, both sweating and freezing, Gesha walked him over to a new corner of the foundry. Something that looked like a metal barrel with handles stood there, with script covering every inch and a few gleaming jewels studding an otherwise unremarkable lid. After close examination, he identified them as crystal flasks.

"This," she said, slapping the barrel, "is mining equipment. You've heard us talking about miners in the Ruins, have you? Well, there's nothing to it. All a 'miner' has to do is go where the aura is thick, funnel madra into the handles, and the script does the rest. A trained dog could do it. When it purifies enough aura, it comes out the other end..."

She flipped a scale into the pan at the bottom, where it landed with a hollow ping. "...as a scale. You see? Scales come out at the bottom."

He thought for a moment, looking over the process. "It seems like it's...cycling."

"Oh, so even a Copper has eyes. Bulky device and all, that's all it is. Just a way to cycle."

He was missing something important here, he was sure. "I'm sorry. Why? Doesn't everyone cycle on their own?"

The scale flew from the pail back into her hands, and she held it up between two fingers. "You don't think this looks familiar? Hm?"

He squinted at it. "I'm untrained, I know, but it only looks like madra to me."

"Close. It looks like *your* madra. It's clean, it's pure. You see? Anyone can use pure madra." She inhaled sharply, and the scale dissolved into what looked like liquid light and streamed straight into her core. She slapped her belly afterward. "For anybody on a Path, cycling pure madra is like adding water to wine. You add a little, and there's more wine, you see? Doesn't affect the flavor much. Add too much, and it's nothing but watery."

She waved a hand. "Mostly you don't absorb them, it's a waste. You use them on your weapons, or on constructs, or you give a handful to young children. Get them to Copper quicker," she said, poking him in the ribs. "Everybody can use scales, and nobody can make them directly, so we use them as coins. Works for everyone that way."

"Nobody can make them..." he began, but she finished for him.

"But *you* can. You start to see, hm? Mining is dangerous work. When you run the equipment, you're helpless, and places with enough vital aura are very dangerous. The aura in the Ruins is so thick you can practically pinch scales from the air, so Remnants and dreadbeasts will be thick as grass down there. If three miners out of ten comes back alive, I'll shave my head."

"Then, if you'll forgive another question, why are you doing it?"

She gestured with her curved sword, which Lindon had come to realize was called a Fisher's hook. "*We* are not. We're trading with those who are. When the Arelius family Underlord comes to visit, he'll take the Ruins and everything inside. Until he does, we're all scrambling to make as much money as we can."

"Underlord?" he asked, but she clicked her tongue.

"Questions? More questions? You're nothing but a little mine." She jabbed him with the dull back of her hook. "When a sacred artist reaches the realm beyond Truegold, we call them Underlord. Or Underlady. If you ever see one in your lifetime, you can thank the good fortune of your ancestors. Now, you want questions? You want more questions? Then *give me some scales.*"

She left him sitting at the bench, figuring out how to Forge madra.

He'd tried before, sneaking tips from his mother as he tried to move his madra in just the right way that meant he was secretly a Forger and not a reject. He'd never had any success, and his failures had always left his spirit exhausted and his body sweating.

This time, he was a Copper.

He started by slipping on his parasite ring and cycling

for a while, running his madra through the burden of the ring until it was as strong and pure as he could make it without exhausting himself. Then he held his palms a few inches apart, focusing on the space between.

He gathered all his madra into that space, packing it thicker and thicker. At first, he could only visualize the flow of madra in the same half-imaginary way he saw when he was cycling. But after his third attempt, he was sure he saw something; a flash of blue against the rough wooden tabletop.

Then he stopped, panting, wiping sweat from his forehead. He had to cycle again, pumping his spirit, generating every scrap of madra he could.

He didn't sleep for most of the night, trying again and again to condense madra into reality. When his spirit failed him, he cycled until he had enough strength to try again.

Just before dawn, he finally collapsed as exhaustion overtook him.

Gesha was disappointed in his failure, but she took it in stride. She couldn't expect much from a Copper, she said. He maintained constructs during the day, but then he was too tired to try Forging at night.

So he used less power.

Instead of spilling his madra into the whole construct and letting it repair itself, he began directing his power where it was needed. If there was a crack, he focused a line of madra and sealed the crack. If it was simply fading away, becoming weak, he fed power directly into it drop by drop until the part was whole again.

After three days, he finally got the knack. He used so much less energy on his chores that he could try Forging again, allowing him more attempts each day. He stayed up that night alternating between forcing his madra out and cycling to recover, over and over until he finally collapsed.

A single scale, round and crystalline blue, gleamed on his lap.

CHAPTER ELEVEN

INFORMATION REQUESTED: THE ROLE OF A SOULSMITH.

BEGINNING REPORT...

Soulsmiths are craftsmen who work with the stuff of spirits. They form constructs, steal bindings from Remnants and transplant them into sacred artists, and forge weapons. The art of a Soulsmith is honored and distinguished, and it requires no qualities more highly than a sharp memory and a dedication to experimentation.

Every aspect of Forged madra and dead matter—the severed body parts of a destroyed Remnant—must be handled differently. Some can only be manipulated by goldsteel tools, others must be chilled, others wrapped. Some types of madra shatter under the least pressure, only to re-form when unobserved. Others dissolve in daylight, or turn to liquid when pierced.

It is the job of a Soulsmith to know which is which. To know what part of a Remnant can be removed and used, and what part is useless.

Experience is the most useful tool in this process, but a drudge is indispensable.

A drudge is a Soulsmith's most valued construct. It is their assistant, their toolbox, their encyclopedia of information. Even two Remnants from the same Path can look identical but be subtly different on the inside—maybe one holds the most valuable binding in the left side of its chest, while the other carries it on the right. A careless Soulsmith may ruin the work by making assumptions, but drudges are designed to scan the structure of a dead Remnant and look for concentrations of power: bindings.

Drudges have many functions, some unique to the Soulsmiths that created them, but most of their abilities are analytical in nature. The more precisely a Soulsmith can determine the structure of a Remnant, the lower the chance of a ruined product.

Before creating their own drudge, would-be Soulsmiths are expected to practice certain core skills. They must familiarize themselves with a Soulsmith's foundry, practice their own Forging—in order to shape dead matter and create a functional shell around valuable bindings—memorize a set of basic scripts, and test dozens of different madra aspects to prove that they can spot the difference.

A Soulsmith's training takes years of dedication, and is sometimes underestimated because the skills acquired do not translate directly to combat. But a sacred artist with some ability in Soulsmithing is a valuable commodity for any clan or sect, and Soulsmiths can often earn the bulk of a family's income.

SUGGESTED TOPIC: SOULSMITH LIFE EXPECTANCY. CONTINUE?

DENIED, REPORT COMPLETE.

●

It had been almost two weeks since Lindon had begun working for Fisher Gesha, and in that time, he'd continued every night until his body refused to continue any longer. Even when he finished his work early, he'd spend hours taking notes on what he'd learned, keeping careful records for the Path of Twin Stars, until he eventually passed out on the page.

As a result, it took more and more drastic methods to wake him. One morning, the Soulsmith had coated his entire hay-strewn nook with uncomfortably warm slime from a binding. Noise didn't work; he'd slept straight through a thunderstorm that rattled the rafters and sent the spider-constructs overhead swinging like chimes in the wind.

So when he woke facedown with some man's shoulder digging into his stomach, he wasn't entirely surprised. Even in his groggy, sleep-wrapped state, he recognized one of Gesha's attempts to wake him.

When the bright green lizard-spirit attached to the man's arm turned and hissed at him, that was when he knew something was wrong.

He scrambled for details. The man's boots were crunching on grass, not dirt, so they'd gone off the path. Smoke in the air. Torchlight flickered against the furs the man wore, and a biting chill lingered in the air.

So a Sandviper had taken him in the middle of the night, and had left Fisher territory to bring him somewhere else.

Still drifting as he was, he initially wondered if he could somehow turn this to his advantage. The Sandviper was an enemy, and therefore an honorable target for robbery. Would he have anything on him? Was there some way Lindon could talk his way out of this? Would the Empty Palm disable him, or just make him angry?

As clarity returned, his thoughts changed. Was he headed back to the Sandviper camp? Was this some sort of revenge against Fisher Gesha, or against Yerin? *He* hadn't personally done anything against the Sandvipers, but now he was going to be treated to a full, painful taste of their powers. Their insidious, venomous powers, which could dissolve flesh like an acid.

He'd dismantled a Sandviper Remnant under Gesha just two days before, and even its dead matter was enough to slowly burn through living flesh. She'd demonstrated on a dead rat.

Worse, she said, the aura they gathered did not kill so quickly. Their Ruler techniques produced a sort of gas that caused seizures, paralysis, and other, less pleasant symptoms. She'd spoken with a shadow in her voice that suggested she'd seen that state entirely too many times.

Now Lindon started to struggle. He'd tried not to, in order to avoid giving away that he'd regained consciousness, but it had become too much. He kept seeing the corpse of the rat, its hair hissing and sizzling away as the flake of Sandviper madra had steadily drilled its way through.

That same madra, in the form of a legged serpent, stared at him from a few inches away. It hissed again, but the sacred artist gave no indication that he cared what Lindon was doing. He trundled along with the consistency of an ox, though with considerably more speed.

It would have been more interesting to Lindon under other circumstances, but while the Sandviper man gave the impression of moving slowly, ground passed beneath him with alarming speed.

He started slowing when sounds of laughter and chatter cut through the night. It had to be the Sandviper camp, though even craning his neck, Lindon couldn't see much more of it than a few temporary buildings and some torch-smoke.

The man walked past the laughing crowd, taking him to one of the only buildings Lindon had seen in the entire Five Factions Alliance that *wasn't* made of rough, freshly cut wood. Instead, it was entirely constructed from iron bars, with rings of script spiraling up the length of the bars like creepers on tree trunks.

Hinges squealed as the door opened, and Lindon hit the ground hard and rolled before he came to a stop on his back.

Even the ceiling was made from bars, which must get unpleasant when it rained. If Lindon were left here, where Fisher Gesha and Yerin couldn't find him, he'd have to survive those rainstorms huddling in the corner and bunched up against the cold.

Before the Sandviper closed the door, Lindon scrambled for it. He kicked at the dirt, launching himself forward.

The Gold still didn't say a word. He grabbed Lindon with one hand like scooping up a squirming puppy, then tossed him back inside. The door shut faster this time.

None of the other prisoners made a break for it.

There were only five others inside this cage, though there were other cages on the left and right. He couldn't begin to guess how many total, which he imagined might be useful information if he ever got out of here.

As he rose to shaky feet, trying to get a better look at his surroundings, one of his cellmates raised her head to look at him. She was filthy, shrouded in a ragged blanket, and she stared with one eye. The other was a half-healed mess, shredded by what seemed to be claw marks.

Lindon couldn't meet her good eye. He was too busy staring at her missing one as though it had shown him his own future.

The next one in the cage was a man that revealed a missing arm and, when he turned in his sleep, several missing toes.

The third, a boy about Lindon's age. Half his hair had been seared off, and he stared into the distance with a glassy look.

The fourth and fifth clung to one another so that he couldn't make out the details of one against another, but blood clung to the bars behind them and the floor beneath him.

Wounds surrounded him, a tale of misery and pain etched in flesh. All of these were Golds, he was sure—a weak cloud drifted over the one-eyed woman's head, and one of the couple in the corner seemed to have a tail—

and they had suffered like this. What had wounded them would crush a Copper to paste.

He took a breath, calming his disordered thoughts, though it felt like trying to spit water onto a forest fire. He knelt and examined the door, studying the latch and the script together, but so many of the symbols were unfamiliar to him. He recognized something similar to the circle he'd used to ward off Remnants, but with ten times the complexity.

That was it. There wasn't much else to examine. No other tools to use, no threads to pull, just idle time to pass before whatever had shredded the other prisoners' bodies was used on him.

Though when he spent some time thinking about it, he thought he might know what had happened. These must be miners.

When he looked up, the blocky silhouette of the Transcendent Ruins blocked out the moon and a good half of the stars. They were camped right at the base of it—so maybe this wasn't Sandviper territory at all, because all of the five allied factions would want to share access to the Ruins.

The Sandvipers he'd met before had mentioned miners, and Fisher Gesha had told him the story of how dangerous it was to go inside the Ruins to draw scales from the air. She'd suggested a survival rate of less than thirty percent.

Lindon took another look around him as he imagined what had happened to the rest.

Laughter echoed around the camp until it sounded almost like screams...no, those *were* screams, along with some shouts and the ringing of metal.

He craned his neck, trying to stick his head between the bars—though they were too closely set for that—in order to see down the row of cages and storage buildings.

Another cage, just like the one in which he found himself, was rattling back and forth as its inhabitants threw themselves against the sides. It looked as though it would actually tip over, but a couple of Sandvipers appeared out of nowhere at the final instant. One of them sent two bright green lights flickering into the cage—he couldn't see the details, but it was obviously a technique of some kind—and the other grabbed the cage in both hands.

He heaved, lifting the entire cage off the ground, and then slammed it back down.

The screams had redoubled in intensity, but now other cages were rattling, and more guards were pouring out of nearby shelters.

When the commotion spread closer to him, with Sand-viper guards running past him to help, Lindon stepped back. He was getting too detailed of a look at what the Sandviper techniques were doing to prisoner flesh.

And his cage seemed least likely to join in. Not a one of his fellow inmates even looked up.

He sat himself with his back against the bars, trying to think. What did he have on him? He didn't have his pack, of course, but even his pockets had been emptied. Except...

A smooth, round ball slightly bigger than his thumb-nail sat at the bottom of his pocket, forgotten. He reached in, pulling out the glass marble from Suriel. A single blue candle-flame flickered in the center, pointing straight up no matter how he turned the outside.

The marble had no use, unless he could throw it like a pebble to distract a guard, but it was a comfort. A concrete reminder that the heavens hadn't given up on him.

He rolled it between his fingers as he took further stock.

He was in reasonably good physical condition, and he'd recovered most of the energy in his cores that he'd spent earlier that night. Not that either of those things would help him against the Sandvipers.

Other than the marble, he had nothing but his clothes and the familiar presence of wood against his chest. So they'd left him his Unsouled badge. How considerate.

The badge itself was tied to a ribbon of blue shadesilk, which was bright as day in direct light and absolutely black

in the slightest shadow. The interesting reflective properties of shadesilk had allowed Sacred Valley to keep trading
with the outside world, but now Lindon found himself
considering more about the fabric's strength. Could he
strangle someone with it?

Not anyone who mattered, not with a Copper's strength.
Maybe he could take a toddler hostage, assuming a toddler
passed within arm's length of this cage in a prison camp, but
that would be as cowardly of an act as he could imagine.

But if he stayed, he'd face the Ruins.

The sky began to lighten before he'd come to any conclusion on a strategy, and in the distance, he saw an enormous block sink back into the wall of the Ruins. A small
army filed out, the Sandvipers in the front carrying weapons, and the collection of people in the middle carrying
iron barrels speckled on the bottom with crystal flasks.

They passed close enough for Lindon to make out the
wounds on the prisoners—missing limbs, fingers, chunks
of flesh. The procession turned to a building that looked
like a big, painted wagon...

And Lindon gained his first truly interesting piece of
information. The back of the wagon lifted open, and the
first prisoner—prodded by a knife—dumped his barrel into
the back.

Scales clattered out. They fell into a box specially prepared for the purpose, and then the second miner stepped
up, also emptying her barrel. It took twenty or thirty people before the box was filled up and pushed to the back.

To join dozens of boxes just like it.

Lindon's eyes were glued to the stack of boxes, the blue-
lit marble spinning in his fingers. Fisher Gesha had said
that scales could be used for advancement, but doing so
was like watering down your madra. Well, his madra was
essentially all water.

How many scales would it take to break through to
Iron? Twenty? A hundred? However many he needed, they
were *right there.*

He pushed himself against the bars, eyes stuck on the boxes.

When the prisoners had finished delivery, the door on the wagon slammed shut. Something like an angry trumpet blast sounded, and the wagon actually rumbled forward, sliding out from between a pair of cages.

So the fortune didn't stick around. That was a disappointment, but it was a good policy not to leave their treasures sitting among a group of disgruntled prisoners.

A Sandviper woman walked up, and Lindon backed away from the bars just in time to avoid her slapping her sword against the cage. It rang like a hideous bell, hurting his ears, but not as much as her voice. She propelled her words with the full force of her Gold spirit and Iron body, causing him to clap hands over his ears and his cellmates to scramble to their feet.

"*Wake* up, *wake* up. Feed time, and then it's day shift."

So there was a day shift. Meaning the wagon would show up at sunrise and sunset, for the two mining shifts to deliver their haul.

She pulled the squealing door open, stepping back, and Lindon eyed the gap uncertainly. Was she really trying to fight six people on her own? He couldn't contribute much, but the others were Gold. Even wounded, they should be on her like a pack of wolves.

That was when he noticed the collars, iron and scripted just like the bars.

He touched his neck, in case he'd somehow missed being collared in metal, but his fingers met only skin. He wondered if they'd put one on him later, but he found it unlikely.

He probably just wasn't worth collaring.

Four of the five prisoners shuffled forward at the Sandviper's prodding, but the woman with the missing eye had curled back against the bars. She shook as though weeping, but made no sound.

The Sandviper woman looked bored as she stepped past

the other inmates and into the cage, holding her sword in one hand.

Before she could reach the crouching woman, Lindon bent over and grabbed the prisoner by the shoulder. "Stand up. I don't know what's happening, but I know you'd better stand up. Come on."

He shook her harder, but she didn't respond. The Sandviper pushed him away and raised her sword.

Unlike his imagination, she didn't decapitate the miner in one stroke. Instead, she slapped the edge of her sword against the shaking woman's head with such force that each stroke sounded like a lumberjack axe against a tree.

Lindon winced and took another step back. You probably had to do this much to get through an Iron body, but a single one of those blows would have caved his head in.

A familiar voice came from behind him, sharp and venomous. "There are no pieces of him missing? Hm? This is good for you."

Lindon spun to see Fisher Gesha, goldsteel hook on her back, standing on top of her mechanical spider legs. She looked the same as always—bun tight on her head, expression disapproving—but there was something about her that made him shiver.

The Sandviper guard stopped beating the prisoner and turned to Gesha, leaning her sword on her shoulder. "What do you think our sect is, that you can come in and order us around? Do you think everyone works for you?"

A gentle, invisible force tugged Lindon out the open door so that he stumbled forward until he was standing next to Gesha.

"You need Copper miners that badly, do you?" the Fisher asked dryly. "Tell your young chief his message was received, but I am taking back my property. Can you remember that, hm?"

Green light spidered up the edge of the Sandviper's blade like veins in a leaf. She glared at Gesha and raised her voice. "Fisher—"

Whatever she was going to say next was cut off when Gesha moved like a flickering snake. She suddenly stood next to the Sandviper woman, one arm behind her back, the other holding her goldsteel hook extended. The sharp inside of the blade's crescent was pressed against the younger woman's throat.

"Silly girl. When I was weak as you, did I disrespect my betters? No, I kept my head on my work. And you have a miner to catch."

She nodded down the row, where the one-eyed woman was hobbling away, casting fearful glances behind her.

As Gesha removed the hook, the Sandviper guard tore her gaze between the escaping prisoner and her enemy, muttered something under her breath, and bolted off after the miner. It was probably a jog for a Gold, but her movements blurred to Lindon's eyes.

He turned back to Gesha as the guard seized the miner by the hair and started dragging her back.

"Can we take them with us?" he asked, voice low. They probably heard him anyway, considering their hearing, but he had to ask.

She gave him a look of almost comical surprise. "There are worse things than this in the world, Wei Shi Lindon. These are enemies, captured in battle."

"They didn't quite capture me in battle," he said. "They took me in my sleep." She darkened.

"And so I have taken you back," she said. "*This* time. But you are not my grandson, you hear me? Hm? I cannot come to save you every morning. If you cannot protect yourself, I cannot protect you either. Next time, remember that." She gestured, and his red Thousand-Mile Cloud floated up from behind her. He hadn't noticed it, and he wasn't prepared for the sensation of relief that flooded him at the sight.

"Follow me," she said, and he did.

His neck was tight from the effort of not looking back to see the others he'd left behind.

Gesha spent most of their journey back cursing the Sandvipers for their cowardice, but Lindon remained lost in thought. When he asked her how she'd found him, she simply said "I looked," in the tone of voice that suggested he was an idiot.

When they returned to Fisher territory, his plans had clarified enough for him to ask better questions. "Pardon, Fisher Gesha, but I'd be better able to defend myself with a Path."

Her drudge's spider-legs did not falter in their smooth, rolling gait, and she didn't so much as glance at him. "You think you've earned it? Hm? You think you've given so much to the sect that we must give you something back?"

"I have nothing but gratitude to you and to the Fisher sect," he assured her, though his only contact with the Fishers thus far had been limited to glimpses of customers in the Soulsmith foundry. "I will never repay my debt for your kindness in this lifetime. I'm only impatient to contribute more."

Judging by her pleased smile, flattery had been the right choice. "Why so impatient? If you have not walked a Path so far, waiting until Iron is not so late. Focus on Forging two scales a day. When you can do that, you will keep one."

He wasn't sure if she'd found his successful scale or not, but he was still a long way away from two scales a day, every day. "If I could, then how long might it take me to reach Iron?"

She was silent for a moment, contemplating the question. "If you work hard, one year is not too short. Not so bad, is it? A year is nothing when you're my age, I can tell you."

"Of course not," Lindon lied, thoughts cast back to the wagon full of boxes. "Not too short at all."

CHAPTER TWELVE

Five days after his release from the Sandvipers, Lindon went to see Yerin. She'd spent most of her time with the Fishers helping them hunt down Remnants and sacred beasts, which seemed to be one of the primary businesses of their sect. There were many Soulsmiths in the Five Factions Alliance, and most of them got their primary supply of bindings and Remnants parts from the Fishers. Refiners paid for rare medicinal ingredients or sacred beasts as components for elixirs, and Fishers prided themselves on diving into the wilderness and emerging with whatever their customers requested.

Yerin provided something that the sect had previously found in short supply: overwhelming offensive power. Though Lindon had sunk entirely into Gesha's Soulsmith business since that first night, he and Yerin had seen each other every few days.

According to her, the Fishers were experts at tracking, navigating the wilderness, and extracting natural treasures for later sale. But they were forced to give up on some prizes simply because their madra wasn't as suited for combat.

As such, they treated Yerin like some kind of long-lost younger sister who had returned to usher in a golden age of economic prosperity. Now, when Lindon showed up at the Fisher housing to see Yerin, she had a room of her own. Previously, she'd had to share one long log cabin with twelve other women. Now, she had her own, smaller log cabin, complete with baked clay tiles for the roof and a hearth and chimney.

She opened the door blearily as Lindon knocked, swiping at her eyes with one hand. The silver sword extended out from her back, touching the invisible traps she'd Forged around the doorframe and dissolved them.

He was glad to see that all the traps were on the *inside* of the door this time. He'd hesitated enough just knocking, wondering what lethal tricks were lurking in the air.

"I'm sorry for waking you," he said. "Should I come back later?" He kept moving inside as he asked; the question was a formality anyway.

She shifted that red rope she wore as a belt and stretched, yawning. "Cycling. The snoring doesn't start until about the third hour."

He'd come at sunset, so she may well have been preparing to sleep, but she still looked better-rested than she had when they'd arrived. The Fishers had replaced her old, tattered sacred artist's robe with a new one, and the fine black fabric looked unmarred despite her days in the wilderness. Her injuries had already healed into new scars—one of the many benefits of the Iron body that everyone but Lindon enjoyed—though her hair had grown out, longer and less even than before.

In short, she looked like she'd had two weeks worth of rest and regular food to get her back into fighting shape. While Lindon himself...

She looked him up and down, growing visibly concerned. "You need to take a seat? You look like a dead dog on a bad road."

He took that to mean he looked tired, which was true. His fingers were twitching and he couldn't seem to focus his eyes on more than one thing for more than a handful of seconds, but excitement kept him fueled.

Lindon slung his pack off, throwing off his balance and staggering for a step, then he pulled out a sheet of paper and slapped it down on her one table.

She leaned over for a closer look. "They've been making you take a lot of notes, have they?"

"These are the shift changes of every Sandviper guard working regular duty with the mining teams. I've been following them for most of the last week. I made up some of the names, but this isn't all; I know their habits, their replacements, what they like to drink, which teams they're responsible for, when they deposit their scales, everything I could think of." She lifted the paper as though wondering how he got so much information on there, and he hurried to add, "That's not the only sheet."

"Why?" she asked simply.

"I know where they keep the scales," he said, passion burning away exhaustion. "It pulls in twice a day, they load up the haul for the day, and then they take it away to a secure location back in their main camp stronghold. Their guards are tired, their miners are angry, and everyone's rushing so that they can squeeze the Ruins dry before the Arelius family gets here." His words were tripping all over one another, and he knew it, but he plowed on anyway. "They're too strong when all the Sandvipers are together, but that's almost never true."

He waited until he had her full attention before hitting her with the selling point. "We can free the miners. All I have to do is activate one of Fisher Gesha's spider constructs, take it to camp, have it disrupt the script—"

"That sounds like a tall cliff to climb," she interrupted. "You think you can keep it powered that long? *And* you know how to disable the script?"

Lindon had to clasp his hands together to keep them from shaking. Maybe he *had* been awake for too long. "It's easy, if you know how and where, which I do because they gave me a personal look. It's like breaking a lock."

"Breaking a lock isn't usually easy," she said.

"It is if you have specialized equipment, which we do. We'll have a construct. Anyway, we release enough prisoners, and we can take the wagon. So long as we strike at dawn or dusk, of course, when it's there. If I fill my pack, I expect I can walk away with a thousand scales, and I'm sure you can too."

"And then we fade away like mist in the sun, do we?" She was still eyeing the paper, so at least she hadn't dismissed him completely, but he'd been hoping for a more enthusiastic reaction.

"Fly away on the cloud," Lindon said, gesturing behind him to the Thousand-Mile Cloud. That was when he remembered he hadn't actually *brought* the cloud; he'd left it behind in Fisher Gesha's foundry.

Maybe he could leave some of his work behind today and grab a nap.

"A Thousand-Mile Cloud isn't made of dragon scales. The Fishers have three, and I've seen at least two people zipping around on Remnants. One of the Sandvipers will run us down."

He'd been waiting for that objection. "I've thought of that!" He dug another paper out of his pack, this one a crudely drawn map, and slapped it onto the table as well. "You remember the bathhouse? It's halfway between Gesha's barn and the Ruins. We only have to fly a short distance to the bathhouses, hide there, and head back to the foundry when we're clear."

Lindon had prepared for other objections. For one thing, if they didn't dress as Sandvipers, they would be caught upon entry to the camp. But if they *did*, then the prisoners would attack them when set free. If they weren't being chased, there was no need to hide at the bathhouse, and if they *were* then the bathhouse wouldn't help.

He had counters to these, nuances to his plans that he'd worked very hard on. He hadn't entirely counted on Yerin handing the paper back to him, smile sharper than the blade over her shoulder. "Let's burn 'em."

He took the plan from her, a little taken aback. "You'll do it?"

She rested a hand on the hilt of her sword. "We're working for the Fishers now, and they get along with the Sandvipers like two tigers in one cage. And they kidnapped you." Her hand tightened on the hilt. "You let an enemy take one of yours without response, and you're giving them signed permission to do it again. The Sandvipers haven't slipped out of my memory, any more than Heaven's Glory has."

Her expression darkened further. "They think I'm not coming back to clean their whole rotten house and burn it down, then they're getting a surprise."

She'd agreed to his plan, and even his own family had never fought for him. But some of his warm feelings cooled in the face of her vengeful oath.

He wasn't sure why he felt that way—revenge had always been part of the sacred arts, as widely celebrated in stories as honorable duels—but her whole demeanor changes when she talked about revenge. Something in the air felt dark, and heavy, and wrong.

It was his own weakness. That was what his father would have told him, and Lindon knew he was right. Yerin was wiser, stronger, more knowledgeable and more experienced. He was seeing the world as a child.

Suddenly ashamed of his own cowardice, he bowed to her. "You won't go back alone."

She gave him a look of such gratitude that he forgot all his misgivings a moment before.

Then something crooned, high and desperate, like a mewling baby bird.

They both started, Yerin drawing her sword in a blur of motion. Another cry, and Lindon checked under the table. A third, and he realized where it was coming from: his pack.

Shoving his notes aside, he dug into the main pocket of his pack.

At first, he was looking for a trapped animal. Something that had crawled inside and gotten stuck, maybe a small bird or even a rodent. He had a temporary fantasy of finding the rare cub of a sacred beast before he dug out a glass case.

The case was big enough to hold two pairs of shoes, and entirely transparent. Inside was a miniature landscape of tiny rolling hills covered in grass, even boasting a single tiny tree. A river flowed around the sides of the case so that the land became a green island, and no matter how he turned or shook the box, the water barely sloshed and the leaves hardly shook. It was as though the glass of the case allowed him to look into a tiny, separate world.

And that world had a resident.

The Sylvan Riverseed looked something like a humanoid Remnant the size of a finger, made entirely of flowing blue waves. It didn't seem to be made of water, exactly, but rather madra imitating water, like in the bowl test that had designated him as Unsouled.

He'd all but forgotten about the Riverseed in the weeks since taking it from the Heaven's Glory School. He took it originally because it was supposed to be valuable, but he'd never given it much thought since then, the more useful treasures he'd stolen taking up most of his attention. He'd glanced at it every once in a while as he dug through his pack, but since the Sylvan was usually spritely and energetic, he'd usually just waved to it and left it hidden. It was expensive and he didn't know what to do with it, so he kept it tucked away.

This time, the Sylvan itself had collapsed against the landscape as though dying. Its substance was faded and pale, and it raised its head to let out one more delicate peep.

Yerin whistled. "Well, that's a storm out of clear skies. You're killing it."

"I should bring it to Fisher Gesha," Lindon said, placing his finger against the edge of the glass. The Sylvan Riverseed raised one featureless arm, like a doll's arm, in response. "She'll know what to do with it."

Yerin gave him a sidelong glance. "If you contend that you want to share blood with the Fishers, then I won't be the one to tell you no. But don't think you can hand a treasure to someone and they'll hand it back out of the sweetness of their soul."

"If you know what's wrong with it, by all means tell me."

"It looks hungry," she said, with no basis that he could tell. "What have you been feeding it?"

"I'm not even sure how to open the case," he said, "but I can look into it." Which meant that he could try and smash it open later, hoping that the Sylvan wouldn't run off.

"It came with a label, true?"

It had, though Lindon hadn't taken it. He said as much, adding, "It didn't say much. Sylvan Riverseed, they thought it had some sort of water aspect, and they planned to give it to someone with pure madra." That was why he'd noticed it in the first place.

She spread both hands as though presenting the answer. "There it is, then. Feed it madra."

"Are you sure that'll work?" It was worth a try, he knew, but he had squeezed a lot out of his spirit already, and he hadn't even Forged his scales yet.

"I'm sure that my sword is sharp and the sun will come up tomorrow," she said. "Everything else is a roll of the dice." She'd crossed her arms and leaned in to watch the Sylvan, so she was obviously expecting a show.

With a sigh, he placed both hands against the side of the case and concentrated.

After almost two weeks under Fisher Gesha, his spirit almost felt like it didn't belong to him. The madra responded too easily, moved too quickly, responded to his will too well. While Forging scales was still a chore, he could condense madra now in only a fraction of the time.

A few seconds after he'd begun, a drop of transparent blue liquid materialized in the box. It dropped straight onto the Sylvan Riverseed...

...who animated as though it had only pretended to be

dying all along. Its featureless head split into a mouth, and it gulped down the drop of pure madra like a snake snapping up a mouse.

Immediately energized, the Sylvan ran around, cheeping and crooning intermittently so that it sounded like a song. Once again, Lindon Forged another drop of madra, and this time the Riverseed's color deepened.

"It's like a Remnant," he mused aloud. Maybe it *was* a Remnant, though it seemed both smaller and more substantial than most he'd seen. Remnants gained in power and intelligence by taking in human madra, the purer the better, which was where the legends of Remnants abducting children came from. He'd used his madra as a bargaining chip with Remnants in the past.

But if he treated this being as a Remnant in a cage rather than a stolen treasure...what was it going to become? What was he growing in his pack?

"If it eases you any," Yerin said, "now the scales are even better for you. You're hungry for them, and so is your little baby chick here."

Lindon refocused back on the task at hand. The Sylvan Riverseed was an interesting problem to consider later, but for now, they needed to hit the Sandviper mining operation soon. His information was less valuable by the day, as the guard habits changed, and the Arelius family could arrive any time to put an end to it all.

"I'd suggest you get ready," Lindon said. "We need to go as soon as we can."

Yerin tapped her fingers on her sword, and Lindon felt as though a blade had passed through the air just in front of his nose. His eyes widened, sure that she'd just used a technique.

Then strands of her hair drifted down. It was razor-straight again, hanging down as though it had been measured to end exactly at her eyes in the front and exactly at her shoulders in the back.

"Straight and clean again," she said in a satisfied tone.

"Now I'm ready." She eyed his head. "I can have a try at yours too, now that it's getting a little overgrown."

He held up his hands, hoping she wouldn't start blasting invisible sword madra at his head. "I could use some more time." For one thing, he could get some sleep.

She shrugged and walked back to the corner of her cabin, where she knelt on a cushion for cycling. "Pop in when you're ready. If I'm not here, I'm out hunting."

He left her to it, walking back through the dark, though he almost fell asleep on his feet before he made it back to Fisher Gesha's barn.

●

At first, the plan worked flawlessly.

They crept in just before dawn, in Sandviper sect outfits that Lindon had made himself. The furs came cheap from the Fishers, who would never deign to wear the same clothing as their rivals, and their Goldsigns were faked through pieces of green dead matter he'd scavenged from Gesha's supply.

He was proud of himself for that, actually. The little Remnant-creatures attached to every real Sandviper's arm couldn't be duplicated, but he had buckets full of pieces from Sandviper Remnants. Four green legs and a serpentine tube sewn onto a sleeve, and he had something that— from a distance—would pass as a Sandviper's Goldsign.

Yerin's was harder to hide. She couldn't control the bladed arm on her back as well as he thought she should, so it had taken them almost an hour of bending and folding to get it stuck between her furs and her pack. But with the bear-like head of a dreadbeast over her hair, hide concealing the red rope around her waist, and her sword-arm hidden, even Lindon had trouble recognizing her.

He had to admit, it was satisfying when these all-powerful Golds scurried away at a single sight of his Sandviper uniform and an angry scowl.

They'd positioned the Thousand-Mile Cloud behind a

tent, close enough to be summoned but not so close that it would give them away. His usual pack was waiting with the Cloud, in case he needed anything from within, and the one he was carrying now contained only the spider-construct.

Everything slid smoothly along, even up to the point where they reached the cages.

He'd worried that he might not be able to find his old cage, but he did so almost instantly. This would be his test case, and ideally a way to survive the prisoner uprising.

Glancing around assured him that everything was in place. Yerin was loitering across the lane, close enough to help if needed. The wagon backed into place almost exactly as he arrived, giving him the fleeting joy of seeing elements of a plan slide neatly into place.

Reaching into his pack, he slowly—and with many a glance around—extracted one of Gesha's spider constructs. The spider was inert, curled up into a ball, and though it stored enough energy for independent action, the crystal flask would be swiftly depleted and its actions would be limited. It would be best to control this one directly, before guiding it to cages down the line.

The cage was mostly empty space, with only three dirty figures huddled inside. He ducked to get a glimpse at each one, but the one-eyed woman wasn't there.

He'd known that was a possibility. Gesha put the miners' survival rate frighteningly low, and the last he'd seen the nameless woman, she was being beaten with a sword.

Too easily, the image came to mind of himself, tucked in a filthy blanket just like the rest and sent day after day into the waiting horrors of the Ruins. The pyramid overhead seemed ominous now, like a monster looming over the corpse of its prey.

With a flicker of his madra, the spider surged to life, slicing across two points in the script according to his instruction. The scrape of spider's leg against iron was surprisingly soft and quick, leading him to wonder what the construct was made of. If it cut iron so easily, he could think of a number of other uses for it.

Finally, he directed the spider up the bars and to the roof, where the final loop of the script-circle was located. This had taken him three days of observation to realize; though he was only an amateur scriptor, he could tell that cutting two of the loops wouldn't be enough. Leaving the final link on the roof made sense from the Sandvipers' perspective, given the risk that one of the prisoners knew some sacred art that could cut iron even with their spirits suppressed by collars.

A scripted key would have simplified this process, but he'd never found one unguarded, and stealing it could have risked everything.

Seconds later, a soft whisk came from overhead as the spider sliced through the last of the protective script. Lindon pushed the door open, wincing at the squeal of hinges, and directed the spider back into his pack.

Even that paltry few seconds of action had drained one of his cores almost completely, and he would need to cycle according to the Path of Twin Stars to restore his madra. In the meantime, he drew power from his second core.

The three figures in the cage all moaned and backed away from him, but as the spider clambered into the pack behind him, Lindon sank to his knees. "Look at me," he whispered. "We don't have much time."

Even less than he'd imagined, as he found out immediately when Jai Long stepped out from beside the scale wagon.

The sight of the tall spearman in the mask of red cloth scrambled Lindon's thoughts for a second. He'd already cast his mind forward, to the next steps of the plan, to the things that could go wrong. Jai Long stayed in his tent in the mornings, Lindon had observed that for five mornings in a row, and idle comments from some of the other Sandvipers suggested he'd done the same thing for as long as he'd known them.

But there was still the possibility that he wouldn't notice

anything. If he'd just decided to stretch his legs and get a lungful of morning air, he would just brush past two "Sand-vipers" going about their ordinary chores with hardly a glance.

That hope died when Jai Long turned his head to look straight at Lindon.

"To save face for the Fishers, I will keep you as miners instead of killing you as intruders. You have my word."

Lindon's head was still spinning. They hadn't even *done* anything yet. Where had he gone wrong? Was there an alarm attached to the script-circle on the cage?

No, he was certain there wasn't. The script connected to nothing, it was all self-contained around the cage. It couldn't have activated an alarm, or he would have found it. What, then?

Yerin, meanwhile, had immediately drawn her white sword against young chief Kral. He wore black furs, finer than those of his subordinates, and he still gave off the air of unim-peachable dignity even while holding an awl in each hand.

Jai Long didn't even look to the side, where his young chief faced Yerin. He remained focused on Lindon, spear propped against his shoulder.

"You want to know why?" he asked.

Lindon didn't dare to nod. In his experience, questions like that didn't really need a response.

"Do you know how many Coppers there are in the Five Factions Alliance above the age of six?" Jai Long went on. "There's one. One of my men happened to notice a Copper days ago, when you were sneaking around the camp, and reported you. I knew you could only be the newly adopted Fisher."

Lindon could put the rest together for himself. Jai Long had assumed he'd come *here* because this was where he'd been held captive. Then all he had to do was set a watch with Lindon's description...

That didn't hold up. Even though Lindon had run into the Sandvipers more than once, it wasn't as though he'd been in camp long. He wasn't famous. Jai Long had seen him before, but there was no reason he should remember.

"How did you recognize me?" Lindon asked, then belatedly added, "If I may ask, honored Jai Long."

The spearman studied him from behind the red wrappings as though unsure how to answer. "I had them sense your spirit," he said, as though it were the most obvious thing in the world.

Lindon had been blind. In Sacred Valley, once a person reached Jade, they could use their spirit to sense things they couldn't possibly see or hear. They *couldn't* sense a person's level of advancement without personally witnessing their sacred arts. Somehow, it hadn't occurred to him that sacred artists on the outside *could.*

It was an idiot's mistake. He'd let his own ignorance lead both him and Yerin into an ambush.

Yerin knew what was possible, of course, but he couldn't fault her for not pointing it out—to her, it was common knowledge. She'd have assumed that he would take steps to disguise himself as a Copper, or prevent himself from being sensed.

If those were possibilities—he didn't even know that much.

Something tugged at his spirit, and he opened his Copper senses. The aura around Yerin bloomed into a razor-edged dome, like a thicket of swords surrounding her, and the pale blade in her hand gathered sword aura along the edges. She hadn't said a word, but her body was turned half to the side, her weapon held high and her eyes fixed on Kral.

For his part, the Sandviper heir held his awls to his sides, completely relaxed. He didn't seem to be drawing up aura at all. "You're not even a Fisher, are you? Are you sure you want to be buried for them?"

The colorless blades around her sharpened, but she didn't respond.

"Your choice," he said, lazily lifting a spike to point at her. Green light gathered on the tip, like poison about to drip off. "I am Kral, young chief of the Sandviper sect, and I will instruct you."

As soon as he finished speaking, a line of venomous green light blasted toward her. She ducked, drawing aura behind her sword like a wave as she swung it upward.

Kral had already reached her, the sword almost at his ribs, but he drove his awl down and pushed Yerin's blade into the ground.

The air roared as her technique sheared a hole through the grass, sending dirt and roots blasting skyward. As though following the steps of a dance, Kral moved forward and drove his second awl at her neck. Sword aura tore at his hand, but they didn't stop him, and Yerin had to throw herself back.

The young chief laughed, shaking off his wounded hand. He wasn't even bleeding. There were red lines, but nothing worse than Lindon might get if he brushed against a briar bush.

Kral gestured, and the aura around Yerin surged. She moved out of the way just as a cloud of toxic gas manifested behind her.

But he was toying with her, moving her like a puppet where he wanted. The awl flashed forward again, this time with four green echoes of itself moving along with it—a Forger trick to duplicate the weapon. She smashed them all, but took a scrape along the shoulder for it.

Her Goldsign burst out then, a flashing arm of steel, blurring as it shot straight for Kral's eye.

Before Lindon could register joy that Yerin might have turned the fight around, Kral's own Goldsign scurried into action. The legged serpent ran down the man's forearm, running onto Yerin's shoulder, and opening its jaws to bite down on her neck.

It froze that way, its tail wrapped around Kral's arm and its teeth on Yerin, as her bladed arm came to a quivering stop a foot from the Sandviper's nose.

"If you draw a blade on a Highgold, you should be prepared for the consequences," Kral said, in a tone haughty enough for a king. His expression, on the other hand, said he was enjoying himself.

Lindon ran at the open cage door, on the chance he might be able to do something, but Jai Long looked at him.

Just looked.

The man hadn't moved, but somehow his spear had become more prominent, as though his relaxed stance was a half-second away from becoming a thrust that put the weapon through Lindon's heart.

Like a coward, Lindon slowed to a stop. He should throw himself forward, he knew. He should challenge the impossible odds to save his own, even before certain death.

But he *would* die. At best, Jai Long would simply hold him down and send him into the mines anyway. He could do nothing, and he hated himself for it.

Kral raised his voice without turning from Yerin. "Are the Fishers coming?"

"At least one of them is."

Hope trickled back into Lindon's heart.

"Good," Kral said, and the tiny Remnant on his arm bit down.

Blood oozed from Yerin's neck, but that didn't even cause her to make a sound. She simply glared at the Sandviper, even as the tiny green spirit ran back up to nest on his arm.

A second later, her jaw visibly tightened as she gritted her teeth.

Another second, and she'd fallen to her knees, chest heaving.

Then she dropped her sword and screamed.

With Yerin's screams washing over him, Lindon closed his eyes. He couldn't do anything, but he distracted himself by thinking of options—what did he have? There was still a spider in the pack on his back. What about the Cloud?

At a deeper level, he knew he was helpless. He'd always been helpless. He just had to wait for rescue, and that was the most he could do. He had been a fool to expect otherwise.

"You like it noisy in your camps, do you? Hm?" Fisher Gesha said, and Lindon's eyes snapped open. She looked the same as ever, her bun tightly in place, spider legs jutting out from where her feet should be. Her hands were clasped behind her in the small of her back, her absurdly wrinkled face disapproving. Lindon had never seen anyone more beautiful; he could breathe again.

If only she could help Yerin.

"You don't enjoy the screams of your enemies?" Kral asked, sidling over to stand by Jai Long. "I'm sure you do."

Gesha was giving nothing away. "Enemies? I see none of your enemies here."

It was Jai Long's turn to speak. "Do you not? Two new Fishers sneaking into our camp, dutifully assigned to us according to the Alliance. If they were working for you, then that's an unprovoked act of aggression on your part."

Gesha's gaze flicked to Yerin. Not to Lindon.

"Are children supposed to be placid and well-behaved now? I made mistakes when I was young."

"If they're not yours," Jai Long continued, "I'll work them in the mines. If they are, then I've captured them as the result of honorable combat, and they will still work in the mines. But in that case, you were the ones who worked to undermine us. Only days before the Arelius arrive."

Fisher Gesha didn't respond, and he let out a heavy breath from behind his mask. "We cannot allow this, elder Gesha. You know that."

When the old Soulsmith spoke again, it looked as though her lips had been pried apart with an iron bar. "There has been a misunderstanding between us, hasn't there?"

"It seems there has," Jai Long said.

"I don't see any Fishers here," she said, and Lindon let his eyes fall shut again.

"Only you, honored elder," Kral said, with his respectable expression back on.

"Then I will return." Without the slightest glance in Lindon's direction, she drifted off on a spider's legs.

Yerin's screams continued.

Eithan watched, sipping from a bottle of what tasted like distilled poison, as the old Fisher departed. The drama had largely faded at that point, but he stayed to see the night shift of miners arrive. They dropped off their scales, headed to their cages, and switched for the day crew.

Lindon and Yerin were bundled among them. Yerin wore a collar, but not Lindon. Why waste a collar? If a Copper trundled off alone in the mines, he might as well slit his own wrists.

They had given Yerin the antidote to the Sandviper venom only minutes after her bite, but she still shambled along like an animated corpse. A natural sandviper would have been much less painful; the Remnant madra attacked the soul as much as the body, and she would have a difficult time recovering with the scripted collar around her neck. He should know; he'd been in similar situations, once or twice.

Handled correctly, this excursion into the Ruins could end up being a valuable lesson for her. Even an adventure, if framed properly.

Eithan took another sip of poison. In his experience, practically anything became an adventure if framed properly.

Her spirit was still flawless, her foundation solid. The Sage of the Endless Sword had done a wonderful job with her, as was expected. There was the problematic matter of her past—as some of the Sandvipers had learned when they tried to unravel the 'rope' around her waist—but even that could be turned to her advantage. Like adventure, advantage was so often just a matter of perspective.

It was her character that he was interested in now. If she had the strength of will to go along with her powers, as he suspected she did, she would be perfect.

Which brought him to Lindon, who was simultaneously more puzzling and more intriguing.

Someone had meddled with Lindon, in a way that he couldn't quite put his finger on. Maybe it would occur to him later. Either way, the boy was still a featureless ball of clay just waiting to be shaped.

Would he work out for Eithan's purposes? Probably not. But the shaping process was fun, and if nothing else, it would be something to occupy Eithan's attention for a few years.

And if there was fun to be had, why not start immediately?

He downed the last of the bottle, which he suspected really was poison, and tossed the empty container aside. His expensive clothes, made of creamy sky blue and imported from the Ninecloud Court, would suffer in this next part. But those were the sacrifices one made to stave off boredom.

Just as the procession of miners was about to enter the gaping maw of the Ruins, Eithan hopped over to stand beside Jai Long.

"THEY'LL KILL US ALL!" Eithan shouted into Jai Long's ear.

The spearman's reaction was gratifying. He spun with a sweeping, glowing arc of his spear that would have taken Eithan's head off if he were anyone else. He ducked beneath it, then straightened again.

Jai Long leveled his spear again, though Eithan was just standing there. Sandvipers started to boil out of their surroundings, clutching weapons.

The man in the red mask studied him for a moment before speaking. "What are you doing here?"

Eithan raised his hands. "Surrendering myself into your custody, good sir."

Jai Long's spear wavered. "And why is that?"

"As just punishment for my many sins and imperfections. I am a cursed man, wracked by guilt."

He smiled.

Slowly, Jai Long lifted his spear, then gestured for a Sandviper to come forward. A short man in furs scurried out, carrying a collar.

"I will be placing a restrictive collar on you," Jai Long said, holding out the iron loop. "It is scripted to inhibit your madra."

"A wise and prudent decision," Eithan said, bowing forward to present his neck.

As though fearing a trap, Jai Long crept forward step by deliberate step, collar in one hand and spear in the other. Eithan sighed, but waited with all the patience he could muster.

Finally, cold iron snapped around his throat. "Adroitly done," Eithan said, straightening up and clapping his hands together. "Now, the previous group is already in the Ruins. I'll go on and catch up—we're wasting valuable mining time."

Jai Long stood over him, spearhead glowing with madra. The young man had a decision to make. And Eithan smiled pleasantly at him until he made it.

Jai Long took one step to the side, the light in his spear fading.

Wise decision.

CHAPTER THIRTEEN

The square hallway was wide enough for all twenty miners and their five Sandviper escorts. Three of the guards moved in front, two in back, but most of the prisoners didn't seem to need guarding. They stumbled along with empty gazes, all of them with wounds both old and fresh.

Each of the prisoners, including Lindon, carried one of the scripted iron barrels that Fisher Gesha had called mining equipment. It was light enough for the rest of them, with their Iron bodies, but Lindon's arms began to burn after half an hour of carrying it. By the time he started sweating and pushing to keep up with the rest of the pack, they still hadn't passed the first hallway.

The hall itself would have been worth a closer look, if it didn't take all his concentration to stay upright with the barrel. Script ran along the walls, with runes etched deeper than his fingers and wider than his hand. It must have continued for miles, judging by how long they'd traveled.

He couldn't even comprehend the scale of a circle like that. It must only be a small part of whatever mechanism drew in vital aura from all over the region, which made it more ambitious than anything he'd ever imagined.

They finally came to a stop in a room shaped like a cylinder, where five other hallways identical to their own had ended. The room was smaller than he'd expected, and while they weren't crowded, he could see why the Sandvipers hadn't taken more miners.

His first question, when one of the guards raised a torch, was why this room had been made of a different type of stone. Unlike the blocks of the hallway, these were splashed with darker shades of color, as though the blocks had been spattered with...

He missed a step.

Fragments of bone were more common than pebbles on the floor. All clean, and none larger than his thumbnail. A distinct scent of copper and rot lingered in the air, and the stone was stained twice as high as his head.

Whatever happened here, it hadn't left any bodies. The dead had been blasted apart.

The old miners had begun to huddle together, setting their barrels down in the center and gripping the handles. A handful, including Lindon and Yerin, glanced around as though waiting for instruction.

The same guard Lindon had seen before, the bored-looking Sandviper woman with the sword, tapped her weapon against the stone to gather their attention. "The activation script for your harvesters is on your handles," she said, in the tone of someone who had repeated the same instructions for so long that the words came out on their own. "If you stop mining, we leave you here. If you run, we leave you here. If you harass or disobey a guard, we leave you here. Meal comes at midday. When battle starts, don't panic or run, just trust us to cover you. You panic, and we'll leave you here."

With that, she turned and took up a position covering two tunnel mouths. Three of the other guards did the same, though one continued to patrol among the miners.

Lindon set up next to Yerin, who was still pale and shaking from the venom.

"We'll pay them back for this," Lindon said. "A hundred times over, we'll pay them back." It wasn't the sort of thing that would comfort *him,* but he suspected Yerin would appreciate revenge more than sympathy.

She smiled in one corner of her mouth even as she gripped the harvester's handles. "Master always said I should get captured once or twice. Shows spine when you break free."

The guard shouted at them to work before Lindon could respond, but his spirits lifted. If Yerin hadn't given up, there was still hope.

If nothing else, running the harvester would be good exercise for his madra. If he got his hands on a few scales, he might even be able to advance while he was down here.

Now that he'd settled on a goal, Lindon grabbed the handles and sunk his spirit into the script.

The harvester activated almost immediately, drawing Lindon's senses to the aura in the air around him...

He swallowed back a scream.

It was a silent storm, a chaotic gale of blinding color that flashed and blasted in every direction as though it would tear everything apart. He couldn't pick a single aspect out of the maelstrom—anything, maybe everything. It felt as though it would peel the flesh from his bones with sheer force, though it passed through him harmlessly.

When the harvester began, it pulled the slightest breath of that aura from the air, running it in a corkscrew pattern through the center of the iron barrel. The energy circled between the crystal flasks at the bottom—purifying the aura and converting it to madra, no doubt—and Lindon's spirit was only necessary to keep the script running so that the process continued. The crystals were steadily filling up, and when they were full, he supposed the final stretch of script would activate and pop out a scale.

He wasn't sure, because he had to release the harvester when his core ran dry. He leaned over the barrel, panting heavily.

The Sandviper guard wore the hide of a bear-like dread-beast and had an axe in one hand. Lindon had to flinch as the man stalked closer, growling.

"Back to work," the man spat, jabbing him with the butt of his axe.

Lindon met the man's eyes, trying to look earnest. "I'm sorry, honored elder, but I'm only—"

The man hit him again, hard enough that the room spun in a haze of pain. "Don't give me that look. You think you're getting out of here? The dreadbeasts are coming, and they're going to...Where's your collar?"

He swung the axe harder, and if Lindon hadn't let himself collapse with the blow, it would have broken his shoulder.

"What have you done with it?" the man roared, lifting his axe again. Lindon sputtered out protests, holding up a hand to protect himself. Yerin moved, standing in front of him.

Something skittered across the floor like a stone across the surface of the pond, and the guard tripped.

His foot flew out behind him, and for an instant, Lindon expected him to plant his face in the floor. But he was still a Gold, and he caught himself with one palm against the ground, flipping upright. He spun around, pulling a second axe from his belt.

"Which one of you?" he growled, choked with anger.

A man in the corner lifted his head and met Lindon's eye, winking.

Lindon stared. It was that same yellow-haired man. He'd been captured too? How? When?

The leader of the guards raised a hand. "Be peaceful, Tash," she said. "You tripped."

Tash shouted a protest, but he didn't even get the first word out of his mouth before she spoke again. "And he's a Copper. Collar won't make him any weaker than he already is."

The guard looked back at Lindon in disbelief, and then something brushed gently against Lindon's spirit. If he hadn't been paying attention, he might not have noticed.

So that was what it felt like, having his soul tested by another. He would have to remember that.

Tash shoved him one more time with the butt of the axe, then left him alone. For the rest of the day, Lindon was allowed to stop and cycle whenever he needed, though the first time he was sure Tash would split his head for stopping the harvester. Instead, the guards treated him like he didn't exist. When Yerin so much as glanced up, they shouted her back down. He was an exception.

That had to be an advantage, somehow.

He glanced back to the yellow-haired man, only to find that the man wasn't against the wall anymore. He was right next to Lindon now, though Lindon hadn't heard a thing.

"Isn't it ingenious, this thing?" he said, gesturing to the harvester. "In the Blackflame Empire, we don't have anything like it."

Tash turned around, his skin blooming red. "Quiet!"

"My name is Eithan," he said with a bow. He made no attempt to quiet himself, and even several of the others turned around with looks of disbelief. "And you are Wei Shi Lindon. The Copper. You're famous! Although *infamous* might be more accurate, really."

Tash had an axe in each hand and looked ready to use them. Lindon scraped his harvester across the ground to put a little distance between him and Eithan.

The yellow-haired man followed him. "You know, there's an opportunity for you here. The measure of a sacred artist isn't talent; it's how you respond to risk."

Lindon turned away, trying to make it clear that he wasn't speaking. Tash had arrived, an axe in each hand.

"It's kind of like this," Eithan said, and pivoted on the balls of his feet to deliver an overhand punch.

Straight at Lindon.

Lindon released his harvester, jerking to the side. He slammed into Tash's legs, and no matter how strong the Gold was, he'd been caught in mid-stride. He stumbled, halfway falling, and caught himself on the lip of a nearby harvester.

The guard looked up at Lindon with a face like a furnace.

"What do you *do* when you're met with danger?" Eithan asked conversationally. "Do you fight? Do you beg for forgiveness? Do you listen to me? Now, Yerin."

Yerin's hand shot out, stopping Tash from planting his axe in Lindon's skull. She looked back at Eithan, looking as stunned as Lindon felt.

"One step to your left," Eithan said, and Lindon followed his instructions. In a blur of motion, Tash had already thrown one axe, and it whistled through the air to clatter against the wall.

Now everyone was staring at Eithan, Lindon included.

"Let him go," Eithan said, and Yerin released Tash just as he swiped at her arm with his remaining axe.

"Lindon, take two steps back and then sit down," Eithan said, but by now Lindon was catching on. The man was singling them out for some reason, pushing them into trouble, and Lindon wasn't going to stand for it any more.

Of course, he didn't have to be rude about it.

He took a step forward and gave a shallow bow. "Forgiveness, elder brother, but I don't—"

Something large and snarling passed over Lindon's head, ruffling his hair, and latched onto Tash. The man screamed, and blood sprayed up onto the walls.

"Well done," Eithan said, patting Lindon on the shoulder.

For the first time, Lindon noticed more openings halfway up the walls. They were half the size of the hallway that had admitted the miners, but they were plenty big enough for the dreadbeasts that appeared out of nowhere, hurling themselves down onto the miners.

"Weapons up!" the woman in charge shouted, raising her own sword, but her command had come late. The guards already had their weapons in hand, and the miners crouched by their harvesters.

The creature on Tash looked like a monkey with skin

mottled bruise-purple and meat-red, and by the time Tash managed to pull the dreadbeast away, he wore a mask of blood. He gurgled as he took a staggering step forward, and Lindon looked away.

Only two of the miners stood in the middle of the deluge: Eithan and Yerin. Yerin had lifted the harvester with one hand—it was taking her obvious effort, which must have been the collar's effect—and punched a rotting dog with the iron barrel on her fist.

Eithan was wandering around seemingly at random, taking a casual stroll around the room, but none of the dreadbeasts ever latched onto him. He grabbed Lindon by the shoulder as he passed, which pulled Lindon to his feet just in time to avoid a foxlike beast's snarling attack. Eithan threw his arm across Lindon's shoulder in a fatherly gesture.

"There's a lineage of sacred beasts, you may have heard of them, known as the Heavenly Sky Tigers. It's a bit much for a name, I know, but they're quite famous." One of the miners was being dragged down a tunnel with his arm in the muzzle of a rotting wolf. A casual blow from a nearby guard sent the dreadbeast tumbling.

"These tigers breed every year or two," Eithan went on, ignoring the carnage around him. "Each litter has two, and exactly two, cubs...but only one ever survives to adulthood. Can you guess why that is?"

Yerin had taken a slash across the shoulder, and she was beating a monkey-creature to death with her bare hands. Lindon strained forward to help, but he couldn't escape from beneath Eithan's arm.

"I'd be happy to hear this story later," Lindon said, forcing calm into his voice.

"It's because the cubs fight each other to the death," Eithan said. "As a child, I found it tragic. My family kept a breeding pair of these Heavenly Sky Tigers, and when they gave birth to a brother and a sister, I was determined to save them both. I kept them in separate enclosures, fed them separately, raised them as I would a pair of children."

Blood spattered Lindon's forehead, and it took all his concentration not to scream.

"In the end, they wasted away and died. Both of them. I tried everything I knew to save them, but it was useless. Later, I found out the truth: for a Heavenly Sky Tiger, the body of their sibling is like an elixir. If one does not consume the other, their madra isn't strong enough to support their bodies, and they will inevitably die."

Eithan clasped Lindon with one hand on each shoulder, looking into his eyes with an earnest gaze. The head of a dreadbeast flew behind him, trailing blood. "Do you understand the story, Lindon?"

"It's a parable about overly protective parents," Lindon said hastily, straining his eyes to catch a glimpse of the creatures prowling around him.

"Not *just* parents," Eithan said. "Sacred artists. Without risk, without battle, without a willingness to fight, you will stay weak. And weakness means death. Do you agree?"

Even if he hadn't, he would have wholeheartedly agreed just to get Eithan's help. "Elder brother is so wise!" he said, his words tripping over each other. "This one agrees, and will gladly discuss it with elder brother at length."

Eithan clapped him on the back, smiling proudly. He took one long glance around the room, where the room had fallen into temporary silence. A few miners lay in bloody pools on the ground, as did Tash, but most of them had survived.

The leader raised her sword. *"Run!"* she shouted, and started down the hallway entrance.

Lindon looked up to the tunnels, expecting more dreadbeasts, but none came.

Instead, a rainbow of light slowly bloomed on the floor, and Remnants started to climb up from corpses.

Something seized Lindon from behind, grabbing him beneath both arms. He flailed in blind panic before he was hurled up, sliding perfectly into one of the tunnels into the wall.

It didn't even hurt much; he scraped his chin a bit on the stone floor, and his ribs might be a little bruised, but he'd slid into the tunnel at exactly the right angle to avoid injury.

He scrambled back to the entrance, looking down, where he saw Eithan smiling up at him. The yellow-haired man gave a cheery wave, and then reached to one side without looking.

Yerin swiped at his hand, but he was ready for her.

A second later, she slid into the tunnel beside Lindon. She growled as she stood, one hand groping for a sword, the other held in a fist at her side.

"Who is he?" Lindon asked.

"A dead man, if he doesn't explain himself true and proper."

Eithan landed neatly on the lip of the tunnel as though he'd moved ten feet vertically in one step, fine white-and-blue robes billowing behind him as he walked. "Follow me. Most of those Remnants can climb, and some of them can fly."

A blue wing spread across the entrance to the tunnel, accompanied by a cry that sounded like the song of a zither. Eithan doubled his pace. "Whoops, faster. We should go faster."

Yerin matched his stride, gesturing back the way they'd come. "You don't have the spine for a fight?"

Eithan hooked a finger underneath his collar. "We could find a way to get these off, if that's what you'd prefer. But you should know that I...well, you might say there's only one string to my bow."

"Can you see the future?" Lindon asked. In his own mind, he was already convinced of the answer. Eithan had moved before the guards or beasts did, every time, and he'd known when the dreadbeasts were coming.

"Better! I can see the *present*."

A Remnant cried behind them, like a low horn, accompanied by a human scream.

Before Lindon could express his skepticism, Eithan

continued. "I have a thousand eyes and ten thousand ears. I know everything that happens within range of my spirit, so as soon as an enemy starts to move, I simply step aside. It's like fighting the blind."

"Can't hit too hard with that," Yerin observed.

Eithan bowed to her. "Just so! Superior awareness is perhaps the greatest power of all, but as far as weapons go, knowledge lacks a certain *heft*. Though it does make me frustrating to kill—no one's managed it so far."

"If you don't mind telling me, how did they capture you?" Lindon asked. He kept his tone casual, but he was listening for a lie. If Eithan could do what he claimed, it would have been easier than lifting a hand to avoid the Sandvipers. He'd entered the mines on his own.

But why?

Eithan smiled broadly and reached out a hand to Lindon's head. Lindon tried to step aside, but the older man's palm landed regardless. He ruffled Lindon's hair. "Oh, I remember when I was your age. Young, spirited, distrusting of strangers. They say the years wear your innocence away, but it took me better than a decade on my own to learn the freedom of trust."

"That's not looking much like an answer," Yerin said, which nicely mirrored Lindon's own thought.

"Very well! As a reward for your observational skills, I'll tell you the truth." Eithan spun around, speaking as he walked backwards. "I came from the Blackflame Empire, located far to the east. Not long ago, I happened to sense a great power coming from the west. I brought it to the attention of my clan, who instructed me to investigate. When I arrived here, I found this incredible pyramid had drawn up all the aura for miles. Of course, I wasn't the only one—every sacred artist in the Desolate Wilds had beaten me to it."

"Is there something in the Ruins you want to take back to your clan?" Lindon asked. The spear Jai Sen had mentioned loomed in his imagination.

Eithan waved a hand. "The Ruins are loud and well worth investigating, but a treasure to a wilderness sect is not necessarily worthy of attention from a major Black-flame clan." He glanced up at the ceiling. "There's quite a nice spear in here, but it looks like it would be most suit-able for the Jai clan. It's not useful for me, so I gave up on it a long time ago."

"You can sense the spear?" Lindon asked, suddenly hungry. If Eithan could lead him straight to the weapon everyone wanted...

But he'd said something more surprising. "You don't want it?"

"We have access to Soulsmiths of our own," Eithan said dismissively. "A spear isn't interesting. Far more than a mere weapon, we value talent."

He was recruiting for a major imperial clan, and here he'd singled out the two of them. Lindon found himself for-getting the spear too. With Eithan's resources behind him, he wouldn't have to scrape for every scale. If he under-stood correctly, with a powerful family supporting him, he could reach Gold *tomorrow*.

"Forgiveness, I was blind," Lindon said. "I should have known that treasures in our eyes are just trash in yours. If I may ask, which—"

Eithan cut him off. "I know this is like asking an ampu-tee what happened to his legs, but I'm dying of curiosity. What happened to your core?"

Lindon glanced down at his midsection as though his core had just become visible. "My core?"

"You have two of them. Were you born that way? Is that why you're so weak? Or did someone damage your soul?"

Eithan asked with a tone of open curiosity, but Lindon had never felt that feather-light shiver of someone reaching out to sense his soul. Either he'd missed it, or Eithan was aware of *everything* that happened close to him. Including the strength and nature of souls.

Lindon swelled with questions. How far did his sense

extend? Was it some kind of sacred art that he had to use, or was he just aware of everything? Did he have to focus to avoid being overwhelmed?

But those were questions he could ask later, after he'd earned his way into the protection of Eithan's clan. For now, his job was to make himself valuable to Eithan.

"Pardon my rudeness. I was surprised that you'd noticed. I was born..." He had planned to say 'Unsouled,' but that had no meaning outside Sacred Valley, so he corrected himself mid-sentence. "...with a weak soul. Instead of wasting resources developing me, my clan chose not to teach me sacred arts. I split my core myself, as a defensive measure."

Eithan nodded along to every word, as though he'd expected exactly that story. When Lindon had finished, the man stopped walking—they'd put quite a distance between themselves and the Remnants by this point, though the occasional haunting echo did drift down the hall—and put his palm against Lindon's chest.

"Breathe in to here," Eithan said.

Lindon glanced over to Yerin, but she looked just as confused as he did, so he followed instructions. He filled his lungs until his ribs pressed against Eithan's hand.

"Now breathe out halfway."

Lindon did, until Eithan told him to hold his breath there.

"Your breathing technique helped you split your core?"

He nodded, still holding his breath.

"That explains why it's all focused inward." Eithan waved a hand vaguely in front of Lindon's middle. "Your madra flow is all knotted. It's not a bad breathing technique for pure madra, and you haven't damaged your channels yet, but it's better to correct now. You have a Path manual?"

He glanced at Lindon as though expecting Lindon to produce the book on command, and Lindon finally let his breath out to respond. "It's inside my pack, but unless you know a way out..."

Eithan tapped his chin with one finger, thinking. "Do you have a madra filter? Some condensation elixirs? You must have something to improve madra quality, if you made it to Copper without harvesting aura."

"I have a parasite ring," Lindon offered.

Eithan beamed. "Perfect! Now, where did you leave this pack?"

Yerin cutting in, pushing her way between them and holding up a hand as though she held an invisible sword to Eithan's throat. "Let's not throw our doors wide just yet. You say you're from the Blackflame Empire. Who are you?"

He drew himself up as though proud to be asked the question. "Young lady, I am the greatest janitor in all existence. I am the son of a janitor, last in a long line of janitors that stretch all the way back to the Sage of Brooms...and beyond!"

"Janitors?" Yerin asked blankly.

"Lest you think I'm speaking figuratively, let me clarify. My clan organizes the street sweepers in Blackflame City, we supervise sewer maintenance, we dig ditches and light lamps and sweep chimneys. 'Dirty hands are a mark of pride,' those are the words by which we live."

This from a man who looked as though he'd never held a shovel in his life. His fingers were long, his skin pale, his hands soft, his clothes far more expensive than anything else Lindon had seen in the Five Factions Alliance. In short, he looked more like the spoiled young master of a noble clan rather than any janitor.

"Please excuse me if I still seem...untrusting..." Lindon said, "but surely such a role does not fit your esteemed station. Do you perhaps mean that you keep the streets clean of *crime*, or you're a clan of assassins ridding an empire of the unworthy..."

Eithan was sliding his hands over the wall now, as though feeling the stone for weakness. "I grew up in the sewers of Blackflame City, ankle-deep in what you might call 'sludge.' They used similar scripts to control intake and

outflow, so if this works on similar principles...ah, there
we have it."

A single rune sparked to life, sending a ripple of light
flaring down the line of script in either direction.

With a grating sound, a stone slab slid upwards, revealing an open doorway onto a flight of stairs leading up.

"Maybe this was some kind of ancient sewer," Eithan
speculated. "Anyway, I have a task for you, Wei Shi Lindon."

Now that he thought of it, Lindon realized that Eithan
had known his full name the first time they'd met. Even
the street sweeper of a great empire was infinitely more
powerful than the four Schools of Sacred Valley, so Lindon
bowed deeply over a salute. "I will do my best to serve."

"Your current breathing technique is sufficient if you're
planning to split your core again, but it's building a wall
between you and Iron. To reach Iron, you have to push
madra *out* of your madra channels, forcing it into every
scrap of your flesh. It's very difficult without elixirs, and
your madra is currently focused into your core...and nowhere else. You need a new breathing technique."

Eithan stood straight, facing Lindon. "Inhale as I do,
and as you do so, cycle your madra in wide loops to every
extremity of your body. As you exhale, gather it together
again, all at once. I'll show you how."

Lindon had practiced a simple breathing technique
since the day he first got his wooden badge, until it eventually became his natural breathing rhythm. He'd changed
it according to the instruction in the *Heart of Twin Stars*
manual, but it wasn't any more complex than his original
technique, only different.

Likewise, the technique Eithan taught him wasn't complicated. It didn't use any principles Lindon didn't already
know, which had come as a relief.

But it was *hard*.

He could barely hold the new cycling pattern standing
straight and watching Eithan, and he was sure that he'd
lose it as soon as Eithan stopped giving him pointers. He

said as much to Eithan, who laughed.

"That's the nature of any acquired skill. It will feel like breathing through a wet rag for a while, and your body will tell you to stop. But one day, you'll look back and wonder how it was ever difficult." He pointed up the stairs. "Now, as your first challenge, hold that pattern as you run up to the next floor."

Lindon peered into the shadows at the top. "Do you have a light?"

"You do," Eithan said.

He reached into his pocket and pulled out Suriel's marble. He was somewhat self-conscious holding it, as though he'd been caught in a lie, but there was no way Eithan would know what it was. Even if he'd sensed it, it was just a light in a glass.

Sure enough, Eithan gave the marble a curious glance, but that was all. Lindon held it up, took a deep breath, and began to cycle as he ran.

Behind him, Yerin protested. "He's about as sturdy as a newborn kitten. If there's anything up there, it'll tear him to rags."

"Remember my thousand eyes," Eithan said. "These Ruins may as well be my own home."

The blue light of the marble was faint, but it was enough to show Lindon when he reached the end of the stairs and found himself in a large room. He couldn't see anything beyond the patch of floor at his feet.

The jog hadn't been long, but his lungs were still burning with the effort of holding the breathing technique. He started to shout back that he'd made it, but when something hissed in the shadows, his words died.

It was only about as big as his arm. A tan centipede with a carapace the color of a sandy dune. It had a head like a snake and two rows of insect claws, and its tail arched up into a scorpion's stinger.

He'd never seen one in the flesh, but their Remnants had left him with an impression all too clear. The first sandviper hissed at him, baring fangs...as a second scuttled up, keeping a wary distance from its twin, angling toward Lindon.

Eithan's voice came from the stairs beneath him. "I know what's up there, and he can handle it."

Then came the growl of stone, like a lid scraping over a coffin, as the door slid shut.

CHAPTER FOURTEEN

Lindon's shouts and pleas came muffled through the stone door, and Yerin gathered what little madra she could onto her fingernails. Sword madra gathered onto sharp edges, so her nails were not the best container.

She would have used her Goldsign instead, but the scripted collar was choking her madra at the source, and she was still shaky from the Sandviper venom earlier. Her muscles squirmed like snakes in a bag, and she barely had enough focus to hold the technique together. If she tried to control the steel arm on her back, she might end up cutting her own head off.

But she'd die and rot away before she gave up without a fight.

She held her fingers up like claws to Eithan's eye. "Pop it back open."

He didn't flinch, looking at her like a wronged child. "But he's not finished yet."

She slashed at him, but he'd already started walking to the side, as though he'd picked exactly *that* second to take a stroll. Her technique rippled through the air, almost invisible without her spiritual sight, and madra cracked against the stone.

"I came here to find some promising recruits," Eithan continued, pacing around her. She turned so he didn't have a shot at her back. "I was also bored, but the recruits are important too. You see, the families of the empire compete largely on the strength of the younger generation, because disciples are the indication of a clan's future power. Since we're looking fairly sparse in the disciple department, I'm keeping an eye or two open for outside talent."

Lindon's cries for help were filling the hall now.

"I'll go along with you," Yerin said quickly. Eithan wouldn't have been the first to try and forcibly recruit the Sword Sage's apprentice—even while her master had been alive, every sect and school they'd crossed had tried to make her a better offer. But none of them had taken a hostage.

If she went with him now, she could break out later. Her master would have loved it.

Eithan paid no more attention to Lindon's screams than he would to a chirping bird, brushing some dirt from his shoulder. "It would be irresponsible of me to turn you down. As I said, we've been backed into something of a corner. But there's a saying where I come from: 'a bad student is a weight around his teacher's neck.' I'd rather go back empty-handed than take someone who isn't ready."

Yerin still couldn't control her Goldsign well under the collar's influence; the bladed silver arm wobbled as it rose into the air, and she couldn't keep it straight. But it was ten times easier to funnel sword madra through the blade on the end than through her fingernails.

She gathered her power into it and fixed Eithan with her gaze. "He dies, and I'm not going anywhere."

Eithan's eyebrows lifted. "Oh, you're more than good enough on your own. A Sage is a Sage after all; he had the good fortune to pick you up early, and your foundation is flawless. It would be an honor to pick up where your master left off." He swept his arm toward the stone door. "But I find myself intrigued by your Copper friend."

Yerin's focus wavered, and some of the madra in her Goldsign dissipated. "What is it you want from him?

"To teach him." Eithan patted the door like a favored pet, even as Lindon shouted on the other side. "It's so rare to find a truly blank canvas."

"You're looking for pure madra? Raise your own kid."

"No no, that's easy enough. The quality I'm looking for, indeed the most important quality for any sacred artist, is *drive*. He needs the resolve to push through any obstacle in his Path, and that kind of focus is very difficult to teach. But here we have someone who split his own core, a Copper working side-by-side with Golds. Something's driving him, and it might be enough to take him to the top."

She found herself speaking through clenched teeth. "He's *blind,* you hear me? The world's all jade beds and silk sheets for him. He's never seen how ugly it gets. He doesn't *know.*"

He'd been mistreated by his clan, that was true. But he'd never fought for his own life. He'd never clawed his way out of a pile of bodies until he was elbow-deep in blood. He'd never woken to find that his only family was dead... and pushed through that crushing weight to draw his sword anyway.

Eithan leaned one shoulder against the wall, considering her. "What do you think I'm trying to teach him?"

Suddenly, he sounded just like her master. It brought up memories she'd just as soon have left buried.

A white forest, long ago. A ring of swords in the snow.

Yerin ran a thumb across one paper-thin scar on the back of her hand, remembering. Her madra dissipated, her Goldsign retreating.

Eithan was smart enough not to crow about his victory. If he had given her so much as a smug look, she'd have peeled his face away. Instead, he spoke as though nothing had happened. "Your foundation is excellent, as I'd expect from a master like yours. But I'm sure you know your advancement is lacking."

She didn't even need to nod. Within Lowgold, she could

call herself strong. But the gap to Highgold was a chasm. She could barely control her Goldsign, much less the powerful madra that had come with her master's Remnant. She'd left it mostly alone so far; when she touched that reserve of inherited power, she felt like an infant strapped to the back of a war-trained stallion. She didn't even like to think of it.

"I'm sure the Sage of the Endless Sword would have had greater insight in regards to sword Paths, but I can offer a few observations of my own."

She looked from his pristine hair to his expensive, unstained clothes. "You think you're a sword artist, do you?"

If he said he was, she wasn't listening to another word from this liar's mouth.

"I prefer not to use a weapon at all. None of them seem to suit me. But sword Paths are common because they're very simple."

She was still trying to figure out if he needed his teeth punched out for that insult when he continued. "You need to push yourself."

She gave that some measured thought. True, she'd felt *something* when she fought off three Sandviper soldiers on the slopes of Mount Samara. Not comfortable, exactly, but like she was moving along a familiar road. And it hadn't been long ago when she'd honed herself to the peak of Jade by engaging in endless battle with the Heaven's Glory School.

Eithan continued, still leaning against the door that held a begging Lindon. "Advancement along sword Paths is very straightforward at this stage. Immerse yourself in the sword, cycle on the battlefield, and find opponents who will push you to the very edge of life and death. There's a reason why it's one of the most common aspects."

Yerin nodded once. Her teacher had said similar things, but every stage of advancement was different. He'd actually stopped her from fighting when she was Iron, for fear that she'd ruin her foundation for Jade. "You know where I can find any of that in here?"

He grinned and pushed off from the wall. "You'll need your sword to really practice, so just sit and cycle until I return. We have to make sure you're in your best condition, don't we?"

Eithan paused for a moment, then added, "If he dies before I get back, you should know that I am sorry. But some Paths are shorter than others."

Before she could respond, he hooked a finger under his iron collar and tugged. With a wrenching shriek, the iron split and tore.

He tossed the ruined metal behind him and left, whistling a cheery tune.

Yerin pulled at her own collar, just in case someone had replaced it with a rusted copy, but it remained firm. She could just barely scrape together enough madra to Enforce herself, but not enough to tear metal with her bare hands. She and Eithan should have been on the same level: left with nothing more than the strength of their bodies. They might as well have been Iron.

How had he done it?

Something smacked against the door from the other side, and Yerin stopped fiddling with her collar. She stared at the scripted line of stone, aching for her spiritual sight. Without it, she felt like she had one eye plucked out.

"Lindon?"

Silence for a moment, then something scrambled on the floor. Seconds later, Lindon's voice came through, ragged and breathless. "Can you open the door? Is Eithan there? How did he close it?"

Yerin sighed. "I'm coming up empty on that count. You're stuck with a rusty patch, that I can tell you."

A muffled sound that she couldn't identify came between her words and his response. "Yerin," he said, "I'm going to die. I can't...I can't do this, I'm running them around in circles, but I don't have...anything."

She wasn't sure that she heard every word, but she got the main thrust of it. She'd said the same things to her master, over and over again, ever since she was a girl.

Yerin sat, leaning her back against the door. "You've got no cards left in your hand, you're staring death in the eyes, and nobody's there to pull you out. That sound true so far?"

"Yerin, please, *it's coming back.*"

She continued. "That's how you advance. When you can't count on anybody else, that's when you know if you've got what it takes. It's painful, it's bloody, and it's hard. You can take shortcuts if you've got a fortune to burn on elixirs and treasures, but if you don't..."

Another scuffle came from behind her, and Lindon didn't respond. He may have been fighting, but she continued talking as though he could hear. "The sacred arts are a game, and your life is the only thing you've got to bet. You want to move up? This is what *up* looks like."

Silence was her only response.

She sat against the door, remembering all the times she'd stared death in the eyes. It had started when she was a young girl, before she'd met her master, and she was sure the heavens would strike her dead for her sins. That had lasted for...longer than she cared to recall.

Lindon didn't deserve anything like that, but here he was anyway. The longer the silence stretched, the more certain she became that he was dead. She couldn't say she hadn't seen it coming; if you bet on the longest odds, you were going to lose more than you won.

But she waited in the endless dark of the Ruins, only the flickering light of the script on the wall for company, straining her ears as time slid by.

When she finally caught a sound, it almost deafened her. The explosion was like a cross between a wolf's howl and the crack of a firework, and it came with a green flash from the gaps around the door.

She was on her feet in a second, slapping the heel of her hand against the door and demanding to know what was happening.

For the first minutes, she heard only scrapes and grunts

from the other side, like a man dragging something heavy across the ground. After an age, footsteps.

"Forgive me," Lindon said, his voice strained and tight. "I was begging like a coward, and I made you listen. I am ashamed."

"Everything steady in there, Lindon?" she asked, straining her ears as though she could hear an injury. "All your pieces still on?'

This time, she thought she heard a faint note of pride. "Sacred beasts are still beasts, after all. I crushed them under a rock. Their Remnants were the tricky part, but I tossed a scale between them and they fought for it until one died. Had to tear the dead one's tail off and use the stinger to finish off the other, but that's nothing to a sacred artist, right?"

"Just one more day," Yerin said, letting out a deep breath and relaxing against the door again. "Don't know why you're crowing about it. Any day where I haven't beaten a Remnant to death with its own limb is a holiday."

He gave a weak laugh. "Forgiveness. I let my head get too big." He hesitated, and then added, "If you could find a way to open the door, I would still be grateful."

For a second, she thought it was a heaven-sent miracle: at his words, the door actually started to grind open.

"I had every faith in you!" Eithan called from only a few feet down the hall, and Yerin staggered to her feet. She hadn't felt him approach at all. She knew it was the collar's effect, but it was still unnerving, as though he'd popped out of nowhere.

Eithan removed his hand from the script, smiling broadly. The Thousand-Mile Cloud floated behind him, sullen and red, with Lindon's pack seated comfortably on top of it. Two packs, in fact: his big one, bulging with all the knickknacks he carried around, and the smaller one he'd planned on filling with scales stolen from the Sandvipers.

And beneath it, peeking out from the edge of the cloud, her sheathed sword.

"If you can get out anytime you want," Yerin said, "let's leave. This place is like a graveyard stuffed into a cave."

"Why leave?" Eithan asked. "Everything we need is right here."

The door had opened completely by then, revealing Lindon standing stunned at the bottom of the stairs. He was leaning with one hand on the wall, displaying a collection of scrapes and bruises, but the corpse of a Sandviper Remnant lay sprawled on the stairs behind him. He held a bright green stinger as long as his arm in one hand, hilt wrapped in cloth so he didn't have to touch the toxic madra directly. He'd torn off one of his sleeves to provide the fabric.

Truth was, he actually looked like a real sacred artist. With his sharp eyes, broad shoulders, and the severed Remnant arm bleeding sparks of essence, he looked like a Jade ready to advance to Lowgold. It was a much better look on him than how she'd found him, all clean and cringing and weak.

Eithan tossed the two packs to Lindon, who had to drop his improvised weapon to catch them. He stumbled back a few steps, almost falling onto the stairs.

"Make sure to take notes," Eithan said, pointing to the pack. "Wear your parasite ring and keep your breathing straight. I put some scales in there for you, but I'm keeping the cloud." He patted the construct with one hand. "I need a bed."

Then he slapped the wall, and the door started sliding shut again.

Lindon lunged forward, but Eithan had already thrust his palm forward. He struck Lindon in the chest, sending him tumbling backwards.

When the door slammed closed, Lindon screamed wordlessly from the other side.

Eithan brushed his sleeves, smiling at Yerin as though he'd heard nothing. "That should keep him occupied for a few weeks. Now, I believe I mentioned something about you needing an opponent."

He tossed her sheathed sword to her and drew a weapon of his own: a pair of wrought iron fabric scissors.

"Best weapon I could find," he said apologetically, snipping them open and closed. "Now, if you're ready, let's begin."

●

Jai Long was having Fisher problems.

Kral's father, the chief of the Sandviper sect, still hadn't returned from his hunt. He'd sent word that he was alive and well, but that was little comfort to Jai Long, because the chief's absence meant that Kral was in charge.

And Kral took responsibility in one way: by leaving it to Jai Long.

So it was that he found himself standing next to the First Fisher, Ragahn, waiting for the old man to say something.

They stood in the shade of an old tree—its leaves were half blackened by the rot of the dreadbeasts, like so much in the Desolate Wilds, but it provided a relief from the sun nonetheless.

Ragahn, the leader of the Fisher sect, looked like a beggar who had chosen that spot to plead for coins. His gray hair hung loose, his feet were bare, his robe brown and stained, and his Fisher's hook—the blade longer than his arm and sharp on the inside—was made of rust-patched iron, dangling carelessly from his belt. He held a net over one shoulder, packed tight with severed dreadbeast parts. They were fresh, still dripping blood, and the stench was almost painful.

But Jai Long stood there, his expression covered by the strips of cloth that masked his Goldsign. He peered out through the gap in the red mask, resisting the temptation to cover the silence.

The First Fisher had come to him before dawn, almost exactly two weeks after Jai Long had sent Gesha's recruits into the mines. He'd assumed that was what the visit was about, but the old man had never said. He simply grunted, indicated that Jai Long should follow him outside, and then left.

For the next hour, they'd stood underneath a tree, as the bloody pieces in the Fisher's net slowly dried.

Jai Long wondered if this patience was perhaps the secret of Ragahn's advancement. The beggar chief was one of the few Truegolds in the entire Wilds, which meant that he'd gained complete control over the Remnant in his core. His Goldsign was very subtle; a stranger may not even notice the webs between his fingers.

Once, Truegold had seemed like the pinnacle of achievement. He'd worked himself half to death to get closer, eventually achieving Highgold himself, only to discover that his *particular* Goldsign would never go away. His face would remain hideous no matter how far he advanced.

Now, he had other reasons to work. The Jai clan wouldn't take his sister back anymore, and she had no one else. To create a home for her, even Truegold wouldn't be enough.

Finally, the First Fisher spoke. "Have you finished your map?"

Jai Long didn't dare to twitch to betray his support. He responded with bland confidence. "My miners keep their eyes open."

Ragahn adjusted his grip on the net. "You have. So why aren't you holding the spear?"

He was right. Jai Long had finished the map over a week ago, but they still didn't understand the script running throughout the Ruins, so he couldn't access the chambers he needed to open the top of the pyramid. The spear should be inside, though he had no independent confirmation of that. If it wasn't, he was going to have some harsh questions to answer when Kral's father returned.

It was frustrating, because Jai Long may have been able to force his way in with a more varied toolset. He had access only to artists on the Path of the Sandviper, as well as his own Path of the Stellar Spear. Neither of them were suited for scouting or breaking seals.

But Fishers adopted a peculiar twist on the aspect of force. In some way that Jai Long didn't understand, they could draw objects in like fishermen pulling on invisible lines. They might have some way to open the doors without manipulating the script.

If the First Fisher was here to strike some sort of bargain, then a little honesty might be in order.

"The script has slowed our progress," Jai Long allowed. "I'm confident that we will make our way inside, given enough time."

"Time," Ragahn repeated, as though chewing on the word. "The Arelius family is almost here. I've seen the black crescent banners myself. Three days, no more."

Jai Long would hardly have met with an enemy without a weapon in his hand, and his knuckles whitened around his spear's shaft. He'd hoped for a little more time. Unless something changed, he wouldn't be able to break the script in three days.

He was about to bend his own pride far enough to ask for help when the First Fisher spoke. "I'll buy your map."

"You want to pay for it?"

"It's useless to you. May as well make a profit. I'll take it, clean out the Ruins before the Underlord gets here."

Leaving nothing for Jai Long, much less the Sandvipers.

The First Fisher would no doubt pay well for the map. He was one of the richest individuals in the Wilds, despite his appearance, and he had his reputation to consider. If he shorted a sect like the Sandvipers, none of the other factions would deal with him.

But that would require Jai Long to admit defeat.

"I would be happy to share whatever bounty we find inside the Ruins with anyone who participates in its retrieval. If you would like to lend me your abilities, I will distribute rewards on merit."

Ragahn chuckled deep in his chest, as though trying to rid himself of a cough. "The bones of the earth will bend before a sacred artist's pride."

He heaved the net of severed dreadbeast limbs off his shoulder and dropped it next to the tree trunk, turning to Jai Long. He spread empty, webbed hands in a show of peace. "We'll compete with honor, to save face for our sects."

"You can't call that a competition," Jai Long said, contempt in his voice. "The other factions will never stand for it." Ragahn was a Truegold, with the power to do whatever he wished, and Jai Long couldn't stop him. But honor and fear for the Fisher reputation should keep the old man from pushing a mere Highgold around.

The First Fisher slowly shook his head. "You question my honor again, boy, and you're taking your life in your hands."

Jai Long carefully did not shiver.

"No, I happen to have a disciple. He's Highgold himself, like you are, and he's more than happy to stand for a traditional duel. Aren't you, Lokk?"

He raised his voice on the last word, and Lokk of the Fishers stepped out of the trees a hundred yards away. He raised a hand in greeting, then dashed toward them, covering the distance with impressive speed. Jai Long had met the man before; he was early in his second decade and had already reached Highgold, which made him a peer with Kral and Jai Long.

He was short but thin, with disproportionately long arms and a pair of steel Fisher's hooks on his back. He and his sister were the only two Fishers who used a pair of hooks in battle, as far as Jai Long knew.

He wondered if the man had been waiting in the woods for over an hour, just in case his name was called. With a man like the First Fisher as his master, he probably did a lot of waiting.

Lokk bowed over his fists to Ragahn. "The disciple greets his master," he said, then bowed again to Jai Long. "We could settle this debate by exchanging pointers, as fellow travelers on the path of sacred arts."

This move of the First Fisher's didn't surprise Jai Long. Sects and Schools dueled one another as often as clans did, for any and all reasons: for pride, for trading rights, to settle disputes, to avoid wholesale slaughter. The faction capable of raising the best disciple was considered to be the strongest, and the strongest got what they wanted.

He had no problem with the logic, but Ragahn was trying to get him to draw his weapon. If he did...well, it was rare to emerge from a duel unscathed. And since Jai Long was currently the de facto leader of the Sandviper sect, any wound on his part would result in a weakening of the Sandvipers as a whole. Win or lose, the First Fisher would get what he wanted. And if Jai Long refused, his reputation would take a hit that might be more fatal than a physical wound. Even the Sandvipers would turn on a coward.

Fortunately, Jai Long had planned ahead. He gestured, and a watching Sandviper relayed his signal.

Kral emerged from a nearby building, standing tall and proud. His fine furs were as rich and dark as his hair, and his sandviper Goldsign twisted around his arm. He covered the distance between them in seconds, arriving before Ragahn in a gust of wind.

The two Fishers exchanged looks with one another, but Jai Long couldn't read their expressions.

"Fisher Lokk," Kral began, his tone imperious. "I, Kral of the Sandvipers, request an exchange of the sacred arts. Let the words of the stronger sect be heard."

The old man crossed his arms. "You'd risk your young chief?"

Jai Long almost laughed. Ragahn knew full well who guided the Sandvipers in Gokren's absence. "The Fishers are worthy of facing our best."

Kral swelled at the praise, though he knew it wasn't sincere. Though they were both Highgold, Jai Long had never lost a sparring match to the Sandviper heir.

But that didn't mean he wasn't good enough to deal with a beggar's apprentice.

Fisher Ragahn nodded as though he thought Jai Long was speaking good sense. "Very well. Fight until the winner is clear. If there is danger, I'll step in."

It traditionally fell to the elders to intervene in a fight and stop injuries on either side, but there were usually elders representing both halves of a duel. If Lokk was in danger, Jai Long had no doubt that Ragahn would move like lightning, but Kral was almost entirely on his own.

Not that you would know it from watching him. The Sandviper heir cast his furs onto the ground behind him, slowly sliding each awl from his belt as though expecting the mere sight of them to daunt his opponent. He ran green madra along the edge of each spike, displaying them like a street performer.

Lokk, by contrast, drew a curved blade in each hand and stood there. If purple madra flickered somewhat between the hilts and the blades, it looked like an accident. His expression was placid as still water.

If Jai Long was honest, he found the Fisher's display more intimidating.

No one signaled the beginning of the match, but both men sprang into action nonetheless. The first exchange was sudden and violent; hooks flew out from their handles as though attached to invisible ropes, whipping toward Kral. The Sandviper gathered green madra into a swirl around his awl, stabbing forward.

Three spikes of Forged Sandviper madra condensed around his weapon, driving forward with him.

The Sandvipers called that move the Four Fangs of the Serpent, but it was really a very ordinary Forger technique. It was only the most basic type of Forging—the madra would stay solid for a few seconds, and then dissipate—but it was still effective. It would be like facing four attacks at once.

Lokk's hooks crashed through the Sandviper technique, sending fizzing shards of green madra spinning to the ground. The grass fizzed around the venomous madra. The tips of his blades landed on Kral's back, puncturing the skin, but the Sandviper chief had taken the move in order to land a move of his own. He continued driving the awl forward, aiming at the Fisher's chest.

Just when Jai Long started to hope that Kral was really pointing at the other man's shoulder—because he didn't want to have to defend the young chief from an angry First Fisher—he learned why Ragahn had chosen to wait under a large tree.

A rope of purple madra flashed into existence behind Lokk, connecting his spine to a branch of the tree. It shrunk rapidly, hauling the Fisher up and away from Kral's attack.

Hauled back by a rope of his own madra, Lokk landed neatly on the lowest branch. He held only a pair of hilts; the bladed hooks were still stuck in Kral's back.

"Thank you for going easy on me," Lokk said, his tone polite.

Ragahn turned to Jai Long as though asking if the duel was over, but Kral's expression was distorted in fury. He dropped one awl, and the aura around the tree rippled green.

"Down!" Fisher Ragahn shouted, making a beckoning motion to his disciple. Invisible force caught Lokk, pulling him away from the tree.

He stopped in midair, hovering only a few feet from the trunk. He hadn't undone his own Forged tether, and now he was bound in place.

The First Fisher leaped into the air, but Jai Long's senses were already overwhelmed by bright green aura.

Sandviper madra drew on aura from toxins, poison, and corrosion of all kinds. It was a Path born in the swamp, originally created as an adaptation to the dread corruption of the Wilds.

And this tree's leaves were half blackened.

Ruler techniques were faster and more powerful when the necessary vital aura was ready to hand, and the tree was riddled with poison. It burst into a harsh green cloud as though exploding in emerald flame, covering both Fishers.

Jai Long dashed over to Kral, seizing one of the bladed hooks as best he could without slicing his own hand open. He tugged one out of the flesh, leading to a pained moan from the Sandviper chief.

"It's only pain," Jai Long said, pulling the second free. "Your ascension to Iron was worse."

"I beat him," Kral panted.

"Let's see if it was worth it."

Ragahn had emerged from the toxic cloud—unscathed, of course—with an unconscious apprentice in his hands. Lokk twitched wildly as his master drifted down to the ground, as slowly as if he were lowered on a wire.

Jai Long stood straight, grinding the butt of his spear into the ground. "Your disciple fought well," he said.

The unspoken words floated in the air: *...but he lost.*

Fisher Ragahn turned a gaze on him, and though his expression was still blank, his eyes held a deeply banked anger.

He was a sacred artist too, after all. His pride was more dear to him than his life.

Fortunately, that same pride was keeping his anger in check.

"The Fishers will honor our debts," he said. "You'll have my best for the next three days. But if Arelius shows up and takes everything, I'll hold you accountable."

He flew off, lashing himself to the trees with a long line of purple madra and pulling himself forward.

"They aren't the most grateful losers," Kral said, wincing as he straightened himself. The wounds would pain him for a few days, but Sandvipers were tenacious. He'd heal quickly.

"We haven't won yet," Jai Long said.

There were still three days to go.

CHAPTER FIFTEEN

Lindon levered himself up to a seated position, the flare of pain letting him know that he may have a cracked rib. He set the pain aside. It was nothing to the damage in his legs, which lay swollen and useless on the ground in front of him. He hadn't been able to walk for days.

He reached over and slid the glass case closer, using the three un-broken fingers on his left hand. One of his eyes was swollen shut, but through the other he watched the Sylvan.

She spun in place, arms swaying as though dancing to some music he couldn't hear. He'd started to think of it as female, though he had no reason to think she had a gender at all. Maybe it was the flowing madra of her lower half, which made her look like she was wearing a dress.

Regardless, the Sylvan had been his only companion these two weeks besides Yerin's voice through the door. He'd fed her what dribbles of his spare madra he could afford to Forge, and she'd grown almost half an inch. Her translucent blue form looked more solid, though that could have been his imagination, and she expressed a greater range of actions. Just yesterday she had swum a full lap of her tank inside the ever-flowing river.

Lindon looked up from the case to regard his fortress.

It was a slipshod attempt at defense—he'd used the claws of the spider-construct in his pack to cut dead matter away from the Remnants that regularly attacked him. With those pieces, those bright blue shells and shimmering green limbs, he'd boxed himself in. His back was to the door, and his fortress was piled up against the stairs. He'd backed himself into a corner, which had led to a few tense moments as he had nowhere to run, but he refused to move his fortification to the top of the stairs. If the door ever opened, he wanted to be able to run through in an instant.

Though he was starting to lose hope that the door *would* ever open.

While watching the Sylvan, he reached over to a binding shaped like a twisted blue seashell. He had to replace the dead matter in his walls every day or two, as it bled away regularly, but he used his own madra to supplement his few useful bindings. He'd been fortunate to find this one, which Gesha had demonstrated for him a few weeks before: it produced water.

He drank only a few swallows; he didn't have any more madra to spare. Most of his power each day went to refreshing the essential bindings and his weapon, the severed Sandviper stinger with the cloth-wrapped hilt. He cycled the rest of it, pushing madra through every square inch of his body.

Despite the haze of agony that hung over him constantly—and the series of sudden, vicious attacks that had driven fear so deep into his soul that he thought it would never leave—he was pleased with the weeks of work. The razor-edged tension had done wonders for his advancement, since there was nothing to do here but cycle and prepare to be attacked. And the slightest moment of inattention would result in his inevitable death.

One of his cores was at the peak of Copper, almost ready to overflow and pour through his body in the transition to Iron. He'd finally raised his second core to Copper as well, but focused most of his effort on one. That had been Yerin's advice.

Eithan's breathing technique had almost gotten him killed in the first few days, when he lost his breath in the middle of a fight and his madra fell out of control. Now, he rarely lost the rhythm, and he'd started to see the advantages: his madra recovered much more quickly, and he was sure he could advance to Iron any day he wanted.

That wasn't entirely true. He *wanted* to advance right now, because breaking through the barrier to Iron completely reforged the body. Advancing to Copper had cleansed him of scrapes, cuts, and bruises, and Iron was supposed to be a more thorough transformation. When Yerin told him that it would heal his broken legs, he'd almost cried from the effort not to force an advancement now.

But if he advanced before he was ready, he would damage his own foundation. That was the only thing that held him back. If his Iron body wasn't perfect, he wouldn't be guaranteed Highgold, much less the heights Suriel had challenged him to reach.

The blue marble sat in a corner, its flame straight and steady inside the glass barrier. He stared at it every day as he cycled, meditating on it. Suriel had believed he could do this. She'd known he would meet suffering even worse than this, and he would come out on the other side stronger.

He seized on that like a mantra, clutching it like the edge of a cliff.

Only one problem remained: his progress was too slow.

He'd only pushed madra through half of his body at most. He could execute a basic Enforcer technique now, making himself stronger for short periods of time, which he had hastily scrawled into the *Path of Twin Stars* in excitement. But he needed to suffuse his body with madra, soaking it completely, and he was at least another week away from that. Probably two.

And his body was done.

With two broken legs, one eye swollen shut, two broken fingers on each hand, a cracked rib, and more wounds and complaints than he could even remember, he wouldn't survive another attack. The day had been quiet so far, which was a blessing from the heavens as far as he was concerned, but something else would come. A twisted dreadbeast, a sandviper, a Remnant. At least he stood a chance against the Remnant, thanks to the scripts he'd left scraped into the top of the stairs.

But even if he survived today, he'd never last until he finished laying the groundwork for Iron. If nothing else, he'd starve. Sandvipers tasted like chicken livers soaked in acid, but they were the best thing he'd found to eat in here. On the fourth day, he'd even been fortunate enough to find a binding that produced fire.

As injured as he was, he couldn't catch food anymore. He'd burned through Eithan's supply of scales in a week, using them to push the barrier of his core further and further, and then he'd started Forging his own.

At first, he'd wondered how a scale he'd Forged would help further his own advancement. It felt a bit like eating your own arm for sustenance. But it was quite simple, in practice: he Forged the madra, condensing it into a scale and setting it aside. Then he cycled to restore his madra to its peak condition and swallowed the scale again. Pushed beyond its capacity, his core stretched a little.

Gradually, by repeating that process over and over, he'd stretched his core to the limit of Copper. When his body was ready, he'd push the core just a *little* further, and then it would spill over and run through all the channels he was patiently preparing.

But that brought him back to the original problem.

He'd poured out his concerns to Yerin, who listened until the end. She'd kept him sane during these two weeks, though she was never as impressed with his accomplishments as she ought to be. To her, any sacred artist should be able to survive for a few weeks under constant attack.

Finally, when he'd finished explaining that he couldn't possibly finish driving madra through his body before he died, and she *had* to convince Eithan to release him, she sat in silence for a moment.

Then she said, "Have my eyes gone soft, or is it getting bright in there?"

At first he assumed that was one of her expressions, and 'bright' meant his situation was getting more hopeful. Then he looked at the walls.

Between the glow of Suriel's marble and the soft luminescence of the Remnant bodies piled around, it was actually quite bright in his little nook. So it took him a moment to realize that there were faint sparks playing inside the script that wrapped the chamber.

He contained his excitement. It really meant nothing to his situation, though any sign of change thrilled him. "Have you asked Eithan? Is he there, by chance?"

Eithan had said nothing to Lindon directly over the past two weeks. Not a word. Yerin had consulted with him a few times on an answer to one of Lindon's sacred arts questions, but otherwise he might as well have left. He spent his days with Yerin, locked in combat that Lindon could hear crashing through the door, and more than once Lindon had shed actual tears of envy.

Now, the light in the script meant the possibility of hearing from Eithan. And that conversation could be the key that opened the door.

Yerin left, and only minutes later, a new voice came through. Lindon closed his eyes, for a moment just savoring the sound of someone else's voice. It had been so long.

"I'm sorry to cut this phase of your training short, Lindon, but it looks as though someone has lit a fuse for us. They're fooling with the script, so power is flowing into empty chambers. Bad news is, this door's going to open soon."

Lindon's spirits soared.

"But don't worry. The power is being drawn to the top

of the pyramid, so every dreadbeast and Remnant in the Ruins will follow us."

His spirits crashed back down to earth, and he almost cried.

The wait for the door to slide open felt longer than the previous two weeks. Lindon stared at the blank stone slab, every twitch of his body sending notes of pain through him like a symphony of agony.

Finally, the lines of script running along the wall flared brighter. Light grew along the bottom, and the door lifted away from the floor.

Tears welled in Lindon's one good eye, and he swiped them away. Better if they saw him as a grizzled survivor of suffering, rather than a boy waiting to be rescued. Though gaining a reputation as a coward would be worth it so long as they took him away.

When the door opened, Eithan was holding an arm over his nose. "I didn't expect you to smell of rosewater and lavender, but it would have been considerate of you to bathe."

Lindon stared at him over the crude splints binding his two broken legs.

Yerin advanced without comment. Her hair had grown slightly uneven again, and the new sacred artist's robe that she'd received from the Fishers was little more than a collection of black tatters. She smiled at him out of one corner of her mouth and then stepped past him, gripping her sheathed sword.

With a grunt, she hauled one of the half-ruined Remnant corpses away from his wall and peered out. "Still scarce for now," she said. "But we should scurry."

Eithan looked Lindon up and down. "It's been hard on you."

Lindon held his eyes very wide so he didn't tear up.

Lowering his sleeve, Eithan revealed a curious expression. "Was it worth it?"

With his less injured arm, Lindon pushed himself up straighter to slowly execute a seated bow. Sweat beaded on his forehead from the pain in his ribs, but he forced himself through it. "Gratitude, elder. This one cannot repay the favor."

These two weeks had been the worst in Lindon's life, but half a month of agony was nothing compared to a lifetime of helplessness.

Now, he was on the verge of Iron. Iron might be nothing but a child's accomplishment out here, but his *parents* were only Iron. He hadn't even turned sixteen yet, so he'd surpass his sister.

If he returned to Sacred Valley, the Wei clan wouldn't just welcome him back. They'd reward him. He would be their new idol, the one they paraded in front of the other clans to show their superiority.

The idea was so sweet that it almost choked him.

Far more important was that he'd taken his first steps on the Path Suriel had shown him. He might really surpass Gold, and Eithan had helped him.

For that alone, he really did owe the yellow-haired man a debt he couldn't repay.

Eithan smiled broadly, pleased with his answer. "That's good," he said. "Because it isn't over yet."

Yerin glanced back over her shoulder, giving him a look of pity.

"You're only halfway through pushing madra channels through your entire body, so if you advanced to Iron now, you'd be crippling your own future. Lowgold would be difficult, and you may reach Highgold in your old age."

Never would Lindon have thought that reaching Gold would be the *lowest* he would aim for.

"Even if you had finished, you will have reached only the most ordinary sort of Iron. If you were very gifted or lucky, perhaps you could reach the peak of Truegold. Underlord would be a distant dream."

"Pardon my rudeness, but does that mean there's another option?"

Eithan's smile widened further. "You need a perfect Iron body."

Lindon liked the sound of that. "Yerin mentioned that sacred artists prepared for each stage, but I'm afraid my family didn't have such a custom. To us, Iron was Iron."

"Well, contrary to what your family may have taught you, Iron comes in several flavors. Every *serious* sacred artist trains their body before advancing."

Once again, Lindon was acutely aware that he'd missed something that everyone else considered common sense. "I'll do whatever I have to," he said. And then, a bit late, "... what do I have to do?"

"How did your master prepare you, Yerin?"

"I was probably seven, maybe eight," Yerin said conversationally. "Master dropped me in a black pool, and it stung like fire. Water drilled right down into me until I thought I was dead for sure. Three days and three nights I squirmed like a worm on a frying pan, breathing through a reed. Then he let me out."

She slapped one arm. "Steelborn body, he called it. You don't see much out of it until you're past Gold, but once you hit Underlord, it's supposed to be the best Iron body in the world for pure brute strength. Same one my master had."

"And a wise man he was," Eithan said. "A fine choice for you, and for your Path. Me, I was born with eyes faster than my hands, so to speak. I needed the reaction speed to keep up with my detection, so my family put me through the training for the Raindrop body. Poetic name; you're supposed to be able to thread through drops in a rainstorm without getting wet, though I've never found that to be true."

"What did you have to do for *that?*" Lindon asked.

"I played games. Catching birds as they ran off, running as fast as I could, hitting balls back with sticks, that sort of thing."

Yerin and Lindon both remained silent for several breaths.

"What can I say? Not everyone grows up suffering in the wilderness." He leaned closer to Lindon, though he did pinch his nose as he did so. "We could give you your choice, if we had a month or two. But we don't, we need to move you very soon. Today would be ideal, since tomorrow I'd give you even odds of being devoured alive."

"Ideal," Lindon said. "Yes, I agree, that does sound *ideal.*"

"I thought your schedule would open up. Ordinarily I would give you options, as I said, but now we have to forcibly create more madra channels *and* prepare you for Iron in a single day. That narrows our conditions somewhat, so I would suggest the Bloodforged Iron body."

Lindon perked up at the name. This one sounded like a legendary technique, something worthy of a powerful sacred artist. "We can do it here?"

"It's the same one the Sandviper sect uses for its initiates," Eithan said, "though of course they call it the Sandviper body. They've really run themselves a rut when it comes to naming their techniques, I can tell you that. They use it to avoid killing themselves with their own venom."

"If it makes you immune to poison, I can see how that might be helpful," Lindon said. It wasn't as exciting as he'd imagined something called the 'Bloodforged body' would be, but he guessed it was practical. Especially if he had to cross through more Sandviper Remnants on the way out.

Eithan considered the statement for a moment. "'Immunity to poisons' is really an impossible concept. Any compound that harms the body is a poison, and there's no one solution for them all. What this *will* do is naturally draw on your spirit to accelerate your body's ability to restore and protect itself. It should help you against poison, parasites, diseases, infection, and so forth, as well as small wounds."

Anything sounded good to Lindon compared to lying here in pain. "If that's what you recommend, then I humbly accept your advice."

Eithan held up a finger. "Before you agree, you should know that there are two ways to create this body, but we're going to have to do it the fast way. And the fast way is terrible."

Steel rang as Yerin's sword left its sheath. An instant later, a Remnant cry followed like a high note from a flute.

"Back to work for me," she said. "But you want to speed things up, that would be golden."

She dashed out of view, and the Remnant screamed again.

"I think it's time for the fast way," Lindon said to Eithan, who nodded.

"That's what I thought too." Then he pulled a squirming sandviper out from behind his back.

Lindon recoiled, pushing himself against the wall to get as far away from the creature. Its centipede legs kicked at the air, its serpentine head baring fangs as it hissed. Its carapace was tan and bright, exactly the color of a desert in the sun.

Eithan held it calmly, regarding the monster with something like fascination. "This isn't one of the corrupted dreadbeasts of this region, you know. It's a perfectly natural sacred beast, it just happens to be hideous. For the first step, you must allow it to bite you. Once the venom is in your blood, you can use your madra to guide it, and it will actually burn channels into your body that madra will be able to follow later. It's *unbelievably* painful, but it's quick, and you will heal once you advance to Iron. But you have to guide it yourself to keep it from running wild, which means you have to stay conscious."

Lindon's mouth was hanging open in horror, but he didn't close it.

"It gets more disgusting," Eithan continued. "As the Sandviper sect found out so many years ago, you also must drink the blood of the sandviper itself. It helps slow the venom's progress into your organs, making it easier to control. And slightly less likely that you will die."

Fumbling for his pack, Lindon pulled out the sheaf of yellow papers that was originally the *Heart of Twin Stars* and was now his personal Path manual. A small brush and portable inkwell followed. He flipped to one of the later pages, filling in the details that Eithan had shared. The motion gave him time to think, with each stroke steadying his shaking hands. Even the pain in his damaged fingers faded as he worked.

Eithan waited patiently even as Yerin fought in the distance.

Finally, Lindon had finished recording, and his own heart had settled. If this was the path forward, he was going to walk it. He'd come too far to turn back now.

But first, he gathered up one of the straps on his pack and placed it between his teeth.

"I'm ready," he said, voice muffled around a mouthful of padded leather. With eyes squeezed shut, he extended his wrist.

"Breathe carefully," Eithan said. "Cycle."

As Lindon did so, pain flashed like someone had stabbed through his arm. Then the venom came, and his blood burned.

If anything, Eithan had understated the pain.

Venom cycled in his veins along with every pulse of madra, and Eithan poured coppery blood through his clenched teeth. Lindon bit down on the leather strap through a mouthful of sandviper blood, and bit down just as hard on memories.

The mountains of Sacred Valley, knocked over like towers of sand. Everything he loved, washed away.

Li Markuth, like a monster in a world of children, and Suriel who could pack him up like an old toy.

If this pain was all it took to approach them, it was a small price.

Lindon pushed the venom everywhere he hadn't already worked his madra, forcing it into his muscles, his skin, even the very center of his bones. It was an endless moment, but still over sooner than he'd thought.

His aching jaw went slack, the blood-stained leather strap falling from his teeth. He panted, losing control of his cycling technique just to fill his lungs with oxygen.

He tried to open his good eye, but the lid wasn't cooperating. Now that he noticed, his limbs were moving out of his control; his fingertips twitched and his back arched as though someone else had tied strings to him and started to pull.

Finally, he wrenched his eye open and was distracted by his own flesh. Black veins stood out along his skin, tracing lines like a map over every inch of himself he could see.

"Is that all?" he croaked out, and Eithan stared at him for a moment.

Then he gave a pure, rich laugh.

"You tell me," the man said finally, wiping a tear from his eye with one finger. "Not even I can sense your insides better than you can."

Lindon closed his eye again, cycling madra to get a sense for his own condition. The venom had indeed permeated his own body...but not as thoroughly as he'd expected.

"I think I could fit some more in," Lindon said, though half of him couldn't believe the words were coming from his own mouth.

Eithan shrugged. "I'm no Sandviper. I've only read about the Bloodforged Iron body. But if you don't think this is enough..."

He tossed the mangled corpse of the sandviper aside and reached into his outer robe, producing a second live specimen.

Lindon recoiled again, just as he had the first time. "Would you mind telling me where you're getting those?"

With his free hand, Eithan lifted the bloody strap to Lindon's mouth. "Once more," he said.

Again, Lindon bit down on the padded leather and squeezed his eyes shut.

●

Five of the little sacred beasts had been all that Eithan could scrounge from the Ruins—it seemed that once they knew he was hunting them, they'd started to run away.

The fifth was still alive, squirming in his hand and sending out its madra to try and burn away his hand, but he kept it suppressed with his own spirit. The other four were dead, having been drained of both venom and blood. The husks rested on the ground at his feet, twisted and broken.

In that respect, they looked much like Lindon.

His body wasn't moving much anymore, as he'd run out of energy sometime in the night. When he twitched, it was like lightning moving through dead flesh more than any conscious attempt at motion, and his skin was all but invisible beneath swollen black veins. Sandviper blood ran from his teeth as his own blood ran from his ears, the corners of his eyes, and even sweated through his pores.

He'd lasted more than a day, which had left even Eithan astonished. His standards were high—too high, really—but this Copper had still surprised him.

Yerin had done well for herself too. She'd fought almost without rest for a full night and most of the next day, and was even now finishing off a pack of twisted dreadbeasts. He kept his eyes on Lindon, but it almost didn't matter; he could still see Yerin, shoulders slumped in weakness, dragging her sword behind her as she limped back to their little enclosure. She passed through their barricade on the stairs, eyes moving to check Lindon's condition...

...and Eithan stepped aside to avoid the sword plunging into his back.

"You *buried* him," she snarled, heat in her eyes and aura gathering around the edge of her sword.

He held up both hands to show his innocence, forgetting for a moment that he held a live sandviper in one. That didn't paint the best picture.

"He asked me to!" Eithan protested.

The sword-arm on Yerin's back stabbed in Lindon's direction. She really was getting better with her Goldsign, thanks to his guidance. "He asked for *this?*"

Under other circumstances, Eithan would have had

trouble believing it too. "I'm performing as instructed. If it helps, I'm as horrified as you are."

Her eyes filled with disgust, and she drew her sword back, flooding it with madra for a strike that would be...at best, inconvenient to avoid.

Instead of dodging, he seized Lindon's wrist, holding up the boy's blackened hand. It was curled into a fist so tight that blood leaked out of the palm. Eithan scrubbed away dried blood and grit from a line of metal on Lindon's finger: a halfsilver ring.

"Do you happen to know what this is?" he asked, and before she could respond, he answered for her. "This acts as a filter for madra, refining madra quality during the cycling process. But it makes cycling twice as hard, and it takes twice as long. Like running with weights strapped to your legs."

Yerin's narrowed eyes moved from him to the ring. "He put that on himself?"

Eithan released Lindon's arm, wiping his hand with a cloth he happened to carry in his pocket. It was difficult to do with only one free hand, the other still clutching a sandviper, but he managed. "I'll admit, I shut Lindon in this room without concern for his will. But he has kept that ring on every day since the door first shut. And now..."

Lindon spoke precisely on cue. "One more..." he grunted, his voice scraping through a ruined throat. "One more."

Eithan shrugged at Yerin's look of astonishment. "As soon as he asks me to, I'll stop."

Then, before the girl could react, he turned and thrust the sandviper's fangs into Lindon's arm.

He tore the creature's head half off with one hand, preparing to drip the blood into Lindon's mouth as he had done before, but the boy's back seized up. His eyes—well, the one eye not hidden by swelling—rolled up into its socket, and foam bubbled up quickly at the mouth.

"Ah," Eithan said, setting the sandviper corpse aside. "That was too much."

Yerin dropped her sword and fell to her knees, pressing fingers against Lindon's throat. "What's the cure?"

Eithan wiped his bloody hand off on Lindon's clothes, then fished around in his pocket until he grabbed the scale waiting at the very bottom. "The venom has escaped his control and passed into the heart, so he's dead." He withdrew the blue crystal coin, holding it up for her consideration. "*Unless* we trigger the transformation to Iron."

He hesitated a moment, considering the accuracy of his own words. Honesty was very important.

"There's always the possibility that it will take too long, and then he'll be brain dead," he clarified. "He can't breathe like this, you see."

Yerin snatched the scale from his hand.

Clutching it in her fist, she broke the structure and reverted it to madra, using her spirit to force a flow of blue-white energy into Lindon's mouth.

That wouldn't be enough. His madra wasn't cycling at the moment, and her soul wasn't strong enough to do it for him. Not quickly, anyway.

So Eithan did it for her.

He pushed his palm against Lindon's core—the one swollen with energy, ready to spill over and advance into Iron—and guided the scale's madra within. It flexed, resisting for a second before cracking like a broken dam.

The madra flooded all through Lindon's body, expelling all physical impurities and transforming him with the power of the soul. His core would condense and restore itself into a smaller, denser form, transmuted from Copper to Iron.

Eithan took a quick step back.

The Iron transformation was never neat or pretty, as the body expelled impurities through any medium, but this was particularly gruesome. Black blood oozed through Lindon's skin, his muscles convulsing beneath as though they were liquefying and pouring out. Black tears ran from his blood-shot eye, and apparently his throat wasn't quite as far gone as Eithan had thought, because his screams were deafening.

The black substance oozing from Lindon's body carried a stench like bodies rotting in a cesspool, so Eithan headed up the stairs to the relatively pleasant air. There were only a few corpses decomposing up here, so at least he might get a whiff of something clean.

He left Yerin to watch over Lindon. If the boy died, that would be shame, though it wouldn't set Eithan back much.

But he expected a better result.

CHAPTER SIXTEEN

As one of the highest-ranking representatives of the Sandviper sect, though he wasn't a Sandviper at all, Jai Long had the honor of supervising a young man's advancement to Iron.

He'd reluctantly bowed to tradition, on the condition that the ceremony could be conducted in a tent at the entrance to the Ruins. If the Arelius family had continued at their current pace, they'd be arriving sometime tomorrow. He and the Fishers believed they had figured out the last of the script around the final floor, but they wouldn't know until they tried.

It was a delicate time, but tradition wouldn't wait.

The boy's whole family had gathered to see this paragon of their younger generation receive his Sandviper body at the tender age of eight years old. It was an impressive sign of dedication for such a young boy. Jai Long himself had reached Iron before that, but he'd had resources the Sandviper sect did not.

Jai Long clutched the sandviper in one hand, his spirit clamping around the creature's powers just as his fist imprisoned its limbs. With the other hand, he delicately squeezed the gland around the serpent's fang.

A drop of venom swelled, and he wicked it off with a needle.

The needle went onto a jade plate prepared for the purpose. He set the plate aside and withdrew a bowl the size of a thimble. With one stray whisk of Stellar Spear madra, he sliced the sacred beast's skin.

A few drops of blood filled the bowl, and Jai Long replaced the sandviper in its cage.

This whole process was supposed to be accompanied by a ceremony as the boy learned the glorious history of the sect and his own place within it, but Jai Long went about his business in cold silence. No one corrected him. They were afraid of him, one and all; afraid of his status within the Jai clan, afraid of the stories that surrounded him when he'd been banished. Afraid of his strength.

Kral stuck his head into the tent, grin blooming. "Bren! You're a man of the Sandvipers today."

The boy—Bren, Jai Long supposed—matched Kral's grin with his own. He seemed only too relieved to look away from the red-masked stranger in his tent.

After a few more compliments for the boy and his family, which instantly put them at ease, Kral walked over to Jai Long. He gave a low whistle at the sight of the blood. "That's not too much, do you think?" he asked, keeping his voice low to avoid spooking the child.

"I'm sure you had more," Jai Long said, not bothering to lower his tone. The most talented young members of the sect received two or three needles of venom, with an appropriate amount of blood to go along with it.

"Most people don't," Kral pointed out. Then he raised his head to look at Bren, and he raised his volume to match it. "But he'll be the pride of the sect in a few years. I'll do it myself."

The boy practically shone with pride, which made Jai Long wonder why Kral hadn't just done this whole procedure himself.

The young chief gave a few ceremonial words, offered

Bren the bowl of blood, and then—when the boy had settled into a cycling trance—pricked him on the wrist with the needle.

Bren's jaw tightened and sweat beaded on his brow, but he only grunted once. His father gave a proud smile.

For Jai Long's Iron body, he'd been forced to undergo a ritual that blistered all the skin on his body, broke most of his bones, and kept him in bed for three months afterwards. For a half-civilized sect that survived in the harsh Desolate Wilds, the Sandvipers were soft.

As Bren cycled in preparation for his transformation, Jai Long pulled Kral aside to give him a report.

"The Fishers have gotten us through most of the doors," he said, and this time he did speak quietly. This was sensitive information, after all. "We think we have a grasp on the rest of the script, but there's still one door between us and the final chamber. I suspect there may be another way—"

The flap of the tent brushed aside, and a Sandviper charged in with his chest heaving and face bright red. No sacred artist would push himself so far beyond the bonds of his breathing technique without a good reason.

Bren's family frowned in disapproval that someone had interrupted their son's ceremony.

"On the horizon," the messenger said, panting. "Come and see."

Jai Long had a good guess what he'd see, and he dashed from the tent without a word. Kral stayed behind to give a word to the waiting family, but Jai Long dashed up the side of a nearby tower. Its unsteady wooden planks creaked alarmingly, but he reached the top in seconds.

With that vantage, he could see the hideous Desolate Wilds spread out before him. The Purelake was a glimmering sapphire, the rest of it a black mess.

Except for a small group on the horizon, which his Iron eyes picked out immediately. They were a motley bunch, dressed in different colors and styles, but it was the banner they carried that caught his eye.

Deep blue and white, with a black crescent in the center. The Arelius family had arrived.

He leaped from the top of the tower, landing next to Kral. "We're out of time," he said, ducking into the tent for just long enough to retrieve his spear. Bren was still cycling, oblivious.

He emerged with his weapon, and heard Kral already issuing orders.

"Gather the Fishers," the young chief said. "Inform the Jai clan. We're going in now." To Jai Long, he said, "And, uh...if we can't open the door?"

Jai Long gripped his spear in both hands. Up to this point, they had tried to avoid unnecessary damage to the structure of the Ruins for fear of disrupting the script. They were dealing with an incredibly powerful script-circle they didn't understand; the slightest disruption could change nothing, or it could detonate the Transcendent Ruins with enough force to obliterate the Wilds.

He had commanded his teams to avoid even chipping away at the walls, for fear of hidden scripts. Until he gave the order.

"We will make a new one."

⬡

Lindon woke to a splash of icy water.

He jerked upright, gasping, hands raised to defend himself from the blow he knew was coming. But the first thing to hit him was the stench—it smelled like a dead pig rolled in rotten eggs.

He rolled blindly away from the stink, but it followed him. His hands were resting in a putrid pool of black sludge and red blood, and more of it caked his skin.

His sister Kelsa had been covered in something similar when she advanced to Iron. Did that mean...all this came from his own body?

The puddle of filth had filled the entire space at the

bottom of the stairs a finger's width deep, and it trickled out the open door. He couldn't believe it all came from his own body.

Another splash of water landed on him, squirted from the twisted seashell binding in Yerin's hand, and Lindon hurriedly rose to his feet. His pack rolled off his stomach, one leather strap severed in the middle.

He'd bitten through it.

He staggered as he stood, his balance shifting strangely. Every step seemed to take him too far, too quickly, and his body felt like it would drift off the ground and float to the ceiling.

"Cut that out," Yerin ordered. She sent another stream of water splashing over him from the binding in her hand. "I'm trying to clean you off, and you're jumping around like a chicken."

"You made it," Eithan said, in a tone of clear surprise. He watched like Lindon's mother examining a new breed of Remnant. "A flawless transition to Iron. Amazing. I'd like to say you have my extraordinary guidance to thank, but... well, how do you feel?"

Lindon glanced at his hands, turning to consider the unbroken flesh. A dreadbeast had fallen on him, leading to twisted fingers, but you couldn't tell now. He took another step, gingerly testing for pain on his formerly broken ribs. He breathed deeply, cycling according to the technique Eithan had taught him.

Once again, his eyes filled with tears and he had to blink them back. But this time, it was because the pain was gone. He could stand.

Another spray of cold water blasted him, scraping away another layer of black.

Eithan rested his hand on a brown backpack sitting on the stairs beside him, safely away from the pool of sludge. "I transferred your belongings over. It's not quite as big as your original, but I...doubt you'll want to use that one anymore."

His original pack, empty and slack, was soaked in blood and sludge, one of its straps dangling in two severed ends. His mother had made him that pack, slaving over bits of leather and patches of canvas for weeks as she would have a particularly complicated construct.

If she knew it had helped him reach Iron, she would have been overcome with joy, though it still felt like leaving another piece of home to die.

He walked over to his new pack—actually the one he'd taken from Fisher Gesha, used to store her spider-construct—and staggered as a single step launched him five feet closer. He caught himself in the stairwell, face-to-face with Eithan.

The yellow-haired man carefully pinched his nose and stepped up a stair.

Lindon reached up his hands to catch Yerin's next blast of water, scrubbing his skin on stone until it was clean. Then he rifled through his pack, looking for the spare clothes he'd packed.

When he reached the bottom, next to the tank of a happily playing Sylvan Riverseed, he remembered that *these* were his spare clothes. He'd never had the previous set cleaned, and they were missing from the pack. Eithan must have gotten rid of them, and Lindon couldn't blame him. But that still left him without anything to wear.

Lindon looked up to see Eithan holding something out to him: an expanse of pastel pink fabric embroidered with metallic thread-of-gold flowers.

"I noticed your deficient laundry situation, and I thought to offer you something of mine."

Only then did Lindon notice the...elaborate curtain...was actually a sacred artist's robe. It didn't have an outer robe to it, but was all one piece, with loose sleeves and enough room in the legs that it wouldn't inhibit movement.

Under the circumstances, he couldn't complain. It didn't matter what the robe looked like, it was better than one he had on.

He glanced between the pink and gold ensemble in Eithan's hand and his own ruined set of bloody rags, considering.

"Yerin, if you don't mind," Eithan said.

Her silver sword-arm flashed, briefly overlaid with light in Lindon's spirit-sense, and his clothes were slashed to ribbons. He snatched at them, trying to preserve some level of modesty.

She turned quickly, which surprised him to some degree. He'd thought of her as a Gold first, but she was still a girl his own age. Now that he thought of it, that might have been a blush coloring the back of her neck.

Eithan grabbed the twisted blue seashell from Yerin's hand and activated it, sending a flood of water gushing out. It didn't end until Lindon spluttered at him to stop, minutes later, every inch of his body scrubbed clean by the force.

Something bright fluttered toward him, and he caught the pink-and-gold robe out of the air.

"It's surprisingly absorbent," Eithan said, "and it will dry before you know it. The threads are plucked from the mane of a sacred beast known by the natives as a 'Celestial Lion-Horse,' and it is both comfortably warm and pleasingly cool. I had to hire a whole family to work on it for months. It's supposed to be worn as the inner part of a set, but I'm forced to waste it on you."

"Gratitude," Lindon said, wincing as he wrapped it around his wet body. If it was that expensive, he hated to ruin it. He could sell it instead. How many scales would this buy him? Come to think of it, how many scales would it take him to reach Jade?

He chided himself for thinking of Jade so soon after reaching Iron, his hands moving automatically to fold and tie the robe.

Maybe it was the expensive fabric, but something felt strange.

He stopped halfway, considering. The robe was tight

across the shoulders, and the robe—which he'd expected
to reach the floor—only stretched to his ankles. He looked
back up to Eithan.

"Do I seem taller to you?"

Eithan glanced him up and down. "Older is the word, I
think, more than taller. Your muscles have developed further, and we need to get some food in you, because you've
burned most of your fat in the transition. You don't look
like a child spoiling for a fight anymore, but there's still...
what do you think, Yerin?"

Yerin turned back around and considered him. "Like
he's ready to tear into someone with his bare hands." Coming from her, that sounded like a compliment.

Eithan moved his hand back and forth. "Eh...I'd say he
looks like an evil sect leader's rebellious son." He thought a
moment longer and added, "Wearing his mother's robe."

Lindon's response was cut off by something flying
through the air toward him; his hand blurred as he caught
it, body responding as fast as thought.

"I thought you might want that," Eithan said, and Lindon opened his hand to see the wooden badge carved with
the symbol for empty.

He stared into it as a tide of joy swelled in his chest.

After a few breaths of silence, he spoke. "It doesn't fit
me anymore."

He clenched his fist closed, crushing the badge with no
more effort than it would take to smash a dry leaf.

The pieces spilled from his palm, landing like so much
trash, but he tucked the shadesilk ribbon into his pack. It
was still valuable.

Eithan slapped him on the back. "There's nothing quite
like advancing, is there? It's like you're reborn."

Lindon couldn't agree more, but he gave a humble bow.
"I'm only glad to be past the pain."

"We will have to get you something to eat soon," Eithan
reminded him. "Otherwise, your body will devour itself
from the inside out."

Lindon's look of horror must have been something to see, because Eithan gave him a pat of reassurance. "Nothing to worry about. We have a whole day, probably, before that starts to happen. Plenty of time. More urgently, our break time has ended."

Yerin nodded and drew her sword, running up the stairs.

"The way forward opened while you were sleeping," Eithan told him. "The only way out is now at the top of the pyramid, which just so happens to be where the Jai clan spear awaits. What fortuitous chance!" He flourished his wide sleeve, gesturing the way forward. "And a small army of dreadbeasts and Remnants stands in our way. What a wondrous opportunity for training!"

Lindon slid his pack onto his back and reached for the weapon he'd hacked from the Sandviper Remnant two weeks ago: the bright green severed stinger, longer than his own limb, with white cloth wrapped around its hilt to serve as a grip.

He grabbed it, habitually running madra into it to replace the essence it lost over time. It flickered with color in response, rippling brighter, and the motes of madra drifting upward slowed. He was very careful not to let his madra flow into the binding within; it was as dangerous to him as to anyone else, if he used it carelessly.

The severed stinger had never been a heavy weapon, but it seemed absolutely weightless now.

"I admit, I look forward to finding out what an Iron body is like," Lindon said. That was not nearly enough to describe his feelings. He'd dreamed of Iron his entire life, which seemed to him to be when one *really* learned to use the sacred arts. And his weeks of agony stretched behind him like a long shadow.

He hungered to find out what that suffering had bought him.

"Fortunately for you, a perfect test awaits!" Eithan nodded forward, where Yerin stood with white blade bared in front of another doorway. And another set of stairs leading up.

Lindon had survived his weeks alone in the Ruins according to his usual methods: he'd trapped, dodged, or tricked every Remnant or dreadbeast that slithered close to his shelter. He'd killed his share of creatures for food, for resources, or in self-defense, but they had almost always been restricted by a script circle. He'd used the Remnant's venomous needle to butcher helpless foes, not to fight.

So his heart pounded and his eyes twitched at every movement as they made their way up the stairs. Yerin walked ahead with blade drawn, seemingly unconcerned, and Eithan took up the rear. He was whistling.

These stairs were much longer than the ones where Lindon had set up camp, and wider too. They could have easily walked side by side and had room to swing weapons, but by tacit agreement, they all stayed away from the walls.

There were monsters in those walls.

Each stone block was missing a chunk in the middle, leaving a square tunnel onto darkness, and Lindon could hear things slithering or skittering across stone. It was the first drawback he'd felt in his new Iron body: yesterday, he wouldn't have heard the things crawling in the shadows.

It must be worse for Yerin and Eithan, but Yerin acted as though this were no more dangerous than a hike through the woods. A glance back showed that Eithan was walking with eyes closed as he whistled, palms laced behind his neck and elbows in the air.

They had only walked for one intense minute, the stairs spiraling upwards, when Eithan said, "On your right."

Lindon jumped left and readied his scavenged weapon in both hands. Yerin only turned her head slightly to the right. As something bright red flashed out of the darkness, a Remnant with claws bared, her Goldsign flashed.

The smooth silver blade was a blur as it slashed the Remnant in two. Dead matter hissed as motes of essence escaped like smoke from a flame.

On some instinct that hadn't fully formed, Lindon started to open his Copper senses to feel the vital aura and search for another threat. A hand on his shoulder stopped him.

"Try not to stare into the sun," Eithan suggested, then continued whistling.

After a moment, Lindon understood. The Remnants and dreadbeasts were gathering because of how thick the vital aura had become. Lines of script running along the top and bottom of the wall provided all the light they needed, proving that the script was fully powered. It would be funneling all the aura for miles into the room at the top.

"Behind you," Eithan said, and Lindon staggered forward.

He spun just in time to see a monkey with rotten skin grabbing at his shoulder, its lips peeled back in the grin of a fanged skull. His hands moved before he told them to, swinging the stinger with all his strength.

He smashed the monkey to the ground.

With half a thought, he withdrew the weapon and stabbed again and again, puncturing the monkey's hide each time. It shrieked and clawed at the Remnant part.

And a pulse of red-streaked force billowed out from the monkey, catching Lindon and slamming him into the ceiling.

Like sacred beasts, dreadbeasts were effectively monstrous sacred artists, and every one of them had a level of advancement beyond his. This was not a mistake he would have made before hitting Iron, and for an instant he thought it had cost him his life.

But he hit the back of his skull against the ceiling and landed on his feet. More than the impact to his head, what stunned him was that he was...fine.

The strike to the skull had hurt, but more like being struck by a stick than slamming his head against a rock. And he hadn't had to try to land on his feet, as though his body had known what to do without him.

He shook himself awake—an instant's hesitation could prove fatal, when facing a stronger enemy—but the monkey just scurried back into its tunnel.

Some shrieking followed its exit, as though it had gotten into another fight just out of view, and dark blood splattered onto the stairs.

"Hm," said Eithan. "They're certainly excited."

Lindon and Yerin broke into a sprint at the same time. He didn't check to see if Eithan was following; he suspected the yellow-haired man would survive if he was dropped into a pit of Remnants with nothing but his bare hands.

More Remnants and dreadbeasts boiled out of the walls as they continued, and Lindon learned about his Iron body.

For one thing, if combat before had been like trying to stay alive in the middle of a panicked nightmare, *now* he felt as though he were tearing his way through a lightning-fueled dream. His hands moved faster than his thoughts, his weapon a green blur, and keeping up with Yerin's running pace was easier than walking. His hearing was so acute that every breath of air was a note in a symphony, and he spotted movements he would never have noticed before: the tense of muscles in a wolf's shoulder, the flick of a sandviper's tail.

Compared to his previous self, he felt unstoppable. His blood burned in his veins, and madra flowed steadily from his Iron core, his breathing even and measured.

At the same time, he saw the difference between Iron and Gold.

Just when he was feeling like a dragon in human skin, a pale gray Remnant with six arms boiled up from the depths of the tunnel, howling like wind through a forest. It seized his weapon in one hand, his empty arm in another, and both his legs as its head peeled back to reveal a gaping mouth.

Lindon struggled, but he might as well have still been Copper; it looked insubstantial and blurry, like a weak Remnant, but it still had physical strength far beyond his own. Scrabbling from behind told him that there was a dreadbeast coming from the other direction, and Yerin was dealing with two enemies of her own.

Eithan was still whistling with his eyes shut as he dodged four creatures, but Lindon couldn't count on him.

The hands squeezed tighter and tighter until Lindon's breath came too quickly to fuel his cycling technique. He tried everything he could think of until his wrist went numb, and the Sandviper stinger clattered from his hand. Only then did he scream Yerin's name.

She went from a black-and-red blur with a sword of white to utterly still in a moment. Her Goldsign flashed, and Lindon felt an invisible pulse move through him despite his spiritual senses remaining closed.

It was the technique she'd demonstrated before: the Endless Sword. But this time, she didn't hold back.

The Remnant was blasted away from him, shredded into a thousand shapeless pieces and a cloud of dissolving madra. The dreadbeast behind him didn't even get to make a noise before it was reduced to a chunky puddle, and Eithan quick-stepped forward to avoid the chunks of blood that his own enemies had become.

Five or six cuts appeared on Lindon's arms where the Remnant had grabbed him, flaring to life like fires after a lightning strike, but he was staring at Yerin. She took a deep breath, restoring her breathing before she spoke. "Everybody stable?"

Lindon nodded wordlessly and she took off.

He scooped up his weapon, vaguely ashamed of himself. Just because he'd let the power of an Iron body go to his head, he'd forgotten the sheer force of the sacred arts. Of all the weapons in a sacred artist's arsenal, physical strength was among the least. He might be able to compete with Yerin in the force of his grip now, but she could carve him into pieces with her will.

It was a sobering reminder, but it was also somewhat liberating.

He had something to look forward to.

It wasn't much longer before they reached the end of the spiraling staircase, and by now the constant attacks were taking their toll. He hadn't used much madra, having no techniques in his repertoire that would help against monsters, but Yerin was noticeably weakened. They'd both taken wounds, in contrast to Eithan, who continued whistling as though his surroundings didn't affect him at all.

At the end, with the snarling of monsters behind them, they reached a door.

It was a heavy slab of stone, just like the ones before, but this one was carved with an intricate mural. It was divided equally into four sections, each depicting a different sacred beast: a serpentine dragon on a cloud flashing with lightning, a crowned tiger, a stone warrior with the shell of a tortoise, and a blazing phoenix.

Though Yerin moved forward to place her palm against the door, he froze at the sight.

He'd seen this before.

CHAPTER SEVENTEEN

Yerin removed her hand from the door, readying her sword. "It's some brand of riddle. Script keeps going right on into it, and there's a key buried here somewhere." The howls of Remnants echoed up the stairs from behind, and the edge of her blade gathered force. "Take a step back."

"Wait!" Lindon shouted, then coughed politely. "I mean, ah, please wait, if you don't mind. We've seen this before."

Eithan sat down on a step and began fiddling with his thumbs.

The shrieks from below grew louder, and a Remnant like a giant purple onion squeezed itself out of the wall to Eithan's side. Before it had completely emerged, he kicked it back.

Yerin took a step back and looked at the door. "I do think you're right. That looks more than a little like the picture in the Ancestor's Tomb."

"That's a week away on the Thousand-Mile Cloud," Lindon pointed out.

"Well, that's a head-scratcher," she said, and then drew her sword back again. The edge of the blade distorted as though a haze of heat had gathered around the weapon, and she took a step forward.

Lindon's instinct for self-preservation kept him from stopping her before she smashed her technique into the door's surface.

It struck with a rush of power that was deafening in the enclosed space of the stairway, ringing in his ears as though someone had struck a bell over his head. Madra and aura flooded forward with her strike until his view of the action warped like he was watching through murky water.

When it cleared, a single chip of stone was spinning on the floor. Otherwise, the door was completely intact.

Lindon would have taken this moment to stop her from damaging the door any further—it was connected to some unknown script, and might bring the entire roof down on their heads if they interrupted the circle, not to mention its connection to Sacred Valley—but he happened to glance behind them.

Dreadbeasts scrambled all over each other as they clawed up the stairs, seeming to blend into a multi-headed mass of corrupted flesh.

Yerin braced her feet against the ground, her Goldsign drew back like a snake preparing to strike, and she gripped her sword in both hands. Colorless sword madra rippled around her until it was like he was looking at her through a cage of razors edge-on. As she gathered power, she focused on the door as though she meant to destroy it with the force of her stare.

Without giving himself too much room to think, he picked up his severed Remnant part and pointed it at the oncoming rush of beasts. His madra flowed down the weapon, trickling toward the binding.

"The big one," Eithan shouted, but through his ringing ears Lindon heard it as a whisper. The man was standing now, but he was actually leaning his shoulder against one of the wider sections of wall, completely at his ease.

Lindon listened, adjusting his aim to point at the biggest of the dreadbeasts: a warped purple creature like a bear with heavily muscled arms. When he was close enough to see the bloodshot veins in the monster's arms, the dread-beast hauled itself back on its hind legs. It looked as though it intended to come down on Lindon like an avalanche.

He stepped forward, thrusting the bright green stinger like a spear.

And just as he did, he activated the binding.

He used his weaker core, the Copper one, because it was just barely strong enough to fuel the weapon. The activation drew his core dry, and if that had been his only source of madra, he would have collapsed immediately.

But he pulled on his Iron core instantly, keeping his legs steady even as the binding activated.

Three hazy green duplicates, like less-real copies of the stinger, flickered into existence around his thrust. It was as though he drove four spears instead of one.

The bear fell on top of his weapon, but one of the Forged spears lodged in its hide. Another caught a Remnant in the head, and his actual spear drove even deeper into the bear's belly. The fourth strike missed, dissolving out of existence in a moment, but Lindon threw himself back as soon as his point bit home.

The venom only took an instant to scour the bear with agony, and it went berserk, flailing its paws and roaring so loudly that it hurt Lindon's ears even through the ringing. It turned in a circle, snapping its jaws as though trying to bite out the infection, and every other Remnant and dread-beast fell upon it.

A hand caught him by the back of his robes and pulled him up the stairs just as a bloody, severed limb landed at Lindon's feet.

Eithan plucked at his own sleeve, indicating Lindon's clothes, and then shook his head.

Well, if Eithan wanted to pull him out of trouble to avoid getting blood on his borrowed outfit, Lindon wouldn't complain.

An explosion drummed his bones, and he spun with an arm thrown up over his eyes. Stone fragments pelted him through a cloud of billowing dust, and the remaining half of the door tipped over and slammed to the ground with the speed of a calving glacier.

Yerin's knees buckled as her technique faded, and she fell to the ground panting. Eithan and Lindon ran by her, each grabbing an arm without discussion, pulling her into the room beyond.

It was a broad, featureless hallway with an open doorway at the end. In the very center lay a circle of script.

The dreadbeasts wouldn't continue slaughtering each other for long, but Lindon spared a moment to admire the advanced script-circle on the floor. There were at least ten layers to the circle, lines of runes and sigils wrapping an empty space in the center.

Lindon and Eithan hurried around the edge, though Yerin regained her feet and ran on her own strength halfway through. Though the circle was much more likely to affect sacred beasts and Remnants, none of them were willing to run through the middle.

The outer circles brushed against the wall, so they were running on runes, and each step sent a little shock through the soles of Lindon's feet. His madra trembled as it cycled, as though drawn down to the floor.

He pushed on, and together the three of them reached the open doorway in seconds. There was, in fact, a door on the other side. This was a more ordinary type of door than the stone slabs before, made merely of dull gray metal and heavily caked with a series of script-circles. It had been left propped open, and judging by the dust sitting at its base, it had been that way for a long time.

Yerin and Lindon heaved together, and Lindon couldn't suppress a flash of pride that he was strong enough to help Yerin with something.

The heavy door slammed shut, its scripts glimmering for a moment as they drew power from the ambient aura. He and Yerin fell to the ground, gulping mouthfuls of the dusty air, and generally savoring their survival.

Eithan stood to one side, hands on his hips. "I have to say...this is fairly impressive."

Lindon followed his gaze, taking in the space lit brightly by warm orange lanterns that were surely some kind of rune light. The lights were covered by paper screens to soften their glow, and it was a good thing; some of them shone too bright, uncomfortably bright, while others flickered off and on in a disquieting rhythm. They must have been powered by the vital aura taken in by the Ruins' script, but either the script was broken, or it had been too long since they'd last come to life. The glow was uneven and left half the room bathed in irregular shadows.

The room looked more like a rich clan's library than anything he'd expect to find in an ancient ruin, the colored tiles set with dusty carpets and beautifully carved tables. One of those tables held a collection of jade statuettes, one a cracked dragon with the head of a lion, the others a series of creatures stranger and more hideous. A glass-covered case displayed some tools of halfsilver and goldsteel, as well as more exotic materials that Lindon didn't recognize, but at least half of the spaces were empty.

Books sat open on stands carved for them, their curling pages painted with arcane diagrams and characters. They had browned from age, and Lindon was certain that if he so much as breathed on a corner, the paper would dissolve.

A row of silver hooks hung from the ceiling, which stood out as he couldn't think of a purpose for them. They varied in size, but none of them held anything beyond empty air.

A long glaive made of Forged madra, with a blood-red shaft and a gleaming golden sword blade at the end, sat on a frame halfway up the wall. A circle of script surrounded it, sealing its power and preventing it from dissolving. Beneath the weapon, an image was painted directly on one wall: a circle, blank on one half, the other half complex and twisted with a network of lines.

Lindon stared at the pieces of the room for too long before they fit together into a whole.

This was a Soulsmith's foundry.

When he realized that, he shot to his feet and dashed to a nearby table, rummaging through it. He found nothing likely, despite pulling a few drawers open, so he slid to the next one, frantically shuffling through a pile of sealed ebony scrolls with scripts worked in gold filigree on their cases.

Yerin stepped up beside him, giving him a curious glance. "Looking for the spear?"

"Take the other side of the room, if you wouldn't mind," he said, casting the scrolls and digging in a box on the floor. "A Soulsmith worked here."

"I'm not seeing your point."

A box caught his eye, ornately carved and polished and standing as tall as he did. It was covered in a layer of dust, like most everything else in the room, but otherwise it looked exactly like the sort of wardrobe they would use in the Wei clan. Wider, though. If he stretched his arms out as far as he could, he wouldn't be able to touch both ends with his fingertips.

He shot for the wardrobe before answering Yerin, throwing the doors wide.

White light erupted from within.

Pain shot through his newly sensitive eyes, and he blinked away the blinding light. When he could see again, Yerin was standing in front of him; she'd moved between him and the potential source of danger.

But it wasn't a defensive construct waiting for a victim—though he really should have considered that possibility before throwing the doors open. It was a shining bar of Forged madra, long enough to stretch from one end of the wardrobe to the other. It was held by a set of carved wooden supports, held just below eye level as though waiting for him to take the weapon.

And it was a weapon. A spear, formed seamlessly from madra by ancient Soulsmiths. It shone with the light of the stars, congealed into a weapon whose power he could feel radiating against his skin.

Yerin's breath slowly left her, and even Eithan gave a low whistle as he strode over to take a look.

"In my grandfather's day, Soulsmiths valued beauty as much as function." He moved his hand along the shaft of the spear without touching it. "The script flows with the contours of the weapon, guiding it so even the aura is a work of art. Exquisite."

Lindon could just barely pick out a few lines of script on the shaft, which looked like white paint on white, but the spear had held his attention too long already. He dropped to his knees, searching the drawers at the bottom of the case.

The real treasure should be down here.

After digging through a handful of junk, he withdrew an ivory box wider than both his spread hands together. It was heavier than he expected, for being only about an inch deep, and the lid was etched with a pattern of interlocking leaves.

Carefully, he lifted the lid. There were no notes and no brightly colored bindings inside, so he almost tossed it aside.

Then he realized what they *were*, and suddenly he couldn't breathe.

The badges were slightly smaller than the ones from Sacred Valley, but otherwise they were practically identical. Eight badges sat within the box, each marked with a hammer—the symbol of a Forger.

The first row contained a badge each of copper, iron, jade, and gold. That much he expected. But the second row moved from halfsilver to goldsteel to materials he couldn't identify. One of them was a deep, fiery red, and the other a blue so rich it was like a Forged slice of the sky.

He reached a shaking hand and lifted the iron badge. It was lighter than a feather in his hand, but he handled it as though it were made from glass. Delicately, he threaded one end of his shadesilk ribbon through the loop at the top.

"Well, look what *you* found," Eithan said, and Yerin leaned over his shoulder for a closer look. Lindon paid them no attention.

He hung the iron badge from his neck and closed his eyes.

After a moment, Eithan cleared his throat. "This anthill has been well and truly kicked," he said. "I'm afraid that very soon we will have to share our meal with the...other ants."

Lindon snapped out of his reverie. "Dreadbeasts?"

"Worse. Humans."

The Sandvipers must have found their way through the Ruins, though he supposed it didn't matter much if it were the Fishers or even the Arelius family. Whoever it was, they would strip this place bare.

Lindon slid the ivory box into his pack, shuffling a few other necessities around to make room, and then dug back into the wardrobe's bottom drawer.

In this one, he finally found what he was looking for.

A script-marked box contained three indents in the silk lining within. One of these holes was empty, but the other two contained a pair of bindings. They were bright white, made of the same arcane material as the spear, and shaped like spiraling drills.

Quickly, he scanned the notes near the bindings. *"Generation Fourteen shows all the qualities we'd hoped for,"* they read. *"It demonstrates the capacity to devour and process madra with a high degree of efficiency, though each individual contains only one binding. If a sacred artist could cultivate similar techniques, our efficiency may double..."*

The next page had been scribbled in haste, judging by the carelessness with which the characters were slapped on the paper. *"The failed specimens may be the key to success. Their auras alter as they devour one another, growing faster than we'd ever predicted. Theoretically, there is no upper limit on this growth, but the spirit warps the flesh. Further study needed; could lead to achievement of the primary goal."*

Lindon stuffed those notes in his pack, continuing to

read. The labels confirmed what he'd thought: these were the bindings at the heart of the Jai clan's spear. The mechanisms that drained madra from victims.

The Jai clan could have their spear back. Powerful it may have been, but it was just a single weapon.

Learning to *make* such weapons...that was the real fortune.

Of course, Lindon didn't have such a high estimation of his own abilities. He would learn what he could from the bindings and from the notes, and he may even keep one of the bindings for later examination, but knowledge like this was worth more than a leg to a Soulsmith. Gesha would have sold the entire Fisher sect for something like this.

Tucked away with the bindings were a trio of polished black river stones, each marked with a tiny script-circle that Lindon couldn't identify. He tucked them away, just in case, but as he was making space in his pack for the box of bindings, he was interrupted by a deafening crash.

The door at the other end of the room, on the opposite end from where they'd entered, had buckled and fallen inwards. A pair of fur-clad Sandvipers filed out to either side of the door, weapons writhing with green madra. Jai clan members followed them, with spears and gleaming hair and meticulous blue sacred artists' robes, and then a couple of wary-looking Fishers.

Jai Long's red-wrapped head emerged next, spear held low with its point toward the ground. The sect heir, Kral, followed him with a roguish smile.

"Fan out," Jai Long ordered. "Spear first, then—"

He didn't get the rest of the command out of his mouth.

Yerin whipped a wave of sword madra at him, her Striker binding thin as a razor but with the fury of a storm. One of the Sandvipers met madra with madra on the edge of his axe, green power eroding her technique. The force still pushed him back a step.

Before he'd come to a stop, Yerin had raised her sword. The white blade rang like a bell.

And every blade in the room answered.

Glass crashed, lights flickered, and the air filled with a storm of splintered wood and shredded paper. Lindon's vision blacked out as something grabbed him by the hair and pulled him back just as the spear's display case exploded.

The eruption of sword aura from Yerin's Ruler technique might have killed him, crouched as close as he was to a powerful blade. He struggled to his feet, setting his pack aside, and thanked Eithan in a shaky voice.

"No trouble at all," Eithan said, watching shreds of paper drift down around him like an early snowfall. "It's an honor to save the helpless."

One of the Sandvipers was bleeding and slumped against the wall, struggling to stand, but before Lindon caught sight of the others, a constellation of stars flashed out of the debris, blasting toward Yerin like a flight of arrows.

Her sword gathered a shimmering edge as she wove the weapon in a complex knot, knocking the technique from the air, but her robe still gathered another collection of tears as the lights ripped through her loose sleeves. One gouged the looping ribbon of her red belt, and motes of red essence rose like smoke from the wound before it filled in again, sealing itself.

Lindon dropped back to his knees, scrambling on the floor for his stinger weapon. He considered searching for the Jai ancestor spear, but he'd lost sight of it in the rubble, and he needed something to defend himself while he snuck around the room. Iron he may be, but a fight was out of the question; if he was caught between Jai Long's technique and Yerin's, the only thing left of his Iron body would be his badge.

But this was an ancient Soulsmith foundry, loaded with all the elements of a secret project. There had to be some construct he could use against the Sandvipers. He gripped his stinger in one hand and crawled along the aisle, scanning the wall for the bladed glaive construct he'd noticed before.

He wouldn't be able to use it to fight, but a distraction would serve him just as well.

A boot slammed down on his weapon.

Lindon's eyes crawled up, past the sable fur lining the boot, over the midnight pelt hanging like a cloak, to Kral's face. The Sandviper heir looked down on him gravely, like an executioner gazing upon a condemned prisoner.

He hadn't used a technique yet, so he must want to talk. Lindon had something he wanted: the location of the spear, along with its foundational binding. That gave him leverage. If he kept Kral from joining Jai Long, maybe Yerin could hold out long enough for—

His thoughts were interrupted by the toe of Kral's boot slamming him in the forehead.

He flipped over and landed on his back, skidding into a table of bronze and polished wood. It didn't hurt as much as he thought it should, but he was still shakier than a struck gong, and he rose to his feet like a newborn fawn. The sight of bright green in the corner of his eye reminded him that he'd maintained his grip on the Remnant weapon. That was something, at least.

Kral raised one of his eyebrows. "Iron. I thought you were a Copper."

Lindon lowered his weapon and spread the other hand, showing it empty. "Nothing more than a humble Iron, honored Highgold. There's no blood between us, and I see no reason why any should be spilled."

Kral nodded along with every word, then flipped his hand as though gesturing for a servant to leave his presence. Three liquid drops of green madra appeared in the air in front of him, splashing toward Lindon. He hastily raised the Remnant part, but the Striker technique still landed on the skin of his arms, burning like liquid fire.

He gritted his teeth to keep from screaming, tightening his knuckles around the weapon and forcing watery eyes on Kral. The bites of the real sandviper had been a hundred times worse than this. He focused on that thought.

But Kral had disappeared.

The young chief's black cloak was still dropping like an abandoned shadow, and hadn't yet crumpled onto the floor, but Kral was gone. As Lindon was still registering that fact, something slammed into his back. He crashed into the table across from him, his head smashing through the solid wood.

A thick shaft of vivid green madra stabbed into his shoulder, and his breath whooshed out at the blazing spike of agony. Only a few hours with a new Iron body, and he'd already ruined it.

He struggled up, instinctively trying to escape the pain, but a green haze covered his head. When he inhaled, it tasted like metal in his mouth, and burned like fire in his lungs.

Kral's boots padded away, leaving Lindon face-down in wreckage, pinned to a destroyed table on a spear of Forged Sandviper madra.

"The Copper's dead," Kral said lazily. "Actually, I suppose he reached Iron, didn't he?"

"So he did," Eithan said. His voice was pleasant, as though he was chatting with a friend. "If he died, then he has only his lack of ability to blame."

"I...can only agree. You're more reasonable than I expected."

The voices were hazy through the pain and the lack of oxygen, but Lindon found himself listening nonetheless. After the past two weeks, this level of agony was nothing. It was almost familiar.

In fact, it was fading quickly.

"Why don't we come to an arrangement?" Kral continued, his words almost swallowed by a thunderous crash behind him. Yerin and Jai Long, no doubt. "I've seen your ability, and I can recommend you directly to my father." He paused as another crash echoed through the room. "In fact, I don't think we've been properly introduced. I am Kral, Highgold of the Sandvipers. My father is Gokren, Truegold and chief."

"My name is Eithan."

The Forged spear pinning Lindon's left shoulder to the table had already dissipated significantly, enough that he could push himself up. His head was starting to spin for lack of air, and he staggered to the side, inhaling a breath.

The burning venom in his veins had already subsided to nothing more than an uncomfortably warm tingle. Even his stab wound didn't scream quite so loudly, though his left arm was still dangling useless and blood dribbled down his side to the ground.

He was injured enough that he should have been sense-less on the ground in pain, but every breath cycled madra through his channels and lessened the pain by another notch. In fact, his madra was entering his flesh and simply...vanishing, as though his blood had devoured it. His Iron core was emptying at an astonishing rate.

The Bloodforged Iron body. Sandvipers used it to combat their own toxins.

And Kral didn't know he had it.

The Sandviper heir was standing with his back to Lindon, an awl in one hand and his fur cloak in the other. Over his shoulder, Jai Long was pacing toward Yerin, who was leaning on her sword to stay upright.

"If you have no sect, Eithan, a sacred artist of your skill would be welcome among the Sandvipers."

Lindon rushed over to the shattered wardrobe, dropping to his knees and gouging them on the debris. He didn't care, wrenching the lid open and dividing his attention between the box and the Sandviper leader. If Kral glanced around, Lindon was dead.

Eithan leaned casually against the wall, his gentle smile fixed on Kral. "I'm here looking for fresh recruits. I don't intend to be recruited myself."

Lindon fumbled one-handed at the pile of garbage next to him, looking for the spear, but he grasped his stinger first. It would have to do. His fingers caught it on the bright green material instead of the hilt he'd wrapped, which burned his skin like acid, but this pain was just a breeze next to a thunderstorm. He set it aside, using both hands to lift free a scripted box.

Two white, spiraling bindings waited within. He slipped one into his pocket and picked up the stinger with his other hand.

"Especially not by a sect as weak as yours," Eithan added.

Lindon could practically feel a winter breeze as Kral responded. "I suspect you may have misspoken, my friend."

"I'm afraid not. If I belonged to your sect, which I'm proud to say I do not, I would be *painfully* ashamed of you. What kind of a Highgold fails to kill an Iron?"

Kral's spine stiffened, and he started to turn.

Lindon slammed into him with the end of his bright green stinger, the end digging into Kral's ribs. Blood splashed, and Lindon poured all of his remaining madra into his makeshift weapon. The energy was soaked up like rain in the desert, and the binding activated.

Three acid-green echoes of the stinger flashed into existence, stabbing into Kral from three different angles. They didn't penetrate far, only scratching him before dissipating, but that was enough to release their venom. Lindon knew that from experience.

Not that it mattered.

Kral had an Iron body of his own, and Lindon had hoped to find a better opportunity to attack than *this*. Eithan had rushed him, threatening to expose him with words, so he'd taken the angle he could get.

As a result, Kral steadied himself in an instant. His jaw was set in pain, but he was barely scratched. Madra gathered around his fist, and he started to turn and deliver the technique that would reduce Lindon to a pile of smoking bones.

With the desperation of a cornered animal, Lindon tore the drill-shaped white binding from his pocket and stabbed down.

The white spiral flashed as it touched blood, blinding bright, and drew Lindon's Iron core dry like an alcoholic pulling at a bottle. Sandviper madra rushed out from the wound in Kral's back, visible as bright green lines running up the drill, but Kral himself did not move. He stiffened like a man in the grip of a seizure, eyes peeled unnaturally wide. The technique withered and died on his fist.

The madra flowed into the binding...but not into Lindon. He'd wondered about that. The binding simply drew out the power, but it took the script on the spear to draw it into himself. The white drill rippled green, brighter and richer with every passing instant. It grew more solid, less like an object painted into existence and more real. In only a breath of time, it was so detailed that it looked as solid as a poisonous green seashell.

Then it exploded.

Lindon released the binding just in time to avoid losing a hand, but green light burst like a dying star, and he was launched backward. At the same time, something spattered him that burned like acid.

His vision blurred in the overwhelming sensation of being devoured by insects, and his mind couldn't keep up. He thought he blacked out for a moment, but he couldn't be sure.

When he came to, nothing had changed except the pain lessening slightly. His skin was red and tender, but as the last dregs of his madra vanished, healthy skin crawled into place.

He didn't have the strength to stand, and his spirit felt like a rag that someone had squeezed too many times, and he finally stopped healing when his madra was completely exhausted.

All he could move were his eyes, and he craned them to their limit, searching for Kral.

The Sandviper heir lay in a bloody, crumpled heap on the ground. His feet twitched, and Lindon couldn't tell if they were the last throes of death or if he was about to stand up and end Lindon once and for all.

Yellow hair fell over his vision, and Eithan frowned at him. "That was a very expensive robe." He lifted a scrap of burned pink cloth lying next to Lindon, which dissolved even as Eithan lifted it.

Lindon croaked an apology.

Eithan produced another robe—this one was sky blue, with a pattern of violet birds spreading their plumage—and draped it over him. "This is why I always carry a spare."

Spear-wielding members of the Jai clan had surrounded them by now, shouting demands, even as a pair of Sand-vipers crashed to their knees next to Kral. Some Fishers loomed over Lindon, hooks in hand, but they didn't look any friendlier.

A flash of starlight, and Yerin flew backwards like a ballista bolt. Jai Long stalked toward her, spear readied, but his red-wrapped head turned as though he'd caught a scent of something.

His figure vanished, and then he was vaulting over the members of the Jai clan, landing next to Kral. He shoved the Sandvipers out of the way, placing his palm against the fallen heir's core.

When Jai Long's hand dropped away and his shoulders slumped, Lindon desperately wished for the strength to run away.

The man in the red mask rose like a Remnant, spear clutched in one hand, and his eyes focused on Lindon.

CHAPTER EIGHTEEN

Jai Long's weapon crept so close to Lindon's eye that the gleaming spearhead filled his vision with light.

"His core is shattered. He won't even leave a Remnant. What did you do to him?"

Every word shook with barely restrained rage.

Lindon's eyes were stuck to the point of light inches from his head. "If I tell you..." he began, but his voice failed him.

"I will not let you live," Jai Long said evenly. "I won't even kill you more quickly. You'll answer my questions now, or you'll answer them later, and it won't change your fate even slightly. You killed my friend." He nodded to some Sandvipers on the side. "Bag him."

Lindon squirmed, but that did nothing but make him feel as though nettles were scraping along his skin. He'd run out of madra before his Bloodforged body had finished healing him, so the venom still lingered in his veins and on his skin. His shoulder had settled into a numb sort of distant agony, as though someone had packed the wound with snow.

His imagination chewed on everything they could do to him once they had him in the bag, and Yerin still hadn't risen from where she'd fallen. Had she died? Her Remnant hadn't risen, but she would be in no shape to help him. Nor could he help her.

He only had one hope left.

Eithan stepped in front of Lindon in a rustle of white and blue cloth. "Under other circumstances, I'd let you kill him. I'm a firm believer in self-sufficiency. But this seems just a tad unfair."

Jai Long shifted his gaze to Eithan, and even the aura responded to his intensity. Lindon didn't have to open his Copper senses to see a halo of light surrounding the Highgold, and invisible blades gouged lines from the floor around his feet. "I am Jai Long, Highgold formerly of the Jai clan. I suspect you are a Highgold yourself, maybe even Truegold, but know this. If you stand before me now, you will make yourself an enemy of the Sandviper sect and the entire Jai clan."

"They care so much for an exile?" Eithan asked. He sounded curious.

Jai Long did not pause a beat. "For me? No. For their reputation? Everything. You will have stood before a clansman for the sake of an Iron, and they will only save face by killing you. Stand aside, or we will water your home with blood and sow the ground with salt."

The worst part was how each of his words was delivered flat and absolute. The Jai clansmen behind Jai Long shifted and looked at each other, but they didn't put down their spears. The Sandvipers looked ready to draw blood with their teeth, and even the Fishers glowered.

Meanwhile, Eithan rummaged around in the pockets of his outer robe.

"I don't disagree with you on any particular point," he said, "and certainly I don't wish to impugn the honor of the famous Jai clan." He bowed to the spearmen in blue. "Having said that...in truth, this was my fault. I didn't introduce myself properly earlier."

From his outer robe, he withdrew an intricately filigreed golden badge. It was bigger than the badges used in Sacred

Valley, and far more ornate. There was no ribbon of silk threaded through it, as though it were meant to be displayed by hand.

Lindon couldn't see what was printed on the front, but it made the Jai clan go pale and throw their weapons aside. Even the Sandvipers backed up a step as though pushed back by a heavy wind.

"My name is Eithan Arelius, heir to the Arelius family, Underlord in service of the Blackflame Empire, and the greatest janitor alive. This young man is an agent of my clan, working under my aegis and my protection, and any action against him will be considered action against me."

Eithan relaxed and tucked the golden badge back into his robe, but not before Lindon caught a glimpse of a black crescent moon on white, set deeply into the badge, with sapphires playing around the edges.

Lindon finally started breathing again, and he couldn't quite remember when he'd stopped. There would be no bag for him after all.

But Jai Long's spear didn't waver.

"The Arelius family is still a day out," he said, his voice flat as a lake and cold as steel. "No Underlord moves ahead of his clan, and they have no reason to move in secret. The Arelius Underlord would have taken control of the whole Five Factions Alliance and commanded whatever he wanted."

With a clear lack of concern, Eithan strolled over to the wreckage nearby and bent down. He emerged with a gleaming white spear, which shone like condensed starlight in his hands.

"What I want," Eithan said, "cannot be commanded."

Like a man throwing an undergrown fish back into a lake, he tossed the spear into the debris from which it came.

While every eye followed the arc of the Jai ancestor's spear, Eithan moved to face Jai Long.

And something pressed down on Lindon's soul.

It was like the feeling of having his spirit searched, but ten thousand times stronger. A thousand-pound weight pushed down on his core, weighing his madra, making him feel as though he were being pressed into the ground. He gasped for breath.

Everyone else seemed to have it worse. Several of the Golds around him fell to their knees, some of them screamed, still others gasped as though trying to breathe underwater. The Jai clansmen gripped their gleaming iron hair as though it pained them, and the miniature Remnants attached to each Sandviper's arm went insane. They hissed and twisted into the flesh of their host as though trying to burrow their way inside.

Jai Long's spear wobbled as though it suddenly weighed a thousand pounds, then it crashed into the floor. It came within a hair's breadth of slicing open Lindon's cheek.

A red-wrapped head slowly lifted, pushing against a heavy weight, until Jai Long looked Eithan in the eye.

"You know, you've insulted me more than once now. Some other Underlords of my acquaintance would have you pulled apart, piece by piece, over a month's time. Others would simply obliterate you."

The pressure vanished suddenly, and everyone—from Lindon to Jai Long—took a gasp of breath at once.

"But I'm famous for my good humor and forgiving temper," Eithan said, clapping Jai Long on the shoulder. "You've lost a friend, so I think you've more than earned a few lapses in judgment. And, of course, you've earned a campaign of vengeance against Lindon here."

Every eye turned to Eithan, disbelieving. Including Lindon's.

"He's a part of your family," Jai Long said warily.

"A flower in the greenhouse is never half so beautiful as one in the wild. Don't you find that to be true? I like to think it's the added edge of danger. Nothing reaches its full potential unless it's threatened." He placed a finger along the edge of his chin, considering. "Give me one year with him. After a year of my instruction, if he's not your match, then he has only himself to blame. Does that sound fair to you?"

"He's *Iron*," Jai Long said. "I may as well kill him now."

"Then you're waiting a year in respect for my wishes. In compensation, I *won't* strip this place to the bones and then break it looking for marrow. Everyone will receive the treasures that they have earned, in order of their contribution to the excavation effort."

The sacred artists behind Jai Long brightened at that, especially the Fishers, who almost as one packed away their hooks and bowed to Eithan.

"As the first to arrive," Eithan said, "the new members of my family will select their rewards." He glanced over to the side. "As Yerin can't join us at the moment, I will choose for her." He reached onto a nearby table and grabbed a bag seemingly at random. It clinked as he lifted it.

"Now, Lindon." Eithan reached down and drove a stiffened finger into Lindon's core. Madra flooded into him, and Lindon sat up with a gasp. His newly revitalized spirit flooded through his body, making the pain sharper. He grabbed at Eithan's shoulder, holding himself upright.

But his thoughts were already rushing forward. Before anyone could say anything, Lindon had scooted over to where the last remaining madra absorption binding was waiting in its case. He snapped the lid shut and raised it. "I'm not so proud as to try and take the spear from the experts of the honored Jai clan," he announced. "I will settle for this small binding, to improve my meager skill as a Soulsmith."

Jai Long might already hate him, but that didn't mean he couldn't build up some goodwill.

"Wise choice," Eithan said with a nod.

Lindon scrambled for some of the papers nearby. "...and these research notes, which teach me how to use the binding properly." It would be a waste if he couldn't be a *little* greedy. And he saw no need to mention the badges or the scripted black stones, which he'd already scavenged and placed in his pack.

Eithan turned to Jai Long. "I have no need of anything for myself. I already achieved what I came for. Jai Long, as the leader of the other party to reach the summit of the Transcendent Ruins, what treasure do you claim?"

"Hold a moment, honored Underlord," an old woman piped up, and Fisher Gesha drifted in on her spider's legs. An old man who looked as though he lived on the street followed her, with a rusty iron hook on his waist hanging almost all the way down to his bare feet. Beside them walked a man in a blue sacred artist's robe, with steel in the wings of his gleaming iron hair: a Jai clan member, surely, and one who carried himself with a stately and commanding grace.

Jai Long ground his spear into the floor, knuckles white around the weapon's hilt. Lindon slid backwards and found his pack, where he crammed his prizes. Eithan seemed to have the situation well in hand, but Lindon wasn't about to risk someone taking these treasures away from him.

Fisher Gesha's wrinkled face folded into a smile as she drifted up to Eithan. "It isn't appropriate for juniors to eat before their elders have a taste, is it? Hm?"

The man from the Jai clan inclined his head to Eithan. "Jai Long has served our clan's allies well, but he is not in favor. The Underlord should rest assured that we will reward him appropriately, once we have catalogued the contents of the Ruins and distributed them according to the will of the clan."

The ragged-looking old Fisher said nothing.

Gesha stabbed a gnarled finger in Lindon's direction without looking at him. "Besides, that boy and the Lowgold accompanying him belong to the Fishers. They were soon to take their oaths, and it would be such a shame to have invested so much in their futures, only to have someone else reap the rewards. That deserves some compensation, don't you think? Hm?"

Eithan chuckled good-naturedly, bowing in return. "Honored leaders of the Five Factions Alliance, it's a pleasure to meet you. I was born Eithan Arelius, and thanks to the good fortune of the heavens, I reached the stage of Underlord at quite a young age."

Without warning, all three elders collapsed.

Gesha's spider-legs snapped as her drudge broke beneath her, and she shrieked as she fell to the floor. She barely caught herself with her hands, trembling as she tried to support her own weight. Hair flew free from her gray bun.

The old Fisher had gotten his hook out before he fell to his knees, and he braced himself against the ground with his rusty iron weapon, but his breath came heavily through clenched teeth. The man from the Jai clan remained standing, but only barely.

Eithan walked up to him and rubbed his hands in the metallic hair, running his thumb along the edge of a rigid black peak. "I've always wondered about the Goldsign for the Path of the Stellar Spear. Frozen *hair?* It's astonishing. Does it hurt?"

The Jai elder grunted out something that might have been a response.

"Does it hurt?" Eithan repeated softly, rapping his knuckles lightly on the man's frozen hair. Metal rang like a muffled bell.

"No...Underlord..." the Jai elder managed to force out. .

"Oh, really? How does it feel, then?"

"...helmet..."

That was the only word Lindon understood, but Eithan nodded. "I see, I see. Thank you for indulging my curiosity." He moved on to the old Fisher man, taking a knee in front of him. "Fisher Ragahn, I assume. It's polite to introduce yourself when you're meeting a superior, you know, but I know who you are regardless. It must have been hard on you, reaching Truegold, but you did what you had to. Anything you had to. A kind person couldn't inherit the Fishers, could he? And if he did, he wouldn't remain kind for long."

Eithan lowered his head, making sure that his eyes were even with the Fisher's. "I can respect that, Ragahn. But there are things you should and should not say to your superiors."

He moved over to Gesha, who looked as though she was suffering more than the others. She was Highgold, Lindon remembered, and the others must be a stage higher.

Eithan crouched next to her, fingers laced together thoughtfully. No one else dared to disturb his silence by moving.

"I've dealt with people like you all my life," Eithan said at last. "You earned everything at the edge of a spear, so you've picked up some unfortunate habits. Oh, but you're a Soulsmith, aren't you? You earned it *making* the spears." He picked up a severed edge of her drudge's cracked leg. "I can deal with you like human beings if I take the time to get to know you, to slide into the walls you've built, to slip through the cracks in your pride. But I don't have the patience for that today."

He tapped her forehead with the edge of the spider's limb. "I am picking up the pair that you discarded. Do you have any objection?"

Slowly, Gesha's head shook once.

"Splendid. And the rest of you. You take what you can keep, isn't that the law of the Wilds? Do you have any doubt that I own everything and everyone inside the Ruins right now?"

The Jai elder choked out a few words. "The...clan...head branch..."

"Do I dare to offend the head branch of the legendary Jai clan?" He paused for a moment as though thinking. "Why wouldn't I dare? If I cut off your legs and threw you from the top of the Ruins, I'd have to spend an *hour* writing a letter of apology to your clan's Underlord. Do you think I would back down from such a threat?"

The man just shook.

Suddenly all three trembled with obvious relief as the pressure vanished. They sat, panting, on the floor.

Eithan stood, all smiles, arms spread generously. "But that's so morbid, isn't it? We're all friends here." He ignored the elders, turning to the young man in the red mask. "Jai Long, I believe it's your turn to make your selection. And choose well; I'll want you to pose a healthy threat to my pawn. I mean, ah, the valued young member of my family."

Lindon's eyes seemed to be stuck on Eithan. The man had never lost his smiling, pleasant demeanor. Ever. If he had driven the spider's leg through Gesha's forehead, would he still be smiling?

And what about when he watched Jai Long tear Lindon to pieces in a year? Would he be smiling then?

Jai Long reached over and lifted the shining white spear from the debris.

●

Information requested: Jai Long's future.

Beginning report...

Spears flash as Jai Long tears his way through the halls of the Jai clan. His spear is pure white, and it drinks the power of slain Remnants; with every death he causes, Jai Long grows stronger. As he destroys his family's homes one by one, he draws closer to the Jai Patriarch.

LOW PROBABILITY: in the heat of battle, he steps left when he should have stepped right, and a Jai Lowgold puts a spear between his ribs.

LOW PROBABILITY: In a crisis of conscience, his little sister has a change of heart, persuading him to set aside his crusade. They move to a city at the far edges of the Black-flame Empire, where she meets a local man and raises a family. He trains alone, and eventually dies in isolation.

HIGH PROBABILITY: The Jai cannot stop him without an expense that would cripple the family. As the Patriarch searches for a way to stop this one-man rebellion without causing his carefully cultivated power to crumble, he learns of Jai Long's upcoming duel.

SUGGESTED TOPIC: THE FUTURE OF THE SANDVIPER SECT. CONTINUE?

TOPIC ACCEPTED, CONTINUING REPORT...

Sandviper Gokren returns from his hunting trip at last, full of news from the outside world and hauling prizes that will sustain his sect for months. He brings with him an ancient bracer, scripted and made of a strange material, as a present for his Highgold son.

When he arrives, he finds his son's corpse.

The stories of Kral's death largely do not penetrate the deaf haze of grief, but he grasps the main points.

Kral was killed by an Iron, bringing shame to the entire Sandviper sect and his family in particular.

This Iron was taken away to the Blackflame Empire, sheltered by a young Underlord.

This family is protecting his son's killer. And in one year, Jai Long will take revenge on his behalf. Gokren knows he must only wait.

SUGGESTED TOPIC: FUTURE OF JAI LONG AND WEI SHI LINDON. CONTINUE?

TOPIC ACCEPTED, CONTINUING REPORT...

WARNING: DEVIATION DETECTED.
ENTITY [WEI SHI LINDON] HAS DEVIATED FROM PRIMARY COURSE. FURTHER DATA REQUIRED FOR ACCURATE CALCULATION. BEST ESTIMATES FOLLOW:

HIGH PROBABILITY: The Jai Patriarch approaches Wei Shi Lindon with a proposition. Lindon fills one of his cores with the Path of the Stellar Spear, enjoying the most powerful elixirs and training methods the Jai clan can procure. Jai Long is sabotaged by a series of attackers in the days leading up to the duel, and he begins the fight weak. Lindon manages to score one severe wound before he dies, and the Jai Patriarch uses that wound to suppress Jai Long.

LOW PROBABILITY: Lindon fails to find a suitable Path to supplement his Path of Twin Stars, and runs from the battle. He is caught by the Jai clan and executed in captivity.

LOW PROBABILITY: Lindon devises a weapon specifically designed to counter Jai Long's spear. He acquits himself well in the duel, but dies of his wounds.

SUGGESTED TOPIC: POWERFUL PATHS OF CRADLE. CONTINUE?

DENIED, REPORT COMPLETE.

CHAPTER NINETEEN

Yerin couldn't be sure if she was awake or dreaming. Her body had no weight to it, drifting on the breeze without direction. Must be a dream, then. The last thing she remembered was facing a Highgold, so cheers and celebration to her for surviving. She hadn't so much as torn the wrapping around Jai Long's head, but she hadn't retreated or died either. Her master would call that a win. She floated into memory, allowing it to carry her back to sleep.

Her arm prickled.

She glanced down, just to make sure everything was all prim and proper, only to see a spider the size of a fox suspended from the ceiling, poking her skin with needle-sharp legs.

She tried to jerk away, but whatever kept her suspended in the air also had her tied like a pig for roasting. She was held in an invisible trap with a giant spider clinging to her arm.

Yerin's breath froze, and before she could think, she tore everything apart.

Sword madra blasted out of her in every direction, shredding the spider...and the unseen bonds that held her suspended halfway to the ceiling. She landed in a crouch, spider parts clattering to the ground in a sizzle of escaping madra. A construct, then. Of course it was. She shuddered anyway.

The walls of her room were made of rough wood that still smelled fresh. One door—the only entrance or exit besides a single shuttered window. The hearth in one wall was too narrow to let anything in besides a construct or a tiny sacred beast, and a script-circle helped ward against those. She'd checked those herself, inside an hour of moving in.

She would have recognized the room faster had she not just reduced all the furniture to kindling. This was the little cottage the Fishers had given her, where she'd stayed for less than two weeks. That almost won the medal for the longest time she'd lived in the same place.

Her robe was soft, white, a single layer, and tied at the waist. The sort of thing you'd put on a patient while they were unconscious. Whatever had tied her to the ceiling hadn't left any fragments of rope lying everywhere, which meant it had been a Fisher technique. The spider would have been one of Gesha's constructs.

She'd lost the fight to Jai Long, so by rights she should be dead. Instead, she was receiving healing from the Fishers.

What had Lindon done?

She took a step forward, circulating madra to her feet to keep out splinters, and her body sent her a pointed reminder: if they were in the middle of healing her, it was because something was wrong. That hint came to her in the form of a shooting pain up her leg, which made her stagger and grab the wall.

Footsteps pounded the grass outside, and she gathered madra into the steel blade of her Goldsign. It wasn't as useful a medium as her master's sword, but she could still cobble together a Rippling Sword technique to defend herself. If she could find a real weapon, she figured she had an even shot of cutting her way out of the Five Factions Alliance camp. Though that would leave her alone in the Desolate Wilds with no idea what had happened to Lindon. Or Eithan, but she wouldn't shed an undue number of tears if the yellow-haired man had gotten himself buried.

The door cracked open, and the blade poised over her shoulder, on the edge of slashing down.

Lindon's voice drifted in. "Yerin, I don't want to seem untrusting, but...please don't cut me."

Yerin let out a breath as she sunk to the ground, strength leaking out of her legs. She leaned against the wall and called back, "Two steps closer and I'd have carved you into a roast."

"That's why I waited." He poked his head into the door, showing off a shy smile. He was still too tall for someone so weak. "I thought I might explain what happened before you went looking for the story yourself."

"So long as they answered my questions proper and quick, they were in no danger."

Actually, Lindon may have been the only person in the Fisher camp that she could threaten as she was. Her spirit felt like a guttering candle, her body like a sack of tender meat, and her unwelcome guest had started to strain against its cage. She rested a hand on her red belt, with her as always, still tied into an intricate bow—the shape designed by her master to bind its power.

It twisted slightly beneath her palm, straining against the seal. It was no threat for now, but its restrictions would weaken with time.

Sand rushed through an hourglass; an incense stick burned steadily down. She wasn't sure how many years she had left, but if she didn't advance far enough to keep her guest suppressed with her own power...

Then she wouldn't be herself anymore.

Now that she thought of it, someone had dressed her. Which meant someone had gotten a good look at the 'rope' tied around her waist and had decided not to fiddle with it. That showed strange wisdom; most sacred artists would poke a bear to see if it was sleeping.

Lindon knelt opposite her, the closest thing to a chair in the room being a thumb-thick splinter. He arranged himself carefully, sitting with his back straight true and proper. You could take a kid out of his clan, but you couldn't pull the clan out of him with a set of red-hot pliers.

Then her eyes snagged on his clothes.

He was wearing the typical sacred artist's outfit, which went by different names in different lands: wide sleeves that left the arms free, a loose hem hanging down to the ankles to allow a broad range of movement techniques, a cloth belt tied around the waist. Usually, the sacred artist's sect or clan would determine the patterns and colors of the robe, and this was what had stolen Yerin's attention.

The robe was deep blue in some places, white in others, and marked over the heart with a black crescent moon the size of a palm. She'd seen that symbol before; it had whipped these Five Factions artists into a frenzy.

The Arelius family.

So they'd shown up after all, just as the Fishers and Sandvipers had feared. And Lindon was wearing their colors. He'd joined someone after all.

His explanation of the events that had occurred while she was unconscious—told in Lindon's way, soft and polite—painted the picture clear.

Eithan was an Underlord. She found that the easiest part to believe. He had always treated Highgolds as though they weren't fit for his eyes, and there were times training in the Ruins where she'd caught a shadow of something in him that reminded her of her master.

Not that a mere Underlord could stand in the shoes of the Sword Sage, but he'd rule like an emperor in a distant land like this.

No, Eithan as an Underlord she could expect. But there were a few other points she found too sticky to release.

"*You* buried Kral? A Highgold?"

Lindon brushed her aside with an explanation of the binding he'd found in the ancient foundry, as though he were ashamed by his own contribution, but pride lurked in his eyes and his words.

An Iron taking on a Highgold, whatever the circumstances, was like the sun rising green. That was a story his grandchildren could be proud of.

Which might explain the second sticking point of his story: that Eithan Arelius, renowned Underlord, had wanted *him.*

"He came here looking for recruits," Lindon explained, "and he thinks we'd be...suitable." Something haunted his expression for a moment. Maybe hesitation. But what was there to hesitate about when it came to an Underlord's personal invitation? For an Iron to exchange words with someone like Eithan was enough good fortune for five lifetimes.

What was he worried about?

But there was a more urgent question. She didn't think she'd missed so much—if she had slept for days, she would have expected hunger, thirst, a powerful pressure in her bladder. But besides her weakness, which was plain and clear after a fight, she felt like she'd only slept for a few hours.

"How long was I out?" she asked.

"Only six hours," he said, and that settled that. Still, it tore a new hole in his story, and one that she'd almost missed.

"You've got a fox's luck," she said. "Kral didn't so much as cut you?"

He gave her a guilty look, pressing a hand to his shoulder. "Forgiveness. I didn't mean to suggest that I walked away without a scratch. He ran a Forged spear through, right here."

She stared at his shoulder, which he rubbed as though it ached. Even if Lindon was exaggerating about being run through, which she doubted, he'd still been struck by a Highgold's Forger technique less than half a day before.

"Underlords must have some great medicines, I'd guess."

"It was mostly the Fishers who worked on you," Lindon said, still rubbing his shoulder. "Eithan didn't do much, but they tied themselves into knots trying to serve him. If I hadn't told them they should be gone when you woke up, I'm sure they would still be in here."

"I'm not concerned about *me*," Yerin said. "How are you moving that arm? You should be dead and buried, but you're up and hopping in six hours."

Lindon's brow furrowed. "I have an Iron body now. Just like you."

"Not like me."

Jai Long outclassed her in power, but her skill was the highest card she had to play. She'd managed to avoid too many direct hits, so she'd taken many small wounds, but nothing like a through-and-through stab. Even so, she'd needed the urgent attention of a healer, and she *still* wouldn't be sharp enough to hold an edge for a week or two.

That was all plain and proper, part of a normal life—she'd barely taken a step on her Path without some gruesome injury. But Lindon just walked his off in half a day.

She flashed back to a figure caked in blood and black ooze until he looked like he'd crawled out of a wildfire. She would have bet a pile of jewels that he was dead, and she was prepared to take that price out of Eithan's skin.

Instead, he'd advanced to Iron.

What kind of body had they given him?

He picked up on her response, and his voice shook. "Is that wrong? Should I be worried?"

She gave him a light kick, shaking his perfect posture. "Your new Underlord can handle it."

He winced. "Apologies. I accepted his invitation before you woke up."

"You'd have been cracked in the head if you hadn't," Yerin said, which was true. It was the sort of opportunity that only a madman would turn down.

But that still left the ugly question: where did it leave her?

An endless winter forest stretched out before her, filled with nothing but snow and no one but her.

"No, I owe you more consideration than that." He bent

slightly, giving her a little seated bow. "Forgive me."

She forced herself to her feet, one hand on the wall. "Don't fuss about that. Irons are allowed out of the house without a shepherd. You'll settle in with the Underlord, stable and true."

Her master's sword wasn't in the cottage, and she needed it. When you're alone, first look for a weapon.

Lindon opened his mouth as though to speak, but quickly shut it again. The silence stretched.

Until he jerked back as though struck, eyes widening on the window. She spun around, bladed arm poised and gathering madra.

The shutter had come apart slightly, and one bright eye was peeking through. It was framed by a few locks of yellow hair and about an inch of smile.

The face vanished from the window, and an instant later Eithan Arelius kicked in the door. "I'm sorry to disturb you, children, though I couldn't help but overhear every word."

Yerin's spirit may have been drained down to the bone, but she still couldn't believe she hadn't sensed someone as powerful as an Underlord a mere ten feet away. At least he couldn't have been there for more than a few seconds, or she would lose trust in her abilities completely.

"How long have you been listening?" she asked, not relaxing her bladed Goldsign.

He tapped his chin thoughtfully. "For about...four weeks now," he said, then turned his smile on Lindon. "Now, as unique and special as you are, where did you get the impression that I wanted you and *only* you?"

Lindon's expression showed only confusion, but he rose to his feet in order to execute a bow. His iron badge dangled from his neck. "Forgive me, Underlord." Yerin would bet a stack of silver against a pile of hay that he had no idea what he was apologizing for.

"Of course you're a treasure," Eithan said, placing a hand on Lindon's shoulder. Then his other hand snaked out and grabbed Yerin as well—she stopped her bladed arm just before it stabbed him. "But I'm not looking for a *single* treasure. I want the set."

Yerin exchanged looks with Lindon, and though she gave no outer sign, it was as though her heart unclenched. She wouldn't have to scrape by on her own after all. At least not for a little while.

"So we're a set," Lindon said.

"Sounds like we are," she responded. She gave him a little smile, and he rubbed his head sheepishly.

Eithan cleared his throat.

"Well," he said, "one half of this set is supposed to be embedding bindings into constructs."

Lindon bowed. "Apologies, Underlord. I thought Yerin might need a familiar face when she woke."

"That's kind of you, and of course I have no objection to kindness. If you think kindness might keep you alive. In one year. When a Highgold is decorating the walls with your insides."

Lindon's head snapped up, focused on Eithan. "Honored Underlord, thank you for your consideration, but I must beg you for guidance. How can I defeat a Highgold in one year?" He sounded like a starving man asking for his next meal.

"Under the right circumstances, it's possible for an ant to fell an ancient tree," Eithan said. "So it's certainly *possible*. But this will be the..." He hesitated. "I was going to say 'the worst year of your life,' but you're very young. Let me put it to you this way: if you can hear my name at the end of this year without screaming until your lungs bleed, I haven't done my job properly."

Lindon paled, but his voice remained firm. "I thank you for the kindness, Underlord." He bobbed his head to Eithan, then to Yerin, and left the cottage. Presumably to work on his Soulsmithing.

Eithan watched him leave, arms folded. When the door shut, he chuckled. "You didn't warn him."

Yerin watched the Underlord the same way she might watch a venomous Remnant rising from a corpse. "About what?"

"I know you noticed the...*flaw* in his assumptions."

Reluctantly, she nodded. There was no point in pretending when he'd seen through her already. "In a year, Jai Long won't be Highgold anymore."

He spread his arms wide, radiant with the joy of a man presented with a glorious gift. "My respect for the Sage of the Endless Sword only grows. When he chose you as his disciple, he proved himself the wisest of men."

Though it may not have been the sharpest move, she kept going. If he was going to turn on her, better to know it now than to live with a knife at her back. "You can say what you want about ants and trees, but I'd contend Lindon can't win against a Truegold. Not in a year."

Eithan held up a single finger. "A Truegold or *better*. Remember that he holds the spear of his ancestor now. But otherwise, you're correct: Lindon certainly will not win. He cannot. And yet he must fight anyway. It's exciting, isn't it?"

The yellow-haired man's cheerful demeanor had always scraped her against the grain. She'd somewhat gotten used to it during her two weeks of training with him, but now the old irritation was worming its way back like a splinter beneath a fingernail. And anger came with it.

"So you're setting him up to bleed," she said, without bothering to hide the accusation.

He drummed his fingertips together. "In a remote range of mountains at the southern edge of the Blackflame Empire, there lives a small sect of earth artists known as the Deep Eye School. And they are artists in the truest sense of the word; their stone sculptures sell for millions on the open market. To train in their Path, Deep Eye disciples spend years examining the aura of every rock and every boulder on the mountainside. Only when they've found the *perfect* material will they begin to sculpt."

He moved his hands as though holding a block of stone between them. "Once, I had the good fortune to visit them and observe their process. To me, it seemed as though they spent all day staring at rocks. So I asked them what they were looking for. And they answered me: they were looking for the most beautiful flaws."

Yerin kept her voice flat. "In this story, Lindon's a rock?"

"And he has an *exquisite* flaw. He was born too weak. He has learned to get by as the weak do, tricking and bargaining and scraping his way through a world of giants." He smiled in satisfaction. "If I wish to *make* him a giant, that is the flaw I must use."

"That's your intention, is it? To make him a giant?" She had been leaning toward joining his family—she hadn't been lying when she told Lindon that only a fool would pass by an opportunity like that—but now she understood his hesitation.

Eithan smiled too much.

"Sounds like you're aiming to give us both a gift," Yerin said, cycling madra to her bladed arm. She didn't plan to use it, but it gave her a sense of control. "I don't like gifts when I don't know the why behind them."

His smile took on a wistful hue, and he stared into the distance over her shoulder. "Why?" he repeated. "That's an elusive beast, and one that's difficult to pin down. Let me simply say that being born with too little power is not the worst problem one can have."

She knew where this path was headed now, and she withdrew the steel arm on her back. Her master had given her a similar speech, long ago.

"Fate is far worse on those born with too much," he said. "In the Empire, I've heard it said that only one in a hundred Lowgolds ever makes it to Highgold. The same holds true between Highgold and Truegold. Between Truegold and Underlord? One in a thousand." He gestured as though spreading a fact before her. "By definition, each advancement means you leave behind everyone you know until, eventually, you've surpassed them completely. That's the very nature of the sacred arts; it is the definition of success."

That was a fact she knew well. She may be little more than average now, but that wasn't where she'd started out.

Nor was it where she would end up.

Whether the heavens were kind enough to grant her mercy or not, she wasn't destined to stay mediocre for long.

"I'll admit that's been my experience," Yerin allowed, "but my master used to say that no Path is wide enough for two."

He'd lost his smile somewhere along the way, and he was giving her a look of such intensity that she wondered if she was seeing him for the first time. "And that is *exactly* the problem I wish to solve. I have been looking for people to walk with me every step of the way."

"Where to?" she asked.

"To the end."

He let that hang in the air, resonating with honest yearning like a pure musical note. The end of the sacred arts. It was the definition of a myth, the unattainable goal sought by every Path.

"You think Lindon can keep up?" He had his story about a celestial visitor, but Yerin would think it impressive enough for a lifetime if he hit Gold someday.

Eithan gave a little shrug. "He's a gamble, I'll admit. But if it pays off, then I'm more worried about *you* keeping up with *him*."

Yerin stared at him.

"Unless, of course, you come to terms with your...unwelcome guest."

She kept her hand from moving to the blood-red Remnant she kept wrapped around her waist like a belt. He knew. He'd known, and he invited her anyway.

"I already had a master," she said at last. "I'm not calling you that."

"Eithan will do fine," he said. And smiled.

THE END
of Cradle: Volume Two
Soulsmith

LINDON'S STORY CONTINUES IN

BLACKFLAME
CRADLE : VOLUME THREE

AND

SKYSWORN
CRADLE : VOLUME FOUR

WILL WIGHT lives in Florida, among the citrus fruits and slithering sea creatures. He's the author of the Amazon best-selling *Traveler's Gate Trilogy*, *The Elder Empire* (which cleverly offers twice the fun and twice the work), and his new series of mythical martial arts magic: *Cradle*.

He graduated from the University of Central Florida in 2013, earning a Master's of Fine Arts in Creative Writing and a flute of dragon's bone. He is also, apparently, invisible to cameras.

He also claims that *www.WillWight.com* is the best source for book updates, new stories, fresh coriander, and miracle cures for all your aches and pains!